2

Murder on Peachtree Street

Also by Patricia Houck Sprinkle

Murder in the Charleston Manner
Murder at Markham

Murder
on
Peachtree
Street

A Sheila Travis Mystery

Patricia Houck Sprinkle

ST. MARTIN'S PRESS

Production Editor: David Stanford Burr

Design by Dawn Niles

Library of Congress Cataloging-in-Publication Data

Sprinkle, Patricia Houk.
    Murder on peachtree street : a Sheila Travis mystery / Patricia Houk Sprinkle.
        p.   cm.
    "A Thomas Dunne book."
    ISBN 0-312-05476-9
    I. Title.
PS3569.P687.M86   1991
813'.54—dc20   90-15538
                                                                        CIP

First Edition: April 1991

10   9   8   7   6   5   4   3   2   1

For Anne Strahota, encourager, critic, and friend.

Murder on Peachtree Street

1

MONDAY, *October 15*

7:45 A.M.

Dean Anderson was not a patient man. He perched on the side of his bed—a stocky man just past sixty, of medium height with a shock of silver hair—and tapped a pencil against the edge of his nightstand while the phone purred an eighth ring in distant California. Where could Raven be at this hour?

At last she answered, her voice thick with sleep. "Hullo?"

"Raven? It's Dean. I woke up this morning with a marvelous idea. Let's get married!"

"Ummm." He could almost see her rolling her lovely body over and pushing herself up on her satin pillows, dark hair cascading over her shoulders as she squinted at the bedside clock. "Dean, do you know what time it is? Not even five o'clock!"

"It's almost eight here in Atlanta, darling—I'll be leaving for the office in a couple of minutes. I waited as long as I could stand it. What do you say? Will you marry me?"

"Ummm." Now she was yawning, probably stretching her long arms over her head. Raven always found it hard to wake up.

"Wish I was there in person." He lowered his voice, although he lived alone. "Got on your peach satin pajamas?"

She gave the deep chuckle he loved. "Blue, sweetheart. And maybe I'll marry you, if you'll fly out and ask in person like a gentleman. But don't tell the press until I say yes. Promise?"

"I promise, if you'll promise to marry me soon."

"Not until this picture is finished. How does Christmas sound?"

"Like ten weeks away. But if that's the best I can get, I'll take it. What does your schedule look like tomorrow?"

"Hectic. Filming all day. But my evening is clear. Will you call back then?"

"Better than that. I'm coming to propose like a gentleman. Make reservations for two somewhere you'd like to be proposed to, and I'll be at your place by seven. Suit you?"

"Can you get away?"

"Galaxia doesn't own me, sweetheart. I'll get away." He spoiled the effect by adding, "I have to be in Seattle Wednesday anyway, so I'll swing by L. A. en route."

She yawned audibly into the phone. "You *did* ask me to marry you, didn't you, darling?"

"Sure did."

"Ummm. That's what I thought. Ask me again tomorrow night, when I'm awake. Goodnight, Dean."

The phone clicked, then buzzed in his ear. He bent to scratch the ears of a small sheltie at his feet. "Lady, we are about to become a family. And we are going to live happily ever after."

8:30 A.M.

Bayard Anderson shoved tousled blonde hair out of her eyes and glared at her mother. "This is the first day of my vacation, and already you're bugging me about Daddy."

"I'm not bugging you, dear." Laura dumped frozen orange juice into the blender, added water, and turned it on. She was tinting her hair blond and frosting it to hide the gray, her daughter noticed. The new shade made the most of her tan eyes. She'd shed a few pounds, too. At almost fifty, she still looked great. (She ought to, Bayard thought sourly, with all she spent trying. Her monthly salon bills could more than keep her daughter in groceries.)

Laura, meanwhile, was wishing once again that Bay didn't look so much like Dean. If only Neal had inherited some of his dad's muscle and Bay had gotten her own slimness, instead of the other way around. Bay had Dean's blue eyes, and her hair was the same white blonde his used to be. Even her chin was square with a dimple, like Dean's. Just looking at that chin was enough to make Laura want to hit something, but she resolved to stay calm. Above the noise of the blender she shouted, "I'm just asking you to do me a favor, honey. He'll listen to you. He doesn't even return my calls."

"I'm not surprised." Bayard thought she had muttered too low to be heard, but Laura turned in time to see her lips moving.

She turned off the blender and dumped the juice into a waiting pitcher. "What did you say?"

Bayard leaned on her elbows and gulped her coffee—both calculated to upset Laura to the fullest. "I said, I'm not surprised. You haven't exactly been easy for him to deal with since the divorce. Don't you think ten years of war is enough?"

"Oooh." The syllable was drawn out to its fullest, followed by a pause. "And I suppose *he's* been easy to deal with— gallivanting around the world while I've been raising his children."

Bayard sighed in self-disgust. When would she ever grow up? Now that she was out of college and working, she had promised herself at least six times she would *not* argue with Mama about Daddy during this vacation. If only Laura would let the subject alone!

"She's worse these last three months, Bay," Neal had said last night, sneaking into his sister's room for a talk after their mother's light was out. "Ever since Daddy came back to Atlanta to take that job with Galaxia. He's bought a house in Morningside. The nerve of him!" He had pounded the foot of her bed with one fist, and Bayard saw with a pang how thin he still was. At seventeen, Neal looked at least two years younger. His emotions, too, were still out of control. Tears had rolled down his cheeks as he'd cried, "We need to do something. Mama can't take much more!"

Bayard had shrugged in the enormous T-shirt she favored for sleeping. "I don't know what we can do, Neal. Daddy has a right to live where he pleases, and the parts of Atlanta he likes are all near here. Has she seen him?"

"I don't know. She talks about him all the time. You'll see."

Bayard had seen. She hadn't poured her first cup of coffee before Laura had asked, too casually, "Have you seen your dad yet?"

"I just got here yesterday afternoon, Mama. Came straight from the airport on MARTA and called you from the station." She was surprised how easily she used the acronym for Atlanta's rapid transit system. In New York she always said "the train." But nobody in Atlanta called the trains anything but MARTA. She realized her mother was looking at her carefully, as if weighing whether or not she was telling the truth. "No, I haven't seen him," she said.

"I thought maybe you'd gone to see him for a day or two. You've always been so close. When you do see him, Bay, I've got a little something I want you to ask him about."

That's when Bayard had shoved the hair out of her eyes with the accusation ". . . already you're bugging me about Daddy" and Laura had risen to make the orange juice.

Just as Bayard silently vowed not to say one more word until breakfast was over, Laura turned penitent. Pouring herself a cup of coffee, she sat across the table and leaned forward as though they were two old friends having a confidential chat. As Laura started to speak, Bayard braced herself.

"Honey, I know you love your daddy very much. I don't want to take that away from you. But you've got to help me talk some sense into him. Neal turns eighteen in April, and unless we can reach a new agreement, his child support will stop that very day." Bayard said nothing. Laura continued, rapidly. "Bay, when those documents were drawn up, Neal was a baby—not even seven. Eighteen seemed a hundred years away. I didn't think about his birthday coming in April, before he's even out of high school. Unless your daddy makes a new arrangement, I won't have money for his graduation expenses!"

"Neal will. Daddy's been giving me an allowance since I was eighteen, and I'm sure he'll do the same for Neal. He's already agreed to pay for college. So what's the problem?" Bayard knew, of course, but she wanted to hear her mother admit it. This same old melody was harder to take after earning her own living for a few months.

Laura looked shocked. (She always did when her children failed to understand how much she suffered for their sakes.) "It's not just college bills, Bay. We need a home for you children to come back to while he's in college and until you get"—she caught the glint in Bayard's eye and changed what she was about to say—"settled a bit. It's not forever, but we're going to need help for a few years yet."

Bay sipped her coffee. "You could find a job." She said it with the cruel assurance of youth.

"Doing what? I'm almost fifty, and I've spent my life caring for you children. That's what your daddy wanted—he told the world how much he was paying me to stay home with his children, those children he couldn't be bothered to come home to if a news story broke anywhere on the globe—"

She caught herself. She'd never win Bay this way. "All I ask is that you remind him that you both need a home until Neal's out of college. Meanwhile I can get some training— maybe I'll try real estate. I'll be ready to support myself by the time Neal finishes college. I promise. But until then—"

Bayard shook her head. "Not this time, Mama. I'm not going to upset Daddy during this vacation. I'm not!"

7:30 P.M.

In a penthouse high above Peachtree Street, two women were enjoying a leisurely dinner.

Mary Beaufort, a tiny elderly woman with silver hair, sharp brown eyes and the bearing of a duchess, wiped her lips with a snowy napkin before she asked, "So you think you will enjoy this job, Sheila?"

Her companion was reflected in the mirror above the buffet—a tall lean woman nearing forty with black eyes and thick dark hair that curled and frizzed in spite of all her best efforts. She smiled. "I only started today, Aunt Mary, and the job's a bit vague yet. They've just created the position, you know, and Mr. Hashimoto is certain to add to the job description as we go along. But yes, I'm enjoying it so far."

"What exactly do you do, dear? When Ada Williams asked me this afternoon, I found it hard to tell her."

Sheila rose. "Here—I'll show you what they've sent to the papers." She went to her briefcase and brought back a news release. "And here are your reading glasses."

Aunt Mary perched the half glasses on her nose and perused the text while Sheila started her dessert. " 'Hosokawa International is pleased to announce that Sheila Beaufort Travis has joined the company in the newly created post of Director of International Relations.' " She looked up. "I'm glad they included the Beaufort, dear, so people who knew you in high school can get in touch."

Sheila, thoroughly enjoying her chocolate cake, shook her head. "People who knew me in high school have probably all moved away."

"You never know, dear." Aunt Mary resumed reading. " 'Ms. Travis, who has extensive experience in diplomatic service, will be based in Hosokawa's U.S. headquarters in Atlanta. Her duties will include serving as liaison between U.S. and Japanese staff, orienting staff for short-term overseas assignments, and arranging hospitality for visiting executives and their families.' That sounds very exhausting, Sheila. Do they expect you to do *all* of that?"

"I have an administrative assistant, Masako Nanto, who's been with Hosokawa for several years. I'll rely on her a good deal."

"I would, dear," she murmured, then went on reading aloud. " 'Widow of Tyler Travis who served the U.S. Embassy in Japan until his untimely death—' Now, why do people say that, as if the Almighty made errors?"

"People don't know how to deal with a man dying at forty-four, I suppose. At least this release didn't call him 'a legend in his own time.' Tyler may rise up and haunt whoever coined that phrase."

"Nonsense." Aunt Mary's eyes twinkled with mischief. "Tyler probably coined it himself."

"Now, Aunt Mary . . ."

But Mary Beaufort was again reading aloud. " 'Ms. Travis was born in Shikoku, where she lived until she was sent to Atlanta for high school and college—' That's not right, Sheila. You didn't go to college in Atlanta."

"I know, but what difference does it make?"

"It could have been worse," her aunt agreed. "They could have misspelled your name." She quickly finished the final sentences of the release. " '. . . comes to Hosokawa from the Markham Institute of International Studies in Chicago.' "

She stopped reading, a puzzled frown creasing her forehead.

"Is something the matter, Aunt Mary?"

"It doesn't mention your experience as a detective, dear."

"Perhaps," Sheila suggested, "that's because my days as a detective are over. I never really wanted to get involved in those cases, you will remember. It was always your idea." If Aunt Mary remembered anything of the sort, she gave no sign.

Sheila persevered. She had run a risk just by moving near her aunt. It was not for nothing that Sheila's father often said of his elder sister, "Trouble follows that woman like fleas a dog."

"I know you like a little excitement in your life, Aunt Mary. But I haven't moved here to provide you with excitement. I don't like poking and prying into people's affairs, and I am still trying to get my own life in order. Do you understand?"

Aunt Mary's eyes widened and her voice was full of reproach. "Of course, Sheila. I should never dream of involving

7

either of us in prying and poking. In our last case I felt you did far too much of that."

Sheila smiled. Their last case had involved poking and prying into Aunt Mary's own past. Her smile faded, however, as Aunt Mary continued, "Of course if a situation arises in which we can be of service—"

"It won't," Sheila interrupted ruthlessly. "Read my lips. I have not come to Atlanta to be a detective."

Chinese fortune cookie say:
Beware of Monday resolutions.
By next Sunday they may all be broken.

2

Unlike Dean Anderson, his boss, Jonah Baker was a patient man. He could sprawl on a park bench for hours chatting with an elderly bag lady. He could rock on a ramshackle porch all afternoon without saying a word. It was one of the qualities that made people let him into their lives and had won him, at not quite thirty-three, several awards for documentaries about American society. This morning he had rolled up his sleeves, spread out a legal pad and pencil, and given his whole attention to Craig Stofford as he droned on. But this last idea tried even *his* patience too far.

"A juggler? Come on, Craig . . ." Jonah's voice rose in disgust. He pushed his horn-rimmed glasses up his nose with one finger and peered across the table.

Until then, this could have been any ordinary staff meeting in Encyclopedia Galaxia's film division. Nobody knew it would be the last for one of them. It is hard to anticipate murder.

The entire staff sat (as they had weekly for nearly two months) discussing ideas for what Dean (head of the film division) had recently begun to call "that misbegotten television series." As usual, this morning only Craig had talked and only Jonah had been really listening.

Because it was such a lovely day, they had opened the

9

huge unscreened windows to enjoy the warm fresh air. Muted sounds of traffic rose from far below, while construction noises from across the street proved that someone was building up Peachtree again. A constant breeze stirred the blinds and rustled papers on the table.

Veronica Yates sat with hands clasped lightly before her. Her brown fingers itched to be working on a new needlepoint she was doing for her mother's birthday, but male colleagues never seemed to believe that a woman's mind could think while her fingers sewed. She'd learned years ago that bringing out needlework was the surest way not to be taken seriously, and Veronica wanted to be taken seriously. Her face was pensive, as if engrossed in the conversation, but she was wondering if this would be the day her infant son, Demonde, would learn to sit up, and if so, if it would be before she picked him up at the sitter's. She was missing all his milestones, and nothing she'd heard here this morning was worth missing this one for.

Elise White hadn't even pretended to listen. On a pink pad she had been sketching her boss, Porter Phillips, in turquoise ink. She was pleased that she had exactly caught the devilish slant of his dark brows. She added a wicked mustache. Porter, peering across the table at the sketch, had immediately retaliated by drawing a lightning likeness of Elise as an angel with horns. He was holding it up for her inspection when Jonah's scorn caught their attention. Scorn was so unlike Jonah.

Craig stopped in midsentence, one square hand still jabbing the air for emphasis. He used it to smooth his sleek blond hair instead. "Don't write it off, Jonah, until you hear all about it," he insisted, his face flushed above his beard.

Dean, at the head of the table, had been giving Craig only half his mind. With the other half he'd been thinking of how he would rather spend this morning—hurrying to the airport for an earlier plane. No woman had ever stirred him like Raven Hillis. He could feel a tightening in his groin just thinking of her. When he closed his eyes he could smell her jasmine perfume, conjure up the sensation of her astonishing black hair cascading over his face. He was on the West Coast in spirit when Craig's ludicrous suggestion jolted him back.

He considered his editor in amazement. "Did you say a juggler, Stofford?" When Craig nodded, Dean could feel his blood pressure rising. "You've come up with some dumb ideas so far, but this is the dumbest of all!"

Porter covered his dark eyes with one hand. "Oh, God."

"Don't swear," Elise admonished him.

"I'm not," he assured her. "I'm praying."

Craig held up one hand to forestall further commentary. "Wait. This guy is good—I mean, really good. He can juggle anything. Cameras, chairs . . ."

"I see!" Elise's navy blue eyes widened in comprehension. "He can juggle whatever the show's about. I mean, if it's music, he could juggle violins or something . . ." Her voice trailed uncertainly when she saw Porter wiggle his brows in mock delight.

"Of course, darling! And if it's about travel, he could juggle maps. Or would steamer trunks give a better effect?" He placed one long, thin finger against his temple to consider the matter.

Jonah pulled an apple from the scuffed backpack that served him as briefcase, travel companion and friend. Chewing was better than grinning when Porter was getting the best of Craig. Even the whites of Craig's blue eyes were turning pink.

"I think we ought to go with our original idea. Just let Dean do lead-ins." They all turned, surprised. Veronica seldom spoke in these conferences. Her voice was soft and careful, but her clasped hands clenched with her effort to make her point. "People will love seeing him every week, and he can write his own lead-ins to go with whatever subjects we've chosen." She looked from one to the other, seeking support.

"I'd vote to stop looking for a gimmick and start picking weekly topics."

She got mixed reactions. Dean thanked her. Craig (who persisted in thinking of Veronica as his assistant rather than his colleague) viewed this as treason, and drew sharp-pointed arrows on his pad. Elise nodded tentatively, then more vigorously when Porter clapped and said, "Hear, hear!"

Jonah, wanting to acknowledge the first intelligent remark of the morning, offered Veronica a bite of his apple. She accepted it with a bow and a conspiratorial grin that surprised him. Jonah vowed that someday he was going to buy Veronica lunch and ask why she was so reticent in these meetings when she obviously had good things to say. Was it because she was the only black? The only woman? (Elise didn't count—she was a species from another planet.)

He wondered, as he munched, whether this staff had a harder time than most working together—or did he just think so because he usually worked solo? Perhaps it was the hybrid nature of Galaxia itself that made things so difficult.

Formed three years ago by the merger of five small encyclopedia companies, Encyclopedia Galaxia had risen swiftly to challenge the giant Encyclopedia Britannica. Purchased by Hosokawa International a year after the merger, Galaxia was fast becoming a world-class encyclopedia. Hosokawa intended by the end of the century to publish it in fifteen languages around the globe.

In the past two years, Galaxia news releases had sent shock waves through more than the business community. First, Atlantans concerned for historical preservation had learned with dismay that Hosokawa had purchased the historic Webster Building on Peachtree Street for Galaxia's new headquarters. Would the shabby old structure be demolished, replaced with another glassy high-rise so favored by Atlanta architects? Hosokawa assured them the building would be restored to its original 1910 splendor, complete with pink marble and polished brass. By last July it had joined the Hurt

Building, Candler Building and Healey Building as a monument to a glorious era in Atlanta's business life. Atlanta was invited to tour the building each Thursday afternoon for the rest of the year.

Then an August release astonished national media circles. How had Galaxia lured Dean Anderson, veteran television newsman, out of semiretirement to head up its film division? At the press conference Galaxia held to celebrate that event, Anderson had given the cameras his famous grin and talked a lot of rot about coming home to Atlanta—where he once worked for WSB–TV—to grow roses. Only in the last minutes of the press conference did he hint about a new television series in the offing from Galaxia's film division.

Nothing had been heard from Anderson since. The media waited. His staff met weekly. But they were stuck.

The concept was good—a series aimed at persons over sixty, covering travel, books, special cultural opportunities, tips for healthier living, and financial advice leavened with a weekly dose of nostalgia. Dean as host would certainly be a draw for audiences. Small stations would snap up the series to fill extra air time. And the programs would be cheap to produce—Galaxia had inherited hundreds of reels of documentary footage in the merger.

All they needed was that one good idea—a gimmick, glue—to turn unrelated programs into a series. "What we're seeking," Porter had once remarked, "is a Reading Rainbow approach for the very adult."

But Galaxia's film division had inherited not only films, but people as well. The staff (and the television series) was bogged down in an old-fashioned turf fight. Craig had come from Minneapolis as senior editor and writer; for fifteen years he had written the best films produced by one of the merged companies. Porter had moved from New York, where he was art director for the film division of Galaxia's largest merged company, and had assumed the same position in Atlanta. Elise had been hired to assist him at the same time Veronica had been lured away from CNN to write scripts. Jonah himself had been recruited by Dean, who admired his work. Sometimes, however, Jonah wondered if he'd been hired as a filmmaker or a peacemaker.

He raised one hand and waggled his apple core. "I vote against the juggler, but I don't have a better idea right now. Can we take half an hour?" He raised his arms and arched his back.

Dean stood. "I've got a plane to catch, and some work to do before I catch it. But Elton Dekker is breathing down my neck about this series, so by Friday a week I want you to have something settled, maybe a first script written. Or I'll write it myself."

He'd been addressing the entire staff, but the last remark was directed at Craig. Craig's face grew even redder and his beard jutted at a dangerous angle from his chin. He pulled out a handkerchief to blow his nose audibly and almost rudely.

Elise hurried to create a diversion. "Will you be back in time for the press reception Thursday, Dean?"

Dean nodded. "I wouldn't miss it for the world. Jonah, chair this meeting after the break. See if you can make some progress."

Craig stood and said in a tight voice, "I've got to make some calls." He walked to the door with quick, purposeful steps.

"Is it Craig's bladder or his telephone that keeps him hopping every hour?" Porter inquired. "Ever notice how he can't go longer than that without heading for the potty or the phone? Maybe we should put a phone in the john . . ." He looked brightly around the room, then shrugged. "Okay. Not funny. Who needs a Coke?"

"I do." Elise reached under the table and brought out the turquoise leather purse that matched her turquoise leather flats. Bets were laid in the film division about how many pairs of shoes Elise had. However many it was, she had a purse to match each one.

As they went down the hall, her voice floated back. "Can we take the stairs? I got up too late this morning to run."

And Porter's protest, "Eleven flights? Darling! My poor legs!"

Dean paused, as usual, to look out the window and check the progress on an enormous steel skeleton across the way. A man in a hard hat looked up and recognized the famous stocky figure with its shock of white hair. When Dean waved, the man nearly tumbled eleven stories in his excitement. With a grin, Dean turned back to Jonah. "Come up with something, Baker." His voice was light, but with a pleading tone underneath. "We're running out of time."

Downstairs in his office, Dean rapidly went through his mail. Three more letters, he told himself, and he could go to the airport. He didn't want to work on the plane. He was too excited. He'd pick up a novel. He checked his watch once again.

"Dean, do you have any idea how I can answer this?"

He looked up, startled. Wylene Fowler, the film librarian, was at his side. She had entered so quietly he hadn't heard her until she spoke. He had hay fever, so he hadn't smelled her perfume, and she must have held her bracelets to keep them from jangling.

Wylene was wearing brown today, a funny color that looked as if it had been blended with yellow mustard. She always wore brown, green or shades of yellow. Somebody must have told her those were the only colors a redhead should wear. Dean had overheard Porter (who was without peer in the matter of dress) trying to convince her to try lavender one day. Wylene, as usual, had known best.

As far as Dean was concerned, it didn't matter what she wore. She was skinnier than the proverbial rail, and even her mother wouldn't consider her beautiful without the layers of expensive cosmetics she used. Now, as he took the letter, he thought her hands looked like talons, blood red at the tips as if she had recently been feeding on raw meat. He repressed a shudder as she moved her unlovely body close to his and read over his shoulder.

The letter was only an excuse, of course. Wylene was a nuisance, running to him with every little thing. He tried to be nice, reminding himself that it must be very dull in the film library all day, shut away from the others by heavy glass doors. He'd even suggested that she move her desk so she could see into the foyer. But while she had thanked him with a simper that made his skin crawl, she had insisted that things be left as the architects placed them. She'd even ticked him off—in a playful, bantering manner—for shifting his own desk so he could look out the window while he was on the phone.

He dealt with her letter quickly, then folded up the rest of the mail on his desk and reached for his briefcase. "I really must be going, Wylene. I have a plane to catch."

"I thought you weren't due in Seattle until tomorrow."

He raised a mental eyebrow. The woman even kept up with his schedule? Only his years in front of a camera enabled him to retain a bland smile as he nodded. "That's right. But I've got some business this evening in L. A. Important business!"

She looked disconcerted. She must have read some of the tripe linking his name with Raven's. Fine. Maybe that would shut down her hormones while he was gone. He shifted in his chair, indicating he would stand if she'd move out of the way.

She backed away with a wide-eyed, worried look. "I hope you'll be back for the reception, Dean." Even the way she said his name made his skin crawl. He really needed to get out of here before he threw up all over her lizard shoes. If he had the power to fire her . . . But he didn't. He'd checked. Apparently nobody did.

"I'll be there with bells on. Now if you'll excuse me . . ." He seized his briefcase and walked quickly to the door.

Wylene heard him say to Sally Webster, the receptionist, "I think my daughter Bayard's in town. She may show up wanting lunch. Ask her to have dinner with me Thursday night—invite her to the reception, in fact. Have her meet me there." The elevator bell dinged—he must have pushed the button while he was speaking. In an instant he was gone.

In his office, Wylene's eyes filled with tears. She muttered, "Damn him, damn him, damn him!"

3

THURSDAY, *October 18*

Sheila swung along the sidewalk as fast as her long legs would carry her, scanning buildings for one she knew only by name.

Above downtown Atlanta the sky was a deep, cloudless blue. A late afternoon breeze blew up the gloomy canyon of Peachtree Street, teasing skirts and enticing tourists and conventioneers to take predinner strolls through the warm October air. But Sheila was neither tourist nor conventioneer, and the only attention she paid the breeze was to hold one side of her thick hair against it. Like the White Rabbit, she was late for a very important date.

The building, fortunately, was well identified. Another time she might have smiled at the juxtaposition of the space-age name in gilt on the transom under an older name in marble block letters. She would certainly have paused to admire the thick brass doors. Today she merely mounted three pink marble steps, tugged open one door and sighed with relief. Encyclopedia Galaxia, at last.

Normally she would have stopped, entranced by the oval foyer, curved staircase of pink marble, and two brass warriors guarding a huge brass mailbox just inside the door. Today she rushed through the foyer and, ignoring the elevator, hurried up one flight of stairs. She paused, panting, to check her watch. Almost five-thirty! A printed sign steered her toward the left.

19

She didn't see a kneeling maintenance man until she stumbled over his leg. He dropped an oil can with a clunk and thrust out one gray-sleeved arm. "Hey, watch where you're going!"

"I'm so sorry!" She peered down at him uncertainly. He was pudgy and past forty, with a ruddy earnest face and thinning hair the color of dry Spanish moss. Like moss, it curled wispily around his bald pink crown. His brown eyes looked tiny, condensed by thick round lenses smeared with fingerprints, and they wore a puzzled look as if life were a riddle he had not yet solved. "Are you hurt?" She was relieved when he shook his head, and gave him a penitent smile. "I was hurrying, and didn't see you."

"I was right here," he said angrily. He peered at her for a moment, then his scowl relaxed. "It's okay. I'm not hurt. Just oiling a hinge on this door here." He picked up the oil can and gave an industrious squirt to the bottom hinge. From the way he put unexpected pauses between words, she wondered if he were slightly retarded. She was certain of it when he rocked back into a squat, wiped his oily palm on his shirt and held out a calloused hand like a child. "I'm Woody."

"Hi, Woody. I'm Sheila Travis." She bent over to shake. "Is the press reception in there?"

"Sure is. You're late. I went in and had a bite. Dean said I could. But it isn't much. You get better food at the Varsity."

Sheila supposed so—the Varsity had long served some of the world's best hot dogs, orange drinks and onion rings. On the other hand, she hoped Galaxia wouldn't serve orange drink and onion rings at a major press conference.

"Guess I'd better make my appearance." She tugged the mahogany door and was nearly thrown off balance by its easy swing.

"Oiled," Woody reminded her with gruff pride.

Inside she paused and scanned the crowd with a practiced eye. Across the room, near the television cameras, she spotted a power circle of reporters, camera crews, and executives connected with Encyclopedia Galaxia's latest innovation, Galaxia Online.

"It is a major step forward," Mr. Hashimoto had assured her when he asked her to attend the reception. "It will enable subscribers to access on personal computers any data from the entire encyclopedia and its many subsidiaries."

"Access data from subsidiaries." Sheila rolled the unfamiliar words through her mind. She had spent an hour reading about the new project, but she still didn't understand it—nor why anyone would prefer sitting at a desk reading a monitor when they could curl up on their sofa with a cup of coffee and Volume 3. Hers, however, was not to reason why. Hers was to spot in this crowd of strangers a certain Wylene Fowler, possibly the only person here who cared that Hosokawa International, the parent company, had sent a representative.

"Just take our greetings," Mr. Hashimoto had said. "Introduce yourself and, if they ask you to, make a nice little speech."

Sheila had no intention of making a nice little speech. What could she say about computerized encyclopedias, for heaven's sake! But she was adept at introducing herself. Sixteen years as an embassy wife had taught her that—and a few other things besides. One of them was, the sooner you arrive at a boring party, the sooner you can leave. If she hadn't been so late, she thought with regret, she could probably be leaving right now.

Wylene Fowler had said to meet near the door, so Sheila waited there. Her attention was caught by an exclamation nearby—"Jonah Baker?"—followed by a question that made no sense. It sounded like "Did *you* make please daddy?"

Turning, she repressed a sigh. The young woman who had spoken could be very pretty, if she didn't dress in tacky chic. Her drab beige jacket, which drooped off her shoulders and bulged at the pockets, was too long for her short, stocky figure. Its matching skirt ended a foot beneath the jacket, and creased across her abdomen. Dangling wooden earrings could scarcely be seen beneath hair that looked like a bad perm blown by a storm. There was something vaguely familiar about the square face and pale hair, but Sheila couldn't remember ever having met the woman before. And she had spoken not to Sheila, but to a lanky man bending over her.

He was several years older—past thirty, probably—with short brown hair and a mobile, humorous mouth. Rubbing one ear, he nodded. "Well, yes, I did. Several years ago." He sounded curt, but years of talking with young men at embassy functions made Sheila suspect he was, rather, painfully shy in the presence of young women. If Sheila had been talking with him she would have admired his suit and his courage to wear it in Atlanta's hot October. Off-white linen with narrow gray stripes, it looked cool, and was a refreshing visual change from the charcoal suits or navy blazers of the other men. From the suit he could have been led naturally into talking about clothes, taste, and, finally, himself.

This girl, however, was too young to think of any topic of conversation other than herself. "We used it in one of my classes. It was great." Her face wore an expression of languid interest, but her eyes betrayed her. She badly wanted to make a good impression. She sipped her wine and didn't seem to know what to say next. Neither did he. He held a glass in one hand and pushed horn-rimmed glasses up his nose with the other.

Another man joined them, short and blond, in tan slacks, navy blazer and red tie. He stroked his beard and smiled. "Hi, Jonah. Hi, Bay—I got that information I promised you. You owe me dinner." He handed the young woman a slip of paper with a grin that made Sheila think of the wolf smiling at Red Riding Hood.

The girl he'd called Bay shoved the paper into her pocket without reading it. "Excuse me," she said with dignity to the taller man. "I need to refill my glass." She pushed her way through the crowd.

The newcomer barked a short, unpleasant laugh. "Bay's not very happy with me. She just lost a bet."

"I didn't know you knew her, Craig." The man called Jonah was looking around the room, over the head of his companion.

"I know *all* the women, Baker! Haven't I told you that?

Bay came by to see Dean Tuesday and we went to dinner. If you'd let me, I could fix you up . . ."

"I know plenty of women, thanks."

Craig's laugh was unpleasant. "Sure, all welfare mothers trying to collect child support. I'm talking about real women, Jonah."

Jonah's eyes still roamed the room. "I'll let you know. Right now, though, I need to see Veronica about something." He moved away with an awkward loping gait.

The blond man looked at his watch, and Sheila could almost read his mind. *Have I stayed long enough? Can I get back to my desk for two last calls before it's time to go home?* His blue eyes met hers across his wrist and he gave her a smile more cynical than embarrassed.

She was about to ask him about Wylene Fowler when she heard a voice on her other side. "Sheila Beaufort! What are you doing here?"

She turned just in time to receive the full impact of a glass of wine spilled down her blouse, wetting her to the skin.

"Omigosh! I'm sorry . . . I was trying to get close enough to see if it was really you!" A petite blond woman mopped ineffectually at Sheila's creamy blouse with a maroon paper napkin. It began to leave stains of its own on the silk.

"It's all right." Sheila held up one hand to forestall her. "At least it was white wine. Just show me where the bathroom is."

"Sure." The woman raised a flushed face and peered up at her. Sheila had known only one person in her life with eyes of that particular navy blue. "Elise?" she hazarded. "Elise Van Dyne?"

"You remembered! Except I'm Elise White now. And you're not Beaufort anymore, are you?"

"Travis." Sheila's own pleasure was dampened by the state of her blouse. "Can we chat in the bathroom while I dry off?"

"Oh, sure! I forgot." Elise took Sheila by the forearm and more tugged than led her to another door. " 'Scuse us," she said cheerfully as she collided with a man in her path. "She has to get to the bathroom real fast." Sheila looked the other way.

"Here, let me help." Elise ran a towel under the water and turned without wringing it, but Sheila hadn't gone through high school with Elise for nothing.

"You sit over there"—she firmly steered her friend toward a chair—"and talk while I repair the damages. What are you doing here?"

"I work here, as an artist. I draw cartoons, things like that. Right now I'm doing one about the cutest little blood cells."

As Elise chattered on, Sheila wrung out the towel and managed to get most of the wine and stain out of her blouse. Then she stood in front of the hot air drier until the damp circle faded.

Elise looked in the mirror and fluffed her hair. "I'd have known you anywhere!" she exclaimed for the fourth time. She added, for variation, "You look exactly the same! You must save hundreds a year on perms," she added enviously.

"I had to wait long enough to get stylish." Sheila repaired wind damage to her hair and gave her friend's frosted perm an approving look. "You look wonderful."

She meant it. Thin and pale in high school, Elise was now voluptuous and delightfully feminine in a pink clinging dress with shoes and purse to match.

Elise checked her lipstick. "I thought you were in Asia, married to a diplomat."

Sheila nodded. "Japan."

"Oh," Elise said, dubious. "I thought it was Asia."

Sheila replaced her lipstick to keep from smiling. A smile might make Elise demand an explanation, which could easily take all evening. Sheila remembered her first high school pajama party, and Betty Sue Bates sighing about her favorite television gunslinger, Paladin, "He's so dreamy, I just wish I knew his first name."

Elise had been astonished. "Why, it's right there on his card, silly: 'Have Gun, Will Travel. Wire Paladin.' His name is Wire." All but Sheila had nearly suffocated stifling giggles

24

in their pillows. Sheila, new to the school, thought Elise deserved an explanation. It took her almost all night, with only one result: She herself had joined the class consensus that if Elise were any spacier, she'd have to live on Mars. In that, Elise apparently hadn't changed.

Elise had more catching up she wanted to do. "Why did you come home? Divorce?" She sounded as if that were the only reason a woman moved.

"No, my husband died in a climbing accident last fall."

"Oh, I'm so *sorry*." Her sympathy was as spontaneous and real as a child's.

"It's okay, I'm doing fine," Sheila assured her.

"Are you sure?"

"Very. I've got a new job that I'm liking very much."

Elise was, as in the past, easy to distract. "What do you do?"

When Sheila gave her title, Elise was no more enlightened than before, so with a grin, Sheila provided a few particulars. "Today I've entertained two Japanese businessmen. We lunched at the top of the Westin Peachtree so they could watch the city go by while we ate, then we went to the Cyclorama because they had read about it in their guidebooks, and we wound up at the Botanical Gardens so they could see the Japanese garden. They've been away from Tokyo for nearly a month, and are getting a bit homesick, so I thought that might cheer them up. But they liked the conservatory so much, they lingered. I got caught in traffic taking them to their hotel, which is why I was late getting here."

"That doesn't sound like work at all," Elise said scornfully. "Even I could do that!"

Why should Sheila feel stung? She herself had made the job sound like a glorified travel agent. Nevertheless, she countered with, "How's your Japanese? And your knowledge of how business works in both countries?"

Immediately she regretted the impulse. Elise was about to give a detailed answer to both questions. "It's not a hard job," Sheila assured her. "All it takes is being thoroughly at home in two cultures and able to tolerate an incredible amount

25

of banal conversation in both languages." She felt her blouse. "There. I'm dry now. I'm supposed to be meeting someone named Wylene Fowler—or I was, an hour ago. Do you know her?"

"Wily Wylene? Of course, who doesn't?" Elise lifted one slim nostril in disdain. "She's the film librarian, really, but Mr. Dekker lets her do a lot of other things, too."

Like a small tug she towed Sheila through the crowd toward a chopstick-thin woman in an emerald suit and a bright paisley silk blouse. "That's Wily," Elise murmured over one shoulder. "Porter says she's ugly as sin, but doesn't she have interesting bones?"

Sheila didn't know who Porter was, but she had ample opportunity to examine at least some of the bones. Wylene's scooped neck would have been provocative if she'd had anything to provoke with. Instead, it revealed a vast amount of bony freckled chest below a skinny neck beginning to show its age. Her face was gaunt, mostly freckles stretched taut across wide cheekbones, and it was topped by auburn hair cut very chic and short. With long hair, Sheila reflected, she would resemble one of Modigliani's models.

What surprised her the most, however, was the price Wylene must have paid for that suit and those matching suede shoes. Most film librarians, Sheila suspected, didn't make that much in a month. Was Wylene also married to the chairman of the board?

Her manner was equally confusing. When Elise introduced them, the thin woman's penciled brows rose above tawny eyes. Although surely junior to Sheila in position, Wylene radiated condescension as she inclined her head and stretched her already wide mouth into a smile of artificial charm. "Why, Ms. Travis, we're so glad you got here. I was waiting for you by the door at a quarter to five, but when you didn't come and didn't come, I had to see about a few things . . ." She trailed off, letting the gentle rebuke settle.

"I spilled wine down her," Elise explained. Bless her, Sheila thought, for not explaining when.

Wylene paid no attention whatsoever to Elise. She put

out one thin hand covered with freckles and large silver and emerald rings. "I told Mr. Dekker—he's our president, you know?—I told him I'd bring you over as soon as you arrived."

Elise gave her a push. "See you later, okay?" Sheila nodded and followed the willowy form toward the power circle.

Wylene detached the president from his conversation with a skill that junior diplomats would envy. "Mr. Dekker, this is Ms. Travis from Hosokawa." She paused only long enough to be sure they shook hands (reminding Sheila of a mother waiting to be sure her children showed good manners), then hurried off, obviously burdened by many responsibilities.

Sheila forgot Wylene and regarded Elton Dekker with interest. This ordinary-looking man was hailed by those who should know as the perfect person to lead Encyclopedia Galaxia into a glorious future. He was obviously regarded by Wylene Fowler as a minor deity. And Galaxia Online had been his original idea. He must have a secret, creative side. It remained hidden as he gave her a genial smile, a pudgy handshake and a glass of Beaujolais.

In the next thirty minutes, Sheila earned her pay. She conveyed Mr. Hashimoto's greetings and listened while Elton Dekker explained once again the wonders of Galaxia Online. She murmured to someone from the mayor's office her delight at being back in Atlanta. She met representatives from Emory, Atlanta University and Georgia State, and nodded appropriately when a director of the Carter Center hailed Galaxia Online as "a dramatic leap forward in communications." Finally she spoke briefly into a video camera about Hosokawa's pride at Galaxia's new accomplishment.

There, Mr. H., your little speech, she thought, moving slightly behind Dekker and wishing her Beaujolais was a cup of black coffee.

Suddenly a man detached himself from a distant group and crossed toward her with purpose and a puzzled smile. Planting himself squarely in front of Sheila, he stuck out one hand. "Dean Anderson. Don't I know you?"

Of course he did.

"Hojatolislam Hashemi Rafsanjani," she murmured mischievously.

If Elton Dekker—who had turned to make introductions—was baffled by this reference to Iran's longtime chief of state, the newcomer wasn't. He came up with a ten-year-old name from the pages of his legendary memory. "Susan—no, Sheila Travis! What on earth are you doing here?"

His voice was warm and his eyes alight, as if he had been living only for this reunion. Sheila was not misled. She leaned into the squeeze of his bear hug and smiled up at him. "Hi, Dean. I'm the new director of international relations for Hosokawa, and am representing them at this"—she almost said "shindig"—"celebration. What are *you* doing here? A television special on computerized encyclopedias?"

His grin was still boyish. "Heavens, no. I'm—"

Before he could finish, a thin, worried-looking boy with more pimples than charm pushed his way through the crowd and blurted, "Dad, you aren't taking this seriously. I tell you, Darius is out—they let him out this afternoon. And he's gunning for you."

4

Dean put one arm around the boy's shoulder. "Elton, Sheila, this is my son, Neal." She would never have guessed. The boy was short and slight, with tan eyes and mousy hair. He must resemble his mother. "Neal, this is Mr. Dekker, president of Galaxia, and Mrs. Travis, whom I knew out in Japan several years ago. Her husband was Tyler Travis, the diplomat who died last year."

"Yeah, well, glad to meet you." The boy had little grace. "I hate to break in like this, but Dad just won't listen to reason. They released Darius Dudwell this afternoon, and everybody knows he's going to come looking for Dad as soon as he gets out."

"Nobody knows anything of the sort." Dean pushed the boy away. "Go find your sister and tell her I'm almost ready. We'll talk later."

He turned back to Sheila and Mr. Dekker. "Sorry about that."

Sheila could sense his embarrassment. "You were going to tell me what you are doing here," she reminded him.

Elton Dekker did it instead. "Dean has come aboard to supervise the development of a Galaxia television series. We have him on a two-year contract." He rubbed one hand across his thinning hair with justifiable pride. Sheila gave him an appraising look. Anyone who could pin Dean Anderson down

29

for two years must indeed have a hidden side. "And you two are old friends?" Dekker asked her.

Anderson put one huge arm around Sheila's shoulder. "This lady and I spent a fascinating morning at the U.S. Embassy in Tokyo back in—what was it, 'seventy-nine?—trying to learn to pronounce 'Hojatolislam Hashemi Rafsanjani' so we could say his name right in public. One of the shared joys of journalists and diplomats. Afterwards, she and Tyler took me out for the best sushi I've ever eaten. I was sorry . . ." He fumbled for the right words of condolence.

"Thanks." She cut him short. "Tell me about this new series."

Mr. Dekker nodded. "Yes, tell us about it, Dean. I tried to call you Tuesday, but Sally said you'd left early for Seattle."

Dean's face lit with a grin that made him seem younger than his son. "I went to California, Elton, to see a lady, and I'll be making an announcement in a few weeks. I'd make it now, but I gave her my promise." His chuckle rippled across the room.

From where they stood, only Sheila could see Wylene Fowler, standing just behind Dean. The woman froze, then raised one hand to her lips as if afraid she was going to be sick. Sheila took one step toward her, but Wylene turned abruptly and went to fetch herself some wine.

Elton Dekker was in midsentence when Sheila caught up with the conversation. ". . . a press reception for that series soon?"

Dean rubbed the side of his nose with one big forefinger, a gesture signifying to millions of viewers around the world that he was about to impart news he'd rather keep to himself. "Not yet, Elton. We're running into some delays—"

Wylene Fowler materialized again and cut him off. "Pardon me, Dean, but Channel Five is ready to interview Mr. Dekker."

As Wylene deftly maneuvered Dekker across the room, a man murmured at Sheila's shoulder, "Trust Wily. Heaven forbid that visitors should detect ripples on the glassy Sea of Galaxia."

The light clear voice sounded as if it would sing a good tenor. It belonged to a thin man in his midforties with a swarthy complexion and eyes that reminded Sheila of ripe olives. He wore a black suit and white shirt, but for the party (or just to be different?) had added an ascot of green and gold. His hair was a fluffy black ruffle around the top of his head, relieved only by a few curly hairs at the front. He reached out and clapped Dean on the arm. His wrist, Sheila saw, was thin, covered with thick black hair, and almost in spite of herself she found him attractive. "Introduce me. You're monopolizing this beautiful lady."

"Trying to," Dean grunted. "Sheila Travis, Porter Phillips, art director in the film division. Sheila's with Hosokawa."

"The top brass," Porter reproached him, "and you were going to keep her all to yourself. You must share her, Dean!"

"Looks like I'll have to," Dean complained. "Other people keep butting in. Now I see my children approaching, with fire in Bay's eye. Excuse me for a minute, Sheila?" He moved away.

Porter smiled down at Sheila. "How about having dinner?"

"She's having dinner with me." Elise stood at Sheila's shoulder, peering up at them both. "At least I hope she is." She was slightly out of breath, as if she'd been hurrying. "I came as quick as I could when I saw you alone with Porter," she told her friend. "I forgot to warn you about him."

"You needn't expect a raise anytime soon, darling," he informed her. "I was just building up to my pitch."

"I'd like to go with Elise tonight," Sheila told him. "We went to high school together, and have some catching up to do."

"Elise went to high school? Well, that will give me something to marvel over during my solitary meal." He bowed and glided, graceful as a dancer, toward the wine table.

Elise sighed. "Porter's sweet, but you have to be careful. He's never really tried anything, but he talks simply *terrible*! The only place I go alone with him is down the staircase, because I can outrun him. Can you go now?"

"Let me just make my formal goodbyes."

As they reached the door, Dean blocked their way. With him were Neal and the young woman in the rumpled beige suit.

"Don't go yet. I want you to meet Bayard Anderson, a television reporter." He didn't add "and my daughter" but his face said it for him. Now Sheila knew why that square face, pale hair and clear blue eyes were familiar. "Bay, this is Sheila Travis."

Bayard didn't bother to conceal her impatience to be off. "Glad to meet you," she said, her voice not in the least cordial.

Dean shrugged an apology. "This younger generation," he seemed to say. What he actually said was, "How about dinner next Wednesday, Sheila? Could you make it?"

"I'd like that." She offered one of the brand-new cards Mr. Hashimoto had thoughtfully ordered before she arrived. "Call me."

Before he could reply, Neal had given his arm a tug. "Come on, Dad, let's go."

With a grin Dean let himself be borne away by his children. "You can't blame them," Elise said sadly. "They don't see very much of him."

Since they were parked in different directions, Sheila suggested they eat nearby. "Oh, you mean Dailey's!" Elise agreed.

It sounded like a Chicago sandwich shop, so Sheila was pleasantly surprised to be led into a large upstairs room with heavy white tablecloths and napkins. At Elise's prodding she admired the exposed ceiling pipes (painted black) and oiled wooden floors, then flashed the waiter a smile of thanks for interrupting Elise's raptures long enough to show them to a table for two just beneath an unpainted wooden carousel horse.

When they had perused the small blackboard menus and ordered, Elise surveyed her friend with obvious delight. "Tell all. Who are the men in your life?"

32

Sheila chuckled. "Dad, who's retired in Montgomery with Mother, and Alfred, Aunt Mary's Persian cat."

Elise was incredulous. "That's it?" Sheila nodded. "But why? You're gorgeous—I mean, stunning. And you've been a widow for a year now? Don't you want to be married again?"

Sheila shook her head. "I'm enjoying being on my own a bit. I never was, before."

Elise sipped her iced tea and considered her friend as if she were crazy. "Well, I have been—twice—and I don't like it one bit. Mama says no man is better than a bad man, but I kind of even miss the last one."

"Last one?" Sheila reached for a roll and encouraged her to tell the story of her life.

Elise did it thoroughly, beginning with a marriage her sophomore year in college. ("I got pregnant," she confessed, blushing slightly and lowering her eyes. "I don't know how it happened . . ." She probably still doesn't, Sheila thought wryly.) Sheila had eaten two rolls by the time Elise had described two childbirths and reached her divorce ten years later, then ". . . married Bert mostly because I was lonely, Mama said. We split up last year, and I guess it was for the best. He wouldn't get a job, and he wrecked my car, and Mama thought he was dealing drugs. But I never saw any signs of it," she added loyally.

She wouldn't, of course.

The waiter set salads before them. Sheila gave him a grateful smile. She was hungry enough to eat that wooden horse.

Elise didn't seem to notice the salads were there. "I don't like being single," she said, sighing. "I miss having somebody to do things with and talk to, you know?"

Sheila didn't know. Tyler Travis had been famed for his diplomacy and public charm, not for the time he spent with his wife. She started her salad and changed the subject. "How old are your children now?"

"Jennifer's nineteen and Robby's sixteen." Proudly she handed over school pictures of a petite girl and a thin, gawky boy. "They're with their dad this weekend, so I have some time to myself. But I miss them like the dickens. I get scared somebody will break in or something."

Which of those fragile children did Elise expect to tackle burglars? But Sheila could share Elise's fears, being cursed herself with an unconquerable fear of the dark.

Tucking the pictures back into her wallet, Elise inquired dutifully, "Do you have children?"

"Not unless you count Aunt Mary."

As she had hoped, Elise was diverted. "She's still alive?"

"Lively as ever, living in the same building."

"Didn't it become condominiums? Her penthouse must have cost a fortune!" Sheila didn't explain that Aunt Mary had always owned the expensive old building, had turned it into condominiums to (as she put it) "realize the whole investment in my lifetime."

"Are you living with her again?" Elise asked.

"Heaven forbid! I'm too old to want somebody running my life, and Aunt Mary is too used to running everything around her not to try. I've taken an apartment in Peachtree Corners. Where are you?"

By the time Elise had told where she lived, how far she drove each way to work, how long her children had to be alone each afternoon, and how many things were broken in her house, Sheila had almost finished her salad. Elise had not yet begun hers.

"Just wait," Elise predicted gloomily. "You won't be so glad to be single when everything falls apart."

"I have an apartment," Sheila reminded her. "Now tell me about your work at Galaxia."

"There isn't much to tell." Elise cut her salad into dime-sized pieces, then set down her fork. "I animate cartoons, do artwork to promote films, things like that. I'll work on the new television series, too, if it ever happens. But . . . I wouldn't say this to anybody else, Sheila, but I wonder sometimes if the guys are dragging their feet on purpose. Just to annoy Dean!" She looked properly shocked at her own idea.

Sheila didn't really care, but thought Mr. Hashimoto

might like to know about any problems at Galaxia. "What's going on?"

"We can't settle on something to connect the shows together. Every time I think we're going to, Craig gets another idea."

"Like what?"

"Oh, one time it was old people in rocking chairs talking. I drew a backdrop sketch and Veronica wrote a script, but by then Craig had gotten excited about Dean having a special guest each week. So Veronica spent several days researching old people who are experts in different fields and I drew another background. Then he decided Dean should jaunt around the country, doing shows out of a camper. Dean hated that idea. Said he's just bought a house, and has no intention of leaving it."

"So what's Craig's latest idea?"

Elise's eyes widened, astonished. "How did you know? He just came up with that juggler Tuesday." She shook her head in dismay. "Some of us are getting really tired of the whole idea."

The waiter hovered to remove their plates. Elise, with a stricken look, began to wolf down her salad. Sheila waved away the waiter. "We're in no hurry."

He grinned. "It's okay. She comes in here a lot."

While Elise ate, Sheila let her eyes roam the room. Most tables had small red chairs, but a few of the larger ones sported armchairs with high backs. She was surprised to see, in a distant corner at one of the larger tables, Dean Anderson and his children.

Finally Elise's salad plate was as clean as that of a child promised dessert. Her eyes met Sheila's, more puzzled than worried. "I've been thinking over what you said. Do you *really* think Craig or Jonah would block Dean on purpose?"

As Sheila recalled, it was Elise's own idea, and she was tiring of Galaxia's affairs. She was tempted to bring the conversation to a swift close by shaking her head and saying firmly, "Of course not." Curiosity won instead. "Why should they?"

"Because they think they should be in charge, of course. Craig was furious when they hired Dean as executive producer instead of just as narrator. He ranted for days about knowing more about television writing than Dean does. He kept saying 'No reporter ever knew beans—except he didn't say beans—about writing.' Then Jonah—well, the series was his idea in the first place, and he's had a lot more production experience than Dean has. He's upset, too, about the money thing."

"The money thing?" Would Sheila spend the entire meal feeding Elise one-line prompts to elicit information about Galaxia's internal affairs? Probably. Elise seemed to need to talk about it.

"You may not know him, but Jonah Baker is famous for making documentaries on poverty in America. Homeless people, welfare mothers, that kind of thing. What he had in mind for this series was something to provide practical assistance for elderly people living on limited incomes."

Sheila suspected that was precisely what Jonah had intended. Those phrases could never have originated in Elise's brain.

Elise herself thought they needed some explaining. "He wanted to tell poor old people how to stretch dollars and where to go for help if they need it."

Sheila gave a fleeting thought to how her active, retired parents and aunt would respond if Elise called them "old people" to their faces. Her dad and mom would be tactful about it, of course, and laugh later. But Aunt Mary? She hid a smile behind her napkin.

Elise was too involved in what she was saying to notice. "Dean says most old people in the United States don't want to watch shows about being poor, even poor ones. He said we need a more even spread. But Jonah—well, he seems easygoing, but he likes to get his own way. I've seen him get awfully mad—" She broke off as the waiter whisked away her salad plate and set down a plate of coconut shrimp.

Sheila regarded it with envy. "That looks delicious!"

"I hope so," Elise said doubtfully. "I never can decide what to order, and this came out mo."

"Mo?"

"You know, eenie, meenie, miney, mo." She took a hesitant bite. "I don't even like shrimp."

"Shall we swap?" Sheila, who liked shrimp above all other foods, had only ordered veal piccata because she'd had shrimp for lunch. She started to raise her plate.

Elise shook her head. "I make my kids eat things they don't like all the time. I guess I ought to do it sometimes, too."

She started eating shrimp stoically. Sheila could have wept.

Across the room, Bayard Anderson also looked close to tears. Her face flushed and angry, she pushed back her chair and stood. Her cry rang through the crowded room.

"I hate you for doing that! I absolutely *hate* you!"

She flung her napkin onto the table and glared at her astonished father. Her voice was clear, and carried. "You think you're Mister Nice Guy, don't you? But you never think about how other people feel or what they think. You just go on planning their lives and expecting them to be grateful. Well, I'm not grateful. I hate you!"

She jerked up her napkin and swiped her nose, then turned to leave, tossing a parting remark over one shoulder. "One day somebody is going to kill you. It may be *me!*"

5

Bayard stomped out without looking back. Dean rose and followed her with his eyes while Neal half stood and half sat, uncertain and miserable. Finally he spoke to his father, who nodded. Neal hurried after his sister.

Dean watched him go, his face bleak. As his eyes moved from the door he gave his audience an apologetic grin and a shrug. Sheila gave him a smile she hoped conveyed sympathy. It must have, for he rose and came to their table.

"Would you ladies join me? My table is larger than yours, and I don't feel like eating alone."

When they were settled, he sank heavily into his chair.

"Kids can be so mean!" Elise declared sympathetically. "I've got two, and they can say the cruelest things."

Dean gave a bark of agreement. "And it doesn't get any easier. You think if you can just get them through adolescence you'll have it made. Then they start to drive. You tell yourself, 'When they go to college, my job is over.' So they get out of college and . . ." He wiped one hand across his forehead. "Here she is, in Atlanta on vacation. I invite her to dinner. Two colleagues, she says, not Daddy's little girl. I say 'Fine!' So what happens? She throws this little scene!" He looked genuinely nonplused.

"Want to talk about it?" Elise propped her chin on one palm.

Sheila shuddered. In her book, listening to parents rant about their children rated right up there with getting a root canal.

Dean, however, needed to talk. "I've blown it," he admitted, "and all I did was try to help."

"What did you do?" Elise prodded.

"Nothing much—just put in a good word for the kid. That's all. She graduated from Vassar a year ago and wanted to break into television. Without saying a word to me she sashays into the national offices and applies as a reporter. How the hell did she expect to get a job with a national network just like that?" He snapped his fingers. "The gal in Personnel calls me. 'Will she do a good job for us?' she asks. How should I know? The only writing I'd ever read of hers were letters, generally elaborating on one main theme: send money. But like any good daddy I say, 'Sure. If she doesn't just let me know.' Was that so terrible?"

"Has she kept the job?" Sheila asked.

Dean nodded. "Sure. She's getting the hang of it." Pride tinged the frustration in his voice. "But now somebody's told her she only got the job because of me, and she's livid because she didn't do it all 'on her own.' " His hands sketched the quotes and he looked from one to the other for support. "I've spent forty years busting my gut in this business. Why shouldn't they ask me?"

He picked up the drink the waiter had set before him and drained it, signaling for another. "Fill me up, Charles."

Dean had had two drinks that Sheila had seen, and he'd carried a glass both times she'd seen him at the party. Now his face was flushed, and perspiration beaded his forehead.

She put a hand on his arm. "The coffee here is great."

He gave her a long stare, then a boyish grin twisted one side of his mouth. "Right. No reason to tie one on because of a fool daughter. Make that coffee, please, Charles. Strong and black."

As he tucked into his steak, Sheila could almost see him shifting roles, from Irate Father to Charming Male Companion.

That ability to adjust to situations quickly and publicly had always been one of Dean Anderson's greatest assets. When life handed him a lemon in the form of a recalcitrant interviewee, or a story that didn't break the way he wanted it, Dean made lemonade—in front of millions of viewers. When guards denied him admission to a Chinese communal farm, for instance, after he had announced for weeks that it would be part of his "Inside China Special," he didn't throw a tantrum. He interviewed strangers on the street in his pidgin Chinese and started a love affair with the Chinese people that would eventually grant him access almost anywhere he wanted to go.

"How did you get started as a reporter?" she asked, partly to take his mind off his worries and mostly because she had never heard the legendary story from the man himself.

He reeled it off as if reading from a well-known script. "I got into television by accident," he said through a mouthful of potato. "I got out of Georgia with a degree in journalism, planning to become another Henry Grady, edit a major southern newspaper. Then Korea came along. I went out as a GI with an assignment to cover it for my hometown paper. One day a television reporter was making a story on the front lines. He got shot right in front of the camera. Without thinking, I dashed in and grabbed the mike, started talking off the top of my head, trying to give the cameras something to do besides film the man being carried off the field. The next thing I knew, I had a contract and a camera crew."

Sheila knew the rest. After Korea, for the next thirty-five years, Dean took his cameras "where duty called or danger"—recording from front lines and disasters, shoving that famous streak of silver blond hair off his forehead and squinting pale blue eyes into the sun. He risked his life to report on wars, riots, earthquakes and coups, and gracefully aged from everybody's big brother to everybody's favorite uncle—someone you could count on to be brave, honest, warm and genuine.

Only once had he settled down—here in Atlanta for a few years, to work at WSB. He had made headlines by marrying the lovely debutante, Laura Bayard, years younger than he and the daughter of a local real estate developer. They whirled with Atlanta's social scene until Dean got the itch to travel again. After that, Laura had remained in Atlanta while Dean worked around the world.

Ten years ago Laura had divorced him, saying in several national interviews, "I can no longer tolerate being married to a saint who manages to be there for everybody except his family." Sheila had felt a deep kinship for the woman.

Dean had responded—on the air and like a gentleman. It was true, he had admitted. It was hard to be in his line of work and give enough to the family he deeply loved. Shoving the hair off his forehead so viewers could see tears in his eyes, he recalled why he'd had to be away for the births of both their children. Now, Laura's own pain, he said (tears spilling onto his cheeks), hurt him worse than his own. He hoped the alimony he had had instructed his lawyers to pay her (the amount slipped out by accident, and it was considerable), so that she could remain at home with the kids while they grew up, would make life a little easier for her, but he wished he knew how to show her how much he cared . . .

He left the studios, Sheila recalled, and went straight to the airport to cover the latest Middle East crisis with his usual accuracy and charm.

He had been talking all this time. She wasn't certain if he and Elise were still talking about Bayard, or someone else.

"She is going to have to learn to take care of her own life," he said, setting his coffee cup into its saucer with a firm click. "I'm making some changes in mine." He raised his coffee cup. "To the uncomplicated life."

Sheila raised her cup, wondering whose life he meant.

Charles hovered to invite them to the dessert bar. Dean waved him away. "Just bring that special French fried ice cream for everybody and bring me these girls' tickets."

Sheila gritted her teeth and managed to smile.

Elise greeted her ice cream with obvious ambivalence. Chin on palm, she asked enviously, "You can still eat anything you want and stay thin as a rail, can't you?"

Dean shook his head. "Never was thin in my life."

"I meant Sheila."

If Elise didn't notice his chagrin, Sheila did. "You look fine," she assured him. "Steady work must agree with you."

Elise looked up from her ice cream, which was sliding around on her plate. "Let's don't talk about work, okay? But I heard what you're doing for Woody, Dean, and I think it's beautiful."

Dean waved away the compliment. "Beautiful? Hell, it was just fair. The man was a great photographer. Shame he had to get blown up. I didn't recognize him, of course—he didn't have glasses then, and he's older. Everybody's older."

Elise explained to Sheila. "Woody, one of our custodians—"

Sheila nodded. "I tripped over him coming in today."

"Well, if you didn't notice, he's a bit slow. He used to be a photographer . . ."

"A great one," Dean repeated.

Elise nodded. "Sure. And he and Dean were doing a story together out in Vietnam when the Jeep they were in was blown up."

Dean shook his head. "No, it was a whole truck, plumb full of reporters, camera crews and God only knows who else. Woody and I weren't working together—he was with some newspapermen and I was with a film crew. We just happened to be traveling together when the truck went up—and most of the fellows with it."

"So how did you get Woody's camera? I never did hear." Elise chased her ice cream around the plate with her spoon.

"Damned if I know. I was thrown out of the truck and must have gone around picking up stuff—cameras, bags, even a canteen. You do strange things in shock, they tell me. So I hung them around my neck without realizing my left shoulder had gotten busted, until the pain got to me and I passed out. I was flown to a hospital in Hawaii, and all the stuff I had collected was sent with me. When I got well, I had a hell of a time trying to find out who belonged to what. Some of the fellows even accused me of stealing their equipment!" He shook his head in amazement at the memory. "It was uphill work all the way. So many guys were dead, you see, and some of the stuff wasn't labeled."

He paused to swallow a large bite of ice cream. "So what I did with the ones I couldn't identify was, I had the film developed to see what was in it. Woody's now, it was special." He forgot his dessert in his excitement. "All these pictures, none of them what you'd expect. No battle scenes, or wounded soldiers. These pictures were priceless." He spooned ice cream and repeated himself. "Priceless. I put them together in a book—*Visions of Vietnam.* Maybe you've seen it."

Sheila nodded. "I treasure my copy." It had won Dean several awards, she recalled. "You dedicated it to 'The Unknown Photographer,' didn't you? That was Woody?" She was astonished.

"Sure was. I couldn't find out who the guy was before. Never did know, until this week. I gave him credit the only way I knew how. But you know, the Lord provides. On Wednesday—yesterday—I called Jonah Baker from Seattle and he said, 'I've found your Unknown Photographer.' He'd driven Woody home from work Tuesday night, and Woody's daughter showed him several albums of other pictures Woody had taken—gorgeous things, he says, and no question they were taken by the same man. Jonah would know. So I called the publisher right away and arranged for new printings to carry his name and an explanation."

"You're printing special copies for Woody's family—isn't that right?" Elise's eyes were wide with admiration.

She couldn't have swelled Dean's ego better with hot air, Sheila decided. He beamed under the praise, even though he dismissed her words with a gruff "He deserves it. He was a genius with a camera."

"Poor Woody," Elise mused while Dean drained his coffee and held out his cup for more. "He can't see very well, and he has some brain damage. But the worst part is, his hands tremble too much to hold a camera steady." She considered her own valuable hands.

"He seemed quite a fan of yours, Dean," Sheila volunteered. "He said you'd invited him in to the reception for a Coke."

Dean waved away the implied compliment. "It makes me mad when people leave out the little people of the world—secretaries, custodians. They work as hard as the rest of us, and deserve to get the same perks." He gave Charles a wave of thanks for removing the plates.

"Speaking of little people," Sheila said, "your son seemed worked up about something this afternoon."

He leaned forward confidentially on his elbows. "Neal's a bit of a namby-pamby, I'm afraid. To be expected, of course, given his mother, and the fact that I've been everywhere but home while he was growing up. Laura takes everything too seriously. She's a real worrywart, especially where Neal is concerned."

"It's hard to be the only parent!" Elise retorted, indignant.

"Sure, but I'm willing to be a parent, too, if she'll let me. Take this college thing, for instance. Why send him to some piddly school where he'll get a degree in Cutting Out Paper Doilies, when he could go to Georgia and get a fine education? My brother has a chain of restaurants around Athens and owns several condominiums. He'll set Neal up, watch over him, make sure he studies. But no. Laura wants him sent off to God-knows-where, away from everybody, to study French. French!" He spat it out like it was an obscenity. "What can he do with a degree in French?"

Elise had no concept of the rhetorical question. "Well, he could teach it, or be a translator, I guess. Or he could go to France to work . . ." She stopped as Sheila put a hand on her arm.

"I think Dean has other concerns about the school."

He snorted. "I sure do. For one, they don't even have a football team."

Aha, Sheila thought. At last, his primary objection. Neal would never be a quarterback like his father once was, but at Georgia he could attend the game his father showed up annually to announce. Did Dean harbor dreams of "my son here in the press box with me"?

She couldn't ask, of course, and suddenly it was unimportant. Dean's attention was fixed on the door. Sheila had to turn in her chair to follow his gaze.

At first she was puzzled. All she saw was a tall heavyset man with skin like polished ebony, his eyes closed to slits that scanned the crowd. He was too far away for her to see him clearly, but he exuded the aura of a man who has spent the past hours with his barber, manicurist and tailor. His navy suit was exquisitely cut and his tie both reserved and dashing. As he adjusted it, diamonds flashed from his cuffs and his pinky finger.

Behind him stood two shorter men, dressed in perfectly respectable dark suits and ties. Atlanta's black community had boasted wealthy men for decades, so why did the word "bodyguards" flash into Sheila's mind? These three could be insurance executives for all she knew.

"Don't look now," Dean murmured, pulling his coffee to the center of his place and cupping it with both hands, "but Darius Dudwell, known in his youth as Darius the Dude, just made an entrance. Looks like I get to deal with all my problems today."

"Why is he your problem?" Sheila asked.

"Because twenty years ago, when I was a reporter for WSB, I did a special on organized crime that turned up the evidence to send him away for thirty years. He served sixteen and got out of the Atlanta federal pen today on parole."

As if aware that they were speaking of him, Darius's eyes turned to their table. As they hovered there, Sheila trembled in spite of herself. Those eyes contained no expression whatsoever.

He inclined his head in gracious greeting and waved aside the maître d', who was about to offer him a seat. "I see a friend," he said in a deep cultured voice that filled the restaurant.

With the tread of a conquering hero he crossed the floor to their table and towered above them. "Hello, Mr. Anderson."

"Hello, Darius. I heard you got out today."

"I sure did," Darius agreed pleasantly, "and I plan to stay that way. Any objections?" The men with him moved only a quarter of an inch, but Sheila felt goose bumps rising. She wished Elise hadn't gasped. It distracted Mr. Dudwell's companions' attention to both women. Darius, however, had taken no notice of them.

"None at all." Dean smiled blandly.

"What brings you back to Atlanta?" Darius inquired, as if asking a social question. Nobody except those around Dean's table would have guessed this was anything other than a pleasant chance meeting. But Sheila braced herself, wondering if she was about to see her host gunned down.

Elise must have been having the same thoughts. She was gulping tea, regarding Darius with eyes wide with fear. Dean, on the other hand, seemed perfectly at ease. "I'm working for Encyclopedia Galaxia for a couple of years, doing a television series for senior citizens."

"That's nice. We're all getting up there." Darius smiled, revealing a gold crown, and rubbed one palm over his close-cut hair. It was just beginning to gray. The smile, however, did not reach his eyes, which were as hooded and guarded as a cobra's.

He gave the ladies a nod, then spoke—softly, but sounding each word. "I'll make you a deal, Anderson. You stay out of my road and I'll stay out of yours."

"It's a deal." Dean put out a hand.

Darius acknowledged it only by another nod. Then, turning to his friends, he spoke in a voice meant to be heard. "I don't think I'm hungry right now. Let's go." He swept out the front door like a king, retinue in train.

6

On Monday afternoon just before four o'clock, Woody Robles found Wylene Fowler in the mailroom. His face was ashen and his hands shook more than usual. "Oh, Miss Fowler, Miss Fowler! It's awful, just awful! Dean's dead!"

Wylene was at her best in an emergency. Calmly she told the mailroom clerk she would finish her business later. With one arm at Woody's elbow to provide support (he had shrunk like a very old man) she steered him toward the elevator and got him on it. The door closed before she asked, "What happened? And how do you know?"

"I found him." Woody seemed close to tears. "I went to check on his light. It's been flickering. Oh, Miss Fowler, he was just lying there, shot!"

"Shot?"

Woody nodded, but by now his teeth were chattering too much to answer more questions. Wylene decided to look the situation over for herself before bothering the security guards. Maybe Dean was merely hurt.

Woody refused to accompany her into Dean's office. She left him collapsed into a wing chair in the oval foyer, head in his hands.

She approached the office door cautiously, half expecting Dean to look up and bark, "What do you want?" He had been so cruel since he'd come back from California.

In spike heels she tiptoed into his office, then hurried forward a couple of steps and stopped. One look convinced her. Dean Anderson was dead.

He was sprawled in his chair, a hole in his chest. His blank eyes stared at the ceiling. One hand hung limply over the side of his chair, and beneath it lay a black gun.

Wylene put one hand to the bookshelf to steady herself. As she swallowed down a hot lump that had risen from her stomach, a movement at the window caught her attention— a pigeon, peering in.

"Shoo!" She flapped her hands. It flew away with a whir of wings.

She tiptoed across the carpet and looked down at the gun. She knew little about them, but enough to tell Woody what had happened.

"He's shot himself," she called.

"Shot himself?" Woody sounded bewildered. "How do you know?"

She went to the door. "Don't ask questions, just go up to eleven and get the others. They're in the conference room. I'll call security, and they can call the police."

Not until he was safely away did she permit herself a grim smile of satisfaction.

7

Sheila was beginning to feel at home in her job. She had mastered the layout of Hosokawa's new four-story complex in suburban Gwinnett County. She could greet by name most of those she met on the top floor. She liked the view from her window—a wide lawn dotted with clumps of pansies, a small lake which ducks lazily circled, and a smattering of young maples just turning a brazen gold before flinging off all their leaves to stand bare before the winter sky. Best of all, at lunch she had found a store that carried her favorite Nicaraguan coffee. Masako had been more than willing to brew and share a pot.

About four o'clock Sheila was enjoying her third cup of coffee and reading annual reports to get a grasp of Hosokawa's multifaceted empire. She scarcely noticed the phone's trill in the outer office until Masako glided into her office and set a pink memo on her desk. *Elise White.* Sheila nodded and reached for the phone.

"Sheila? Is that you?" Sheila would never have recognized the voice. It was a full octave higher and much faster than Elise's usual southern drawl. "I saw your card on Dean's desk, and thought you'd want to know. Isn't it awful?"

"What?"

"Dean! Oh, Sheila, I don't know what to do!"

Sheila took a deep breath. She hoped it might inspire

Elise to do the same. "Calm down and tell me what's the matter."

"He's dead! That's what's the matter! He's killed himself!" The last sentence was wailed rather than spoken. Elise's teeth chattered across the wires. "Woody found him." She sounded close to hysterics. Sheila felt like she had her shoulder to a bulging dam.

"Elise, is anybody there with you?" She spoke sharply, the only slap she could administer at this distance.

Elise sniffed and gulped. "Everybody is here . . . somewhere." Sheila could picture her looking about helplessly. "They've called the police, but they haven't come yet."

"What happened?"

"Well, we were in a staff meeting upstairs, and Woody came up to get us. Wylene sent him."

"I meant, what happened to Dean? How did he die?"

"I told you!" Elise's voice was shrill. "He killed himself. In his office. Shot himself through the heart. Sheila, he looks terrible!"

Sheila could feel bleakness creeping in around her own edges, but obeyed other instincts first. "You've been in his office?"

Elise gulped again. "I told you," she repeated. "That's when I saw your card. Woody came to get us, and we all went in."

"Is anybody in there now? That office should be closed until the police arrive."

"That's what Jonah said. He's guarding the door."

Good for Jonah. Sheila was glad somebody on the staff could think clearly under stress.

"Do you know when it happened?"

"I took him a memo right after lunch, and he seemed fine. He even told me he'd enjoyed dinner Thursday and was looking forward to seeing you again. How could he do it? How could he?" This time her sobs made further conversation impossible.

"Elise," Sheila commanded, "go to somebody else's office. You shouldn't be alone. Do you hear me? Go find some-body to be with. And call me again if you need to."

She hung up and pushed back her chair. With a thought-ful expression she carried her coffee to the window, where she gazed at the maples without really seeing them.

Poor Dean, so full of life and charm, never hurting some-one else except unintentionally, never understanding other people at all. What could have driven him to this? Whom had he seen—or spoken to—between the time he talked to Elise and the time he pulled the trigger?

She crossed to her desk and had almost written herself a note to check on that when she caught herself. This wasn't her case! It was in the hands of the Atlanta police.

She stretched her arms high above her head, gave the maples one moment's glance and returned to her desk. If she had no plans to solve the mystery of Dean's death, she could at least pray for his soul.

Thirty minutes later her phone rang again. The voice on the other end was deep and full of gravel, as if from half a century of secret smoking. "Sheila? Didn't you say you had dinner with Dean Anderson last week? He's dead."

"I know, Aunt Mary. I just had a call from Elise. But how on earth did you know?"

"Mildred heard it on the radio. He was well known, you know."

Sheila smiled at the typically Southern understatement. "I know. It's sad. He was a special man."

"What are you going to do about it?"

"Me?" Sheila raised her brows even if her aunt couldn't see. "Nothing. It's not as if he was a personal friend. Besides, what can one do about suicide?"

"Pshaw." Nobody could put as much expression into a "pshaw" as Aunt Mary. "Dean Anderson wouldn't kill himself. Didn't he have a date with you on Wednesday?"

"In spite of my considerable charm, Aunt Mary, I don't think a date with me would keep a person in despair from killing himself." Only secretly would she admit that the same point was bothering her. Was that wisdom—or only pride?

Pride. She knew, as soon as Aunt Mary said matter-of-factly, "Of course not, dear."

Aunt Mary went on. "But it's an indication that Dean was making future plans. I think you should let the police know that, and give them what help you can. After all, you know the people at Galaxia."

"I only met a couple of them," Sheila protested, "and spent very little time with any of them except Elise. You don't think Elise killed him, do you? Or drove him to kill himself?"

"Elise has nearly driven me to kill *her* occasionally, but no, she could never commit a murder without telling the next fifty people she met. Sheila, you should at least offer—"

Sheila interrupted without a qualm. "Aunt Mary, I have no intention of offering anything. I work for Hosokawa, not Galaxia, and I have work to do here. So if you'll excuse me . . ."

Aunt Mary sighed the sigh of the deeply disappointed. "Very well, dear. I'm glad you had the news."

Sheila hung up with a little disquiet. It was unlike Aunt Mary to give up so easily. Nevertheless, in a very few minutes she was buried in a description of automobile production, without a thought for her aunt.

S umanai ga . . ."

She looked up in surprise at the greeting, stood and bowed. "Ah, Hashimoto-san. *Nan desko ka?*" It was more than a polite or rhetorical question. She genuinely wondered what could bring the president of Hosokawa to her office this afternoon.

He moved to one of her gray suede guest chairs, crossed his legs without harming the razor-sharp crease in his dark trousers, and inclined his head. "You are happy here?" he asked in Japanese. "You have everything you need?"

"Oh, yes," she replied. "All is well, and I am beginning to get a sense of the work."

This small formal man commanded respect from many people in high places. In addition to respecting him, Sheila genuinely liked him. She waited quietly for what he had to say, wondering why he had sought her instead of sending for her.

"Yokoyama-san sends his greetings and many thanks for your kindness in showing them the city last week. He said his firm will be delighted to do business with us. I am grateful to you as well." He gave her a small nod of approval.

She bowed with a twinkle. "And I am grateful to you for stressing my executive position at Hosokawa."

He did not smile, but a gleam of amusement lit his dark eyes for a moment. "I thought that might be wise. Yokoyama-san has quite a reputation with women." He paused, and she was lulled for an instant into thinking he had only come to express his gratitude.

He regarded her gravely. "You enjoyed the reception last week at Galaxia? Discovered old friends there?"

She nodded, suddenly wary.

"I have had a telephone call. Dean Anderson, the television celebrity, has shot himself. You were friends, I believe?"

"I knew him slightly." She hoped he noticed her stress on the last word.

If so, he gave no sign. "It occurs to me that this may be a very delicate matter for both Galaxia and Hosokawa. We will need to work closely with the police to see that nothing soils the honor of either company. I think perhaps we should have someone—" He paused, then said in careful English, "on the spot."

She gave him a look of rebuke. There was a perfectly good Japanese idiom for the same thing, and he didn't need to pretend he had just learned that one in English. Surely he had run into it once or twice while getting his Ph.D. in economics from Harvard.

"What do you want from me?" she asked bluntly.

His eyes flickered at her quickness. "Ah! That is the question I have been asking myself these past ten minutes. Do I merely want you to go to Galaxia for a few days as the representative of Hosokawa? You could prepare news releases to explain to this country and my own how this much loved man came to kill himself on the premises of our subsidiary. Or do I want you to assist the police with their inquiries, as you have done in the past?"

Her eyes narrowed. "Who told you about that?"

He raised one shoulder in a small shrug. "It is common knowledge among certain sectors of Tokyo. When police needed an insider to help solve the crime of missing pearls at the embassy, or wanted to discover why one American businessman shot another, they asked Tyler Travis's wife to 'assist them.' " He sketched small quotes with his hands.

Sheila sighed. "That was only because I knew the people involved, Hashimoto-san. I know no one at Galaxia except one old school friend. And I cannot write news releases as well as half a dozen other people on your staff. Most important, I cannot think of a single way I could assist the very capable Atlanta police, who by this time surely have everything well under control."

"Ah, so." He seemed to give the matter some thought. "Very well, perhaps you will not need to stay several days. Perhaps only a day or two will do. But there are, ah, complications. Yes, complications. I believe it will be better if you go for a few days. If you can find out why he has done this terrible thing and, shall we say, gently steer the police toward the answer as quickly as possible . . ."

"Is that an order?"

He stood. "Let us say, rather, an assignment. You should perhaps go now, to be there from the beginning. I will arrange with Mr. Dekker for you to have an office there.

She sighed. "Very well. If you insist. But I don't think there is a single thing I can do . . ."

He waved her objections aside. "For the good of the company, yes?"

She bowed, inwardly seething.

As he turned to go, he took from his pocket a small pink telephone memo slip. He wadded it and tossed it carelessly into her wastebasket. "Swish," he said, with a rare smile.

She waited until he was down the corridor. Then, as he had intended her to do, she retrieved the slip.

It read, as she had expected, *Mary Beaufort.*

8

It was past five when Sheila pulled out of Hosokawa's parking lot and headed toward I-85.

When she'd come to Atlanta, her father had suggested she trade her small red car for a sleek black Maxima, better suited to Atlanta's sprawl. Normally she would have enjoyed driving the twenty-five miles between Hosokawa and Galaxia, especially on such a glorious day. Today, however, she was heading southwest at sundown, directly into the maelstrom of Atlanta's afternoon traffic. Furthermore, she was furious.

She knew she was clutching the wheel too tightly, was squinting as much from anger as from the setting sun. She put on sunglasses, rolled down the window and breathed deeply. But not even the spicy autumn air relieved her mood. She reminded herself she was going against traffic. It didn't help. A courteous driver slowed to let her into the stream of homebound cars, as was Atlanta custom. She was momentarily grateful, then remembered—*that driver* was probably headed home. She turned the radio to the public station and let "All Things Considered" waft out her window to inform the minds of other travelers. There was nothing on the news to improve her own thoughts.

As she approached the interstate ramp, she was tempted

to head northeast, toward Lake Lanier. It was an incredibly lovely day. The trees had matured into richer golds, reds and oranges over the hot weekend. She could explore one of the logging roads that surrounded the lake, shuffle through autumn's first fallen leaves and forget all about Dean Anderson and Encyclopedia Galaxia.

Reluctantly she turned right and headed downtown, speaking her thoughts aloud. "You needn't think you'll get away with this. Calling Hashimoto like I was a second grader needing instructions from home. Do you remember how hard I looked for an apartment ten minutes from my office? Now, thanks to you, I get to drive forty minutes each way through Atlanta traffic for heaven only knows how many days, to do something I don't want to do anyway. I know who's responsible. Don't think I don't."

She was not letting off steam, but rehearsing for a later confrontation with a tiny silver-haired woman who was probably sitting at this moment with her feet up, reading a mystery, looking for what she blithely called "a little excitement in my life."

"If you think I'm going to tell you one blessed thing about this case, think again," Sheila warned her in absentia. A little comforted, she switched to the mellow strains of WPCH and let herself enjoy the fast pace of Atlanta in-bound traffic. Too soon, however, it was time to exit and brave bumper-to-bumper cars.

Galaxia might have private parking near the office, but Sheila had no idea where. She parked where she had last Thursday, in an expensive garage, and scraped the Maxima against a blue concrete pillar getting into a too small space. "Chalk up one more for you, Aunt Mary," she muttered, running her finger along a tiny scratch.

A burly policewoman guarded Galaxia's entrance, impartially turning away both gawkers and reporters who beleaguered the building from every network and newspaper. The officer was also besieged by a short young woman with tousled blond hair and tears streaming down her cheeks.

"I'm his daughter!" she was insisting as Sheila arrived,

for what was obviously not the first time. Cameras rolled and pens scratched all around her. Her father's daughter, she turned straight toward the nearest television camera.

A reporter—perhaps also a friend—signaled the camera to zoom in. "Bay, when did you hear about this?"

She sniffled and brushed the hair off her forehead in a familiar gesture. "I was on my way to the airport in a cab. I made the driver turn right around, of course, but now *she* won't let me in."

"Let her in! Let her in!" The chant was begun by those nearest, and swelled back through the crowd until some of those chanting surely had no idea what it was all about.

The policewoman stood firm. "I have no authorization to admit you. Sorry."

The reporter asked, "When did you see your daddy last?"

"Yesterday. We drove down to Calloway Gardens."

Someone called from the back. "Was your father planning to marry Raven Hillis?"

Bayard turned and glared. "That's none of anybody's business anymore, is it?" The television cameras loved it. Realizing that they were no longer friendly, Bayard took a step backward. They followed. Sheila felt an instant of pity for her.

Bayard was only a fledgling reporter, after all, unaccustomed to being harassed herself. She swallowed hard and turned, raised one arm as if she would strike the policewoman with her fist. "I have to go in. Can't you see? I just have to!" Sheila was reminded of a small lion cub she'd once seen teased by children at a zoo. Its eyes had held the same defiance— and the same fear.

She stepped up and touched the young woman's arm. "Bayard?"

Bayard turned, confused. Her tear-reddened eyes took in Sheila's gray suit, yellow blouse and peacock paisley scarf, then met the older woman's eyes without recognition. "Do I know you? Are you another reporter?" She sniffled, fumbled in the sagging pocket of what seemed to be her only jacket for a tissue that wasn't there. Sheila supplied one.

"Thanks." Bayard sniffled again.

"I met you Thursday at the Galaxia reception. With your dad. I'm Sheila Travis." Sheila fed it to her in bite-size sentences, waiting for recognition to dawn. The reporters crowded close to hear every word.

"Aren't you Tyler Travis's widow?" one called.

Sheila nodded and faced the cameras. "And I'm currently working for Hosokawa International, who owns Galaxia. I've come to say how sorry we are that this has happened, and to offer condolences to the family."

She hoped Mr. Hashimoto and Aunt Mary caught the six o'clock news. That ought to give them a clear picture of her intentions.

She turned to the officer. "Mr. Dekker is expecting me."

The officer eyed her warily. "You got a driver's license?" She perused Sheila's temporary license, unimpressed. "You don't have anything with a picture?"

"I'm afraid not. May I go in now?" At last Aunt Mary came in handy. From her Sheila had learned that quelling tone.

The officer stepped back without another word and jerked her head toward the brass doors.

As Sheila started up the shallow marble steps, Bayard Anderson grabbed her arm. "Please, may I go in with you? May I?"

Sheila hesitated, then nodded. She couldn't leave her standing there with all those reporters around. "It's all right," she told the officer. "I'll be responsible for her."

"Me, too," called one cheeky reporter. "Be responsible for me, too."

She dismissed him with a friendly wave.

Keeping up with Bayard wouldn't be easy. Once in the foyer she bounded forward and dashed into an elevator, which would have risen alone if Sheila's long legs hadn't carried her through the closing doors in the nick of time.

"Don't do that again!" she said sharply. "If I am responsible for you, then please stay with me."

"I've got to get to Daddy." Bayard slouched against the wall and watched the lights flash at each floor. "This is *slow!*"

"You were with him yesterday?"

"Yeah." She shook her head in disbelief. "He had all sorts of plans. He . . ." She turned her face to the wall and said in a muffled voice, "If only he hadn't made plans for other people." She was talking not to Sheila, but to herself.

As soon as the doors slid open Sheila put a restraining hand on her arm. "Make sure you stay with me, please."

Bayard had no intention of obeying. She shook Sheila off, shot through the door and would have darted across the foyer if she had not been held firm by a large pink hand at the end of a policeman's sleeve. An officer was standing by the elevators to prevent just this sort of intrusion.

"Hold up there." His voice was gentler than his grip. "Who're you looking for?"

"I'm Dean Anderson's daughter." She pulled away. "Let me see him!"

"You sit in one of these chairs and let me ask Lieutenant Green about that." He guided her by the shoulder to a wing chair in the center of the foyer and waited to be sure she'd stay in it before he turned to Sheila. "And you are . . . ?"

The face beneath his mop of auburn curls was very young. It was also oddly pale. Sheila wondered if this was his first murder case—or one which, for some reason, he was taking personally. She realized he was still waiting for Sheila to identify herself.

"I'm Sheila Travis, from Hosokawa International, looking for Elton Dekker."

"Mr. Dekker is in Mr. Anderson's office with Lieutenant Green. Why don't you join your friend and let me tell them that you two ladies are here?" He crossed the foyer toward

Dean's door. He was a well-built policeman with kind, but worried, eyes.

Bayard shoved her chair so that it faced her father's door, obviously in no mood for conversation. Sheila took a seat and looked about her.

By now the staff of Galaxia was used to the antique splendor of their workaday surroundings. Sheila, however, seeing them for the first time, was impressed. Instead of the plum carpet and soft gray walls currently in vogue, Galaxia's decorators had opted to return to an earlier era. Four large pillars supporting the oval foyer were painted sky blue. The walls were papered in an Edwardian paper of blue and cream, and rose fourteen feet to a white ceiling encircled by a plaster frieze. Wing chairs flanked a large curved receptionist's desk, while around the walls, silk ficus trees were reflected in Oriental mirrors hung over mahogany drop-leaf tables.

"The unusual floral carpet is woven from a 1910 pattern."

She jumped as Porter spoke softly beside her chair. He was kneeling, his mouth level with her ear. Before she could reply, he laid a hand on her arm and continued. "Step into my office to see how clever they were about preserving the original windows while lowering most of the ceiling."

Sheila hoped Bayard could not hear his absurd remarks. Had the man no sensitivity whatsoever? "Thanks, Porter, but I need to stay here until I hear from Elton Dekker."

"Very well. But you do know, don't you, that you two look like potential martyrs?"

She saw at once what he meant. Several offices and double glass doors labeled FILM LIBRARY opened around the big oval like numbers on a clock face. From almost every door uneasy faces watched, looking very like a coliseum crowd awaiting the lions.

The silence was broken by Elise, who came out of the ladies' room and spotted her friend. "Oh, Sheila! You came! How kind!" She hurried across the foyer and nearly smothered Sheila in a hug. "Isn't it awful?" Her eyes were still red from weeping.

Sheila returned her hug. "It sure is."

Wylene Fowler came from the Film Library doors. Her lashes might be damp and the tip of her long nose pink, but she still claimed the privilege of being hostess. "Have you seen Mr. Dekker?"

"Not yet, thanks. I'm waiting to see him." Sheila wished they would all go away. She found trivial conversation hard to make with Bayard sitting, a lump of horror, just across the way.

The film librarian returned to her doorway, but her eyes asked the same question as all the others: Why are you here? Sheila had no good answer to give.

Porter stood and flicked the creases in his pants to straighten them. "If you came for a tour, they are only offered on Thursday afternoons. We could offer instead, perhaps, a cup of tea."

Elise hurried from the foyer without a word.

Sheila appreciated his attempt to lighten a grisly situation, but Bayard did not. She lurched forward in her chair and glared at him. "My father is dead, and you're offering us a cup of tea?" She sniffled, hard, and dabbed at her nose with a very soggy tissue.

Jonah Baker fetched a box from the receptionist's desk. "Here. Sorry they're almost all gone. If you need more, we'll look around for some."

Somewhere behind her, Sheila heard a woman exclaim softly, "What's he mean, all gone? That was a new box this morning!"

Jonah seemed not to hear. He bent to Bayard and touched her shoulder. "Here, have yourself a good blow."

Now that the young woman looked like a drowned rat, Sheila noticed, his shyness had vanished. Maybe the only young women Jonah knew how to relate to were females in distress.

Bayard regarded him sullenly, then pulled out a tissue and followed his orders. "Thanks."

Elise rushed back in carrying two Styrofoam cups. "Here you are! I had to guess at the sugars, so I put in two each." She handed one cup to Bayard and brought one to Sheila.

Sheila's years of embassy service stood her in good stead. "Thanks, Elise." She smiled, sipped the steaming beverage, then held the cup near her face as she swallowed to hide her grimace. It was a toss-up which she abhorred more—foam cups or sweet tea.

The officer returned, his forehead puckered as if questioning his instructions. "Mrs. Travis, Mr. Dekker says you are to go right in. Miss Anderson, Lieutenant Green will be out to speak with you shortly."

Elise gasped and started to speak, but Bay's body and voice rose in unison protest. "Why her and not me?" The officer started to shake his head (probably, Sheila thought, wondering the same thing). Bayard swept on. "I'm his daughter, and she's . . ."

Her next word was obviously going to be "nobody." Jonah stopped it by putting fingertips to her lips. "You don't want to go in there, Bayard. Not yet." He handed her her cup, and she drank as obediently as a child. Then, with a loud sniffle, she sank into her chair and glared at Sheila over the rim of her cup.

Sheila could feel the eyes of everyone in the room— some curious, Porter's gently mocking, and Elise's blue pools of horror. All were wondering why she alone was being given the dubious privilege of examining the corpse. She felt a sudden urge to jump onto the receptionist's desk and shout, "Don't blame me, blame Aunt Mary!" But who could explain why corporation presidents and an adult niece kowtowed to a tiny, elderly lady? Sheila couldn't. She didn't know either.

Feeling like a branded ghoul, she handed her cup of syrupy liquid back to Elise. "I don't think I should take this into Dean's office."

Elise handed the cup to Porter. "Do something!" she begged.

Porter moved toward the wastebasket murmuring, "Of course, darling, just any little thing I can."

Elise stamped one foot and her eyes flashed. "That's not what I meant, and you know it. I don't think Sheila should have to go in there!"

Sheila agreed. It looked, however, as if she would have to.

9

Dean's office occupied one whole corner of this floor. Two high arched windows overlooked Peachtree Street at the front. Across the way, steel girders stood stark against an apricot sky.

Two side windows were filled with palms to block a view of the neighboring building. A leather sofa and chair occupied the near end of the room, a shelf with more trophies than books covered the side wall. A massive desk was positioned so that, Sheila suspected, Dean could have swiveled to look out when he was on the phone. It was common knowledge that Dean had been partial to views of cities a-building.

She knew she was taking in all these details to avoid taking in one more: the man sprawling in the chair behind his desk.

Elton Dekker sat, pale but determined, on Dean's leather sofa while the police did their jobs. She had to give him credit. Many men she knew would have passed this task on to an unfortunate underling. When Sheila entered, he stood to greet her, then took her arm in such a grip that she wondered if he were giving or receiving comfort. Probably both.

Finally she gathered her courage and looked at the unpleasant sight at the far end of the room. It made her sick. She wished she could run howling from the room, or wake up from a nightmare.

Dean—that vigorous, delightful man—lay back in his chair with one hand dangling and his head at an uncomfortable angle, staring straight at the ceiling. But those eyes would never see again. When a uniformed officer shifted, Sheila saw the hole in Dean's shirt, surrounded by black.

"He shot himself and dropped the gun on the floor," Elton said in a low tone. "I don't know why he didn't come to me if there was something this terribly wrong."

Sheila was about to murmur words of comfort when Bayard darted through the door and flung herself toward her father with a shriek.

"Hey, miss, you can't do that." A hand the color of old chocolate reached out to hold her just before she reached Dean.

A shamefaced young officer appeared in the doorway. "I'm sorry, sir. I was speaking with one of the others and she came in before I knew it."

"It's okay, McGehee. I'll handle it. Get back to your post."

His voice was so like Bill Cosby's that Sheila was startled. But the man resembled Cosby only in voice. In build he was slight and stooped, with a fringe of salt and pepper hair around a soft-brown pate that made her think he was older than his unlined face would indicate. His eyes were the saddest she had ever seen, as if they had viewed the world and found it unbearably tragic. Because his cheeks sagged beneath them, she was reminded of a gentle basset hound in a brown tweed suit and brown and orange striped tie.

Bayard struggled against him. He held her until she grew calm, then asked, "You are the daughter of the deceased?"

"Yes!" Again Bayard pulled against him, again he held her firm.

"So you're going to want to help us, right?" His eyes compelled hers until she nodded. "Then you go out and sit in a chair by the desk until my people finish, and I'll let you have a few minutes alone with your daddy. We got a deal?"

Bayard pointed to Sheila. "Why does *she* get in?"

"She has nothing to do with you." He jutted his lower lip in and out, again holding Bayard with his eyes. "Now will

70

you do like I ask, so we can get on with our work? I'll let you in as soon as we're through. I promise."

She hesitated, then agreed, reluctantly. At the door, she took one final look toward the desk. Her eyes flickered with horror and she crumpled to the floor. "Daddy! Daddy!" she screamed between sobs.

The policeman went to the door. "McGehee? Come carry her out of here. Get her some strong tea, sweet. On the double!"

It was not McGehee, however, but Jonah Baker who came into the room and helped the sobbing Bayard out.

The policeman watched him go, then crossed the room and extended his hand to Sheila. "Mrs. Travis, I was on my way to introduce myself when we were diverted. Now that that young woman is in capable hands, let me do so. I am Lieutenant Owen Green of the Homicide Division." When she stood and shook his hand, he continued. "You are here, I understand, to, ah, *assist* us." There was something she could not interpret deep in those sad eyes. Was he angry—or laughing at her?

She shook her head. "I'm here to assist Mr. Dekker, and to report back to Mr. Hashimoto what you find out."

"That's fine." He spoke mildly and turned back to the desk. She had been dismissed.

She sank back beside Mr. Dekker and looked around the room. "Did Dean leave a note?" she asked softly.

"Not that they've found. Somebody said it could have blown out the window."

She nodded. Those large windows let in a lot of air. Even now a breeze was rippling papers on his desk. She was glad they were open, though. The room smelled of blood and a trace of perfume, even so.

She wondered what had caused Bayard to finally break down. Was it seeing her father? Or something else on the desk? It was hard to see all of the desk from the couch, so—using the excuse of needing a breath of air—Sheila rose and went to one of the side windows. She breathed deeply, turned and scanned the desk.

It was littered with papers and video tapes. A mug covered with the word "Daddy" in many languages sat amid the piles of papers. To one side lay a Chinese vase, on its side as if blown over. Sheila remembered, suddenly, Dean at lunch in Tokyo years ago.

"I've got an old Chinese vase that keeps me lucky," he'd said, shoveling in the sushi. "It's hundreds of years old, and I probably ought to put it in a safety deposit box, but I keep it on every desk I have." She regarded it with a sad smile: It hadn't kept Dean lucky today. But why had it fallen? Surely it was too heavy to be shifted by the wind.

"Was that vase turned over when they first found him?" she asked Mr. Dekker.

He nodded. "I guess so. Wylene said she didn't touch anything, not even the phone. She called the police from the receptionist's desk."

Sheila made a mental note to ask Elise about the vase. Spacey in most ways, she had an artist's eye for that kind of detail.

But now she saw what must have been the last straw for Dean's daughter: in a plastic bag on one corner of the desk, the gun that had killed him.

She was appalled at the way the police were tramping around the room. "I don't suppose this carpet would show footprints," she called to the lieutenant.

"Oh, it could," he nodded. "We've got special foil these days and a static electricity rod that lifts prints from almost any carpet. But it's expensive. We don't use it for a suicide."

"Are you sure that's what it was?" She spoke without thinking.

His eyes narrowed. "Why do you ask that?"

"Not a very good reason, I'm afraid. But will you try to trace the gun, or take prints off it to be certain they are Dean's?"

"Guns are hard to trace, and don't give very good prints—we'd have to take it in to the lab. Might not get much even then. Have you any reason to think we ought to do that?"

Even though his words were mild, she felt the challenge behind them.

She bit her lip, wishing she could shake Aunt Mary. Back in her office at Hosokawa, she had been very willing to let Dean Anderson's death be accepted as a suicide. Here, looking at that familiar face she, like many others, had admired, she couldn't let go without at least an investigation. That was exactly what Aunt Mary had known. That was why she was here.

But no matter how tactful she tried to be, she was about to look like nothing but an interfering busybody. Her explanation sounded thin even to her own ears.

"Dean had just gotten engaged." She felt more than saw his surprise. "And he had invited me to dinner next Wednesday night. His daughter says he was with her yesterday, talking about plans for his future. I don't think his state of mind was consistent with suicide."

He stood there, a small man in brown tweed, and gave her a searching look. "You know anything about suicide and murder?"

"A little," she admitted. "A very little. I'm not trying to butt into your case—"

"But you just butted." His voice was sour and he jutted his lower lip in and out. "I hope you can't name anybody who might have wanted to see Dean Anderson dead. If you can, I'll have to call the state crime lab and get them to go over this room with a fine-tooth comb. Instead of a nice, neat suicide, I'll be investigating the murder of a famous man. The media will love it. My boss will absolutely hate it. And if I don't solve it, I'll be in hot water. Think carefully, now. Are you going to make me go through all that?"

She met his gaze, then nodded ruefully. "I'm afraid I am. At dinner last Thursday night, Darius Dudwell made a special trip to let Dean know he was out of jail."

"Darius." The officer's tan lips worked over the name like it had a sour flavor. "He's got a grudge, all right. But this doesn't look like Mr. Dudwell's work." He turned back toward the desk.

"His last words were, 'You stay out of my road and I'll stay out of yours.'"

"That's no threat." He sounded relieved, but questioning.

"No, but he was accompanied by two men who looked a lot like bodyguards. Their mood was ugly. Mr. Dudwell may have meant what he said—or he may have just wanted witnesses he could call later at a trial."

The lieutenant whistled softly through his teeth and thought for several minutes. "You were actually there?" She nodded. His look of gloom increased and his lower lip worked for nearly a minute before he spoke again. "Mrs. Travis, you *do* want me to have an exciting autumn, don't you? I should have told you before, I like to get my kicks watching television football." He looked at Dean, then back to her. "I'll have to go over this whole room, trying to find just one footprint or fingerprint to link Darius Dudwell or his men to this case."

"Maybe you'll find prints from somebody else, instead."

"Maybe I'll find prints from a hundred somebody elses, trace them all, and then find out the man killed himself. But you've cut my work out for me." His shoulders slumped. "Okay, Mr. Dekker, I need this room vacated. I promised the little lady a bit of time with her daddy, and I'll give it to her, but right after that we're going to have to seal the door until the lab is through." He looked at Sheila and shook his head. "Some help you've been, ma'am, if you don't mind my saying so."

10

When they reentered the foyer, Elton Dekker checked his watch. "I need to run up to my office to tie up a few loose ends and call my wife. Lieutenant Green said he'd want to talk with all the staff in about ten minutes. Do you want to stay for that?"

The temptation was great to say "No thanks" and head for her car, but Sheila really did want to hear what the staff had to say if Lieutenant Green would let her. "If you don't mind, I'll stay."

Porter moved from his doorway. "I'll introduce her around, Elton, while you're gone. Maybe even get her a cup of coffee."

The president thanked him and hurried to the elevators. Wylene bustled to join him, dabbing at her nose. Given its prominence and current redness, Sheila thought she would have done better to artfully conceal it behind her hanky. Wylene, however, seemed to feel that grief deserved to look pitiful. "Has anyone called Dean's poor mother? If you want me to . . ."

Mr. Dekker took a short step back as if to distance himself both from Wylene and her query. "That will be taken care of, of course."

He did not add "it's not your concern," but the way he turned toward the elevators was an eloquent dismissal. Wylene thanked him in a weak little voice, as if he had taken a responsibility off her shoulders, then stood beside him in damp misery while he waited. At last he looked at his watch again and headed for the door to the stairs. "I'll walk up."

"Poor devil," Porter said close to Sheila's ear. "Dean is scarcely gone and already Wily's transferring her lambent drives in his direction."

Sheila gave him a reluctant smile. "Lambent drives? I would have said primitive urges."

Porter shook his head in gentle rebuke. "Too, too cliché, darling."

"Do I forfeit my coffee?" she asked. With a deep bow, he waved her toward the break room. In a few minutes, carrying a steaming mug, she felt equal to anything except sitting still and listening to Bayard Anderson sniffle. "What now?"

Wylene had been standing uncertainly where Mr. Dekker had left her. Suddenly she remembered her self-imposed social duties. Hurrying over, she grabbed Sheila's arm in one talon.

"Oh, Ms. Travis, I forgot you haven't been here before. You really must see our film library. It's the finest in the nation." She more dragged than led Sheila toward the double glass doors. Sheila threw Porter an imploring look and went with Wylene—primarily to keep her arm attached to her body.

"This is it," Wylene announced. Sheila had already guessed. She'd read the six-inch gold letters on the doors.

"Our forerunner encyclopedias made many educational films." Once again Wylene said the obvious. The library took up almost half of the tenth floor and was filled from floor to ceiling with metal racks of film cans and videotapes.

"At least one on every topic of interest to man and woman." Porter moved between the two, forcing Wylene to let go of Sheila's arm.

"Must be at least that," Sheila agreed with a grateful smile.

Wylene warmed up to one of her favorite subjects. "We've turned most into videos and still distribute them to schools. We're also looking for ways to pull out the best footage for various uses. Currently, as you may know, we're working on a television series."

" 'Reading Rainbow' for the very grown up," Porter added, sotto voce. But Sheila noticed he stroked one film can almost reverently as they turned to go. "Wylene," he murmured, putting one hand at the woman's wasp waist, "shouldn't you see if Dean's daughter wants coffee? Jonah's not skilled at caring for young females."

Wylene hovered, uncertain between her duty to this executive from the parent company and duty to a dead employee's child.

"Do," Sheila urged her. "I'll be fine."

As they reentered the foyer, Wylene again remembered she was grieving. With tears in her eyes, she gave Sheila's forearm an affectionate squeeze and hurried to Bayard's side.

"You're a skillful creature," Sheila murmured in admiration.

"At your service." Porter put a hand at her waist.

"I don't need quite that much service." She moved ahead of him past the elevators.

He bowed. "As you wish." He raised his voice slightly and spoke in the tones of a docent. "Our tour will continue with the offices, which—in order—belong to Veronica, Craig, Jonah, Dean, me and Elise. If you notice the absence of secretarial personnel, please put it down in your report. Somebody upstairs has the mistaken notion that writers and artists write no letters. We've endeavored to correct that opinion, but so far to no avail. Note also that each office is unique, because of the shape of this wonderful foyer. But we all have the same space, more or less."

"He has more, we have less." A young woman at the first door spoke with a gleam of mischief in her eyes.

"Don't be petty, darling," Porter replied. "Sheila Travis, Veronica Yates, one of our writers. She is graciously sharing her office with Sally Webster, our receptionist, for the evening since Sally's desk has become a bit too public for her taste."

Sheila shook hands with the two young women. As she admired a chubby brown infant pictured in several poses on the desk, she mused that her own stereotypes would have switched the women's names. Veronica was the name Sheila had given to a favorite doll years ago, a leggy blonde with ample curves and exquisite wardrobe. This Veronica was still plump from childbearing, with large round glasses and a sensible navy suit. Only her voice matched her name—a rich alto that was probably the joy of some choir director.

It was Sally who exuded glamour from every pore. Her body was as long as Sheila's own, slim as a model's. Her skin was a flawless café au lait, her hair straightened and permed. Her clothes, Sheila was certain, had cost a great deal of money. It must take enormous determination to wear a tight skirt and pointed stiletto heels all day, but Sally would obviously rather be beautiful than comfortable. Her nails were so long and enameled that Sheila wondered how she could type, and surely those African earrings must get in the way of the telephone.

Porter interrupted her thoughts. "Craig here is too neat to really be a writer. I think he has a ghost." The office was indeed neat—books shelved, papers in stacks, and, on his desk, a mug of pens lined up precisely with a clock. Craig was on the phone, sleeves rolled to his elbow, industriously jotting down notes.

"Just a minute, Jack." He tossed a toothpick into a wastebasket and put out his hand. Sheila recognized the man she had overheard speaking with Jonah at the reception. As they left, he turned back to his call.

"Craig's not one of the world's players," Porter remarked.

"We have enough players around here," Craig covered his mouthpiece to mutter.

In the third doorway Woody, the maintenance man, clung to the doorjamb, eyes fixed on the police officer. His face was gray and ill. "Woody, go sit down," Porter ordered him, "if you can find a place in this hovel." He shifted a sock and stack of books from a visitor's chair and gently pushed the older man into it.

"Jonah's a living illustration that clutter is the sign of a creative mind," Porter continued, endeavoring to stack a pile of magazines that spilled over half the floor, "but you can count on him for snacks. Want an apple?" He held out a wooden bowl containing one solitary piece of fruit. "No? How about you, Woody? You look hungry."

"I'm . . . I'm scared." Woody shrank into his chair. "What will they do to me? What will they say?"

"They aren't going to do anything to you," Porter assured him. "They'll ask you some questions about finding Dean, then they'll let you go home."

"You promise?" Woody's relief was pitiful to see.

"I promise." Porter clapped him on the shoulder, then led Sheila across the foyer to the office past Dean's. "I perch here, with the pigeons. Normally Winston and Mamie would greet you from the windowsill, but they've gone out for the night."

Sheila regarded the wide windowsill suspiciously. "Do pigeons. really come up this high?"

"I assure you, darling, they not only come up, they would come *in* if I didn't keep them fed outside. Jonah left an open bag of chips on his desk once and we almost never got them to leave."

A drawing table sat beneath his single window, which Sheila calculated must face north. "Do artists really prefer northern light?" she asked.

"Buried this deep among the skyscrapers, I take any light I can get. And I try to do my bit to brighten things up." His overstuffed chair was whimsically covered in bright fuchsia, yellow and royal blue. Two excellent modern watercolors in the same tones enlivened his walls.

She peered closer to check the signature. "You did them!"

"I told you, I do my bit."

"Isn't he good?" Elise stood in the door. "He really ought to be showing in a gallery, but he's too modest."

"Too proud, darling. It would gall my soul to hear strangers making rude remarks about my creations. Here, I only entertain friends who are certain to speak kindly of them."

Before Sheila could think of a suitable reply, Elise slapped one cheek in chagrin. "I almost forgot. The policeman came to take Dean's daughter in to see him, and he said we are to all come sit in the lobby now and bring chairs."

"How about this?" Porter asked her. "We'll bring the chairs first, then sit."

Elise thought that over. "Okay, if you say so."

W hat I don't understand," Elton Dekker said, setting down his mug of coffee, "is why Dean had a gun. He was so vocal about gun control."

"Maybe he wanted to illustrate how dangerous guns can be." Craig wiped cookie crumbs from his beard.

"Not so loud," Jonah cautioned him. "His daughter might hear."

"It won't bother her," Craig replied. "She's tough."

Jonah flushed. "You know so much after one date?"

Craig shrugged. "Sure." He hoisted his own mug to end the conversation.

Veronica turned to the president. "Do you know how long we'll be? I need to call my husband."

"Probably not long," he told her. "They'll just want to get statements about where you all were when it happened."

"We were all upstairs," Elise replied. She looked about the circle and amended her statement. "Most of us, anyway."

They were now sitting in the foyer, "circling the wagons" as Porter had termed it. To augment the wing chairs, he and Jonah had dragged office chairs—and, eventually, Craig with his own chair—to form a rough circle. Elise and Sally had brought mugs of coffee and a tin of cookies.

As Elise took a seat beside Sheila, her chair scraped Sally's wastebasket behind them. Automatically she looked around. "Oh, Sally, here are your Kleenex!" she called across the circle. "There's a bunch of them in here." Sheila looked, too. Sure enough, under a balled yellow memo, a toothpick and a few soggy tissues lay a large wad of dry tissues, crumpled as if they had all been pulled out at once and used si-

80

multaneously. No wonder that now, between Bayard and Wylene, a new box was almost empty.

Sally, who had seated herself as far from her desk as possible, was more interested in other things. "If I'd known we were going to be here all night," she complained, "I'd have brought my nightie."

"But there are no beds," Elise said seriously. "And I don't think the carpet would be very comfortable."

"And what I want to know," Sally continued as if Elise had not spoken, "is why anybody cares where *we* were when Mr. Anderson killed himself?"

"Maybe if you'd been at your desk, he wouldn't have done it," Craig taunted her.

She put one hand on her hip and cocked her head to one side. "And how do you know I wasn't? Were *you* here?"

"Only a fool would kill himself with somebody in the outer office."

"N—n—nobody was here when I came up to fix the light," Woody offered.

"That's what you'll need to tell the police," Jonah advised him, draping one arm around the shaking man's shoulders.

"I don't want to talk to the police. They have"—Woody struggled with the word before he could get it out—"guns!"

"They won't use them if we are very good," Porter told him. Then he caught Jonah's eye and subsided.

"You were very brave." Elise gave Woody a little pat.

"He looked like death warmed over when he found me." Wylene sniffed and wiped her nose again. She didn't look so good herself.

While they were waiting for the chairs to be set up, Elise had confided to Sheila, "When we first came downstairs, Wily was dissolved in a perfect puddle of tears. Veronica and I had all we could do to make her stop. She was in love with him, you know." By now, Wylene was in control of her tear ducts, but still wore a bereaved, soggy look. (Which did not, however, prevent her from telling the others how chairs should be placed in the circle.)

Dean's door opened. Lieutenant Green ushered Bayard to the elevator. All color had drained from her face, and she walked like a zombie, eyes straight ahead. Jonah rose, then sank back to his seat as the lieutenant said to Bayard, "There's a police car waiting downstairs to take you home. I'll see your mother tomorrow. You try to get some rest, now." When she had left, he went to Sally's telephone and apparently continued a call he had begun inside. Only Sheila was near enough to hear what he said. "Get on it right away. Vacuum it, dust it—the works. I want every print and every scrap of paper."

He went to lean against a pillar, one foot propped across the other. Officer McGehee handed him a piece of paper. "This is a plan of offices and current seating, sir, with each name written on it."

Green looked at the plan, occasionally looking up to match a face with a name. "Good work, McGehee." He turned to the circle. "In a few minutes I'm going to need individual statements from some of you. But could I just see a show of hands, first, from those who were on this floor this afternoon, so I can sort people out?" He flicked one hand, and the red-headed officer pulled out a notebook and moved to stand behind Woody. Woody shuddered and moved his chair forward a bit.

The only hands raised were Wylene's and Sally's. Craig spoke. "Most of us were together this afternoon. We have a big deadline coming up"—he slid his eyes toward Elton Dekker and back to the officer—"so we met from lunchtime until Woody came to get us."

Woody cringed and hunched even further forward in his chair. "I don't like that gun," he confided to Elise.

"He's not going to shoot you," she said.

"Guns do shoot people." Woody's eyes, which had been merely wary, filled with tears. "A gun shot Mr. Anderson. I'm afraid of guns!" Sobs began to shake his body.

Elise patted his arm again. Jonah, behind Bayard, put a hand on his shoulder. "Hey, Woody, you're going to be all right. Why don't you swap seats with Porter?"

82

"Sure," Porter replied. "Let me sit by that charming gun instead." But he moved to change places.

Lieutenant Green marked the change on his map and spoke without looking up. "Were all of you upstairs?"

There was a pause. Sheila had the feeling some silent decision had been made. "Not Sally or Wily." Elise replied.

"I was in the mailroom almost all afternoon, seeing to the shipping of orders," Wylene reported.

"And I was here and there." Sally waved one hand and three gold bracelets jangled. Where *did* a receptionist get that kind of money? She and Wylene, Sheila decided, must have rich lovers or private sources of income. She martialed her thoughts back to what Sally was saying. ". . . letters to type, then I had to take an express letter to the mailroom. Wily saw me then."

Wylene nodded confirmation. "But that was just at three. Where were you after that?"

Sally tossed her head. She didn't have to answer to Wylene, and wanted the world to know it. But Mr. Dekker was looking her way, too. "I stopped to visit a friend. We went on break together."

"So after three, there was absolutely nobody on this floor except Mr. Anderson?" Lieutenant Green sounded as if he were merely confirming what he had heard, but Elton Dekker turned to them with astonishment and not a little anger.

"Who was covering the phones?"

They all looked at Sally, who played with one of her earrings. Her voice was sulky. "We hadn't gotten any calls after lunch but one, Jack Somebody for Craig. So Mr. Anderson told me he'd answer the phone while I took his express letter down. It was to Raven Hillis," she added, as if that explained everything.

"And you extended that offer to cover your break?" Wylene challenged her. "I got here just before four, and you—"

Mr. Dekker put out a hand of protest. "We'll discuss this later. These officers don't need to get bogged down by internal affairs."

The lieutenant pursed his lips. "But as I understand it, no one was on this floor when Mr. Anderson got shot?"

Sally tossed her head, setting her earrings swinging. "I don't know when he *was* shot. I didn't hear anything, if that's what you mean, but he could have shot himself anytime after two and I wouldn't have heard it. That's the last time I was in his office. He gave me that letter and said get it downstairs by three-thirty. I had some typing to finish first, so I put my Walkman on, listened to music. I couldn't hear much except the phone. And I don't go in his office, unless he calls me. Not like some people." She recrossed her long legs and her eyes flicked Wylene. "He could have been dead most of the afternoon and I wouldn't have known it."

"When did you leave the floor?" the officer asked her.

"About three, like Wily said. I finished what I was doing, put all the telephones onto his, and left."

"You didn't speak to him? Tell him you were going?"

She shook her head. "Mr. Anderson didn't like to be bothered with every little detail. He wouldn't even *need* to know I was gone unless he got a call. If the phone rang on his desk, he'd know."

"Was Miss Webster the last person to see Dean Anderson alive?" Green looked around the circle.

There was a moment of silence.

"He was okay at one-thirty," Elise contributed. "I took him a memo then."

The officer gave her a baffled look.

"Don't mind her," Porter told him. "She's just being helpful."

The officer tried again. "Did anyone see him after *two* o'clock?"

Sally licked her lips. "I think . . ."

Green waited, then prompted, "You think what?"

She polished one nail against her skirt and shook her head without looking up. "Nothing. I . . . It was nothing."

Lieutenant Green looked around the circle, meeting every eye. His lower lip worked in and out. Finally he pushed away from the pillar and headed back to Dean's office. "I will want a complete statement from you, you and you." He pointed out Sally, Woody and Wylene. "The rest can go." He entered Dean's door.

Woody trembled. "I don't know anything. I just found him."

"All we want is your story of finding the body," the young officer told him. "So we can write it down." He was trying to be soothing, but as he spoke he leaned forward. Woody's eyes fixed on his gun.

"I don't know anything!" he cried.

Jonah walked around the circle, bent down and gave Woody a hug. "I'll stay with you, fellow," he promised.

Lieutenant Green came back out, accompanied by a young Hispanic officer. "You've got that, now? I want you to look for Darius Dudwell and bring him in for questioning."

Someone in the circle had caught a quick breath at the name, but Sheila did not see who. Probably Elise, remembering Thursday night. Green was still talking. ". . . those thugs he keeps with him, too. I've received information he sought Anderson out on Thursday. I'd like to talk with him when we're through here." The young man nodded and took the elevator down.

Green turned back to the group. "Anybody here have anything to add before I let you go home?"

He was met with headshakes and blank stares.

The phone shrilled on Sally's desk. Green nodded to McGehee, who moved to answer it.

"It's Woody's daughter." His voice was a bit hoarse. He cleared his throat and added, "Maintenance called and told her he's involved up here. She's downstairs and wants to come up."

Lieutenant Green jingled the change in his pockets and considered Woody, who was bent almost double in his chair, weeping. "I think that might be a good idea," he said. "Send her up."

He looked around the circle. "Okay, except for the three I mentioned, good night to you."

Craig rose first. "I've got some work to do. All right if I stay in my office?"

Lieutenant Green nodded. "We'll use one of the other offices for our interviews."

"You can use mine." Elise sprang to her feet. "I've got a class." She scurried to her desk for the yellow purse that matched her pumps.

Porter caught Sheila's eye. "Don't go imagining it's third year Greek." She grinned.

Elise reappeared. "Coming, Sheila?"

Sheila hesitated, torn between a desire to escape and a desire to hear anything she could. "Not just yet, Elise. Thanks."

"Let me get my purse, and I'll come too." Veronica had already moved to her door, and returned soon with a bag large enough to hold diapers and bottles.

One elevator had scarcely closed behind them when the other opened. A tiny young woman, with a face almost as careworn as her jeans and her brown hair skinned into a ponytail, perched at the door, ready to run out. She looked from one policeman to the other, at her father, and back to the red-haired young officer.

"Frank McGehee! What have you been doing to Daddy? Why is he so upset?"

"We're not upsetting him, Crystal." The young officer blushed.

Lieutenant Green looked from one to the other. "You friends?"

"We went to Grady High together," McGehee replied, still pink, "and had a math class together last year at Georgia State."

Sheila began to understand why this case had upset the young policeman so. He was not the first young man who preferred having his own adventures to having his girlfriend involved in them.

The young woman ignored him. Moving to her father's side, she asked, "What's the matter, Daddy?"

Woody raised red-rimmed eyes to hers. "He's got a g—gun, Crystal." The name suited her, Sheila thought. She looked as fragile as fine porcelain.

She was tough as ironstone, however, as she wheeled back toward McGehee. "Couldn't you take it off and put it somewhere? He's terrified of guns."

"Why don't you come in this office with him?" Lieutenant Green had strolled between the girl and the officer. He put one hand at her elbow and turned her back toward her father. "I need to ask him a few questions." He looked over his shoulder at his colleague. "You can stay out here with the others."

They were almost in Elise's door when McGehee said in a baffled voice, "Where's that other black woman?"

Green turned. Sheila and her companions scanned the foyer, bewildered. Then they stared at one another, knowing what must have happened. When Crystal had left the elevator, Sally had gotten on. Unnoticed, she had escaped.

11

"And they never found her?" Mary Beaufort's dark eyes were speculative above the iced tea she held.

Sheila sipped her coffee before she shook her head, grateful for fresh coffee in a china cup. In spite of her vow not to keep Aunt Mary informed, her car had seemed to drive of its own accord from Galaxia to this comfortable penthouse and the one person in the world to whom she could talk freely about the case. Now Mildred, out in the kitchen, was putting together "a bite to eat," and Sheila could feel the tension draining from her body. She shifted her position in the huge, soft chair with matching ottoman—"her" chair since high school days.

"Lieutenant Green called down to have all exits watched and IDs checked, but Sally was clever. She borrowed another woman's driver's license and slipped out in a crowd. The other woman got caught, but she could easily prove who she was. She said Sally didn't say why she needed it, and several others backed her up. By then Sally had melted into the city."

She let her head drop against the chair back. How tired she was! And all she'd done was sit in Elise's office while the men carried out Dean Anderson's heavy body and Lieutenant Green questioned Wylene and Woody.

"You have no idea why the woman thought she had to

disappear." It was a statement, but Aunt Mary raised her silver brows in query.

Sheila shook her head wearily. "None at all. She must have been downstairs when Dean died." She adjusted her legs on the ottoman. "Why couldn't I just have an ordinary job? Why did you insist I get mixed up in this?"

There. She'd finally asked it, put the blame squarely where it belonged. But the tiny woman across from her didn't seem to have heard her. Aunt Mary came from a long tradition of Southern ladies, who learn in infancy to avoid unpleasantness—or ignore it.

Her forehead was creased in thought. "Well," she finally pronounced in her deep, gravelly voice, "we can't locate her by sitting here." She cocked her head in thought and suddenly brightened with an idea. "I wonder if Jason could be of any help."

Jason Findlay was Aunt Mary's driver, errand runner and devoted servant. He was also, in his off hours, well known to the partying segments of Atlanta's black population.

"He might know something about her—where she lives, perhaps," Sheila agreed, "if I could remember her last name. I'm drawing a blank."

Aunt Mary pursed her lips with the expression of one who never forgot anything important. "Try Elise dear, she may remember, although it's hard to predict just what Elise *will* remember. Then I'll set Jason the task of finding her. She won't go home, of course. Not with the police looking for her, too."

"A race to the finish," Sheila murmured, reaching for her purse. "The police against one lone chauffeur."

She rummaged through scraps of paper and tissues while Aunt Mary shook her head and made "tsk" noises. "I would have hoped by now you would have developed some order in your life, Sheila."

Sheila held up the number. "I have, see? Elise's number."

Elise was at aerobics class, and her daughter did not know Sally's name or number. She could, however, provide Jonah's number.

He answered on the fourth ring, out of breath. "Sorry, I just got in from taking Woody and Crystal home. We ordered a pizza and I stayed, to be sure he was going to be okay." Sheila asked her question. "Sally? Sure. Her name is Webster, like the building. Maybe an ancestor built it. She lives in southwest Atlanta."

Along with half a million other people.

Aunt Mary was not daunted. While Sheila moved into the dining room for beef tips over toast and a crisp fresh salad, she called Jason. "He doesn't know her," she reported, accepting a refill on tea from Mildred and carrying it to join Sheila, "but he says he has ways to find her. He'll let us know."

Aunt Mary never discussed unpleasantness at meals, so while Sheila finished her dinner and a piece of Mildred's pecan pie, they chatted about people they both knew and the latest sale at Rich's.

"Of course it's never been the same since Yankees bought it out," Aunt Mary lamented, "and those Canadians have nearly ruined it. But if you look hard, they still have good buys."

Sheila cocked one eyebrow. "Since when have you ever looked hard for anything in a department store?" Aunt Mary belonged to the school that still ordered by phone and expected home delivery.

"I had to return the last dress they sent twice before they got it right," her aunt replied with unshaken dignity. "First they sent a navy one, and you know I never wear navy. So elderly, I always think. And the second one was the right shade of rose, but the wrong length. It took them nearly a week to get it hemmed."

Sheila hadn't known Rich's still did alterations, but Aunt Mary took it for granted—as she did many services she expected (and got) from merchants she had patronized for nearly fifty years. Some things, Sheila mused, regarding her aunt fondly, never change.

When Sheila finished dinner, she settled again into the big ivory chair with her long legs on the soft ottoman while

Aunt Mary curled into one corner of the couch, feet tucked beneath her.

"Now, dear, tell me all about this case."

"Well, as I've already said, Dean was shot at close range while sitting at his desk. He may have shot himself, or whoever did it wanted the police to think so. He was found by a maintenance man who went to the office around three-thirty to change a light bulb."

"Did he touch anything?"

Sheila shook her head. "Woody says not, that he could tell Dean was dead right away. Then he burst into tears and had to be escorted out. He is brain damaged—the result of being blown up in Vietnam."

Sheila sipped her coffee, remembering the distasteful scene: Woody blubbering and sniveling until the policemen told Crystal to take him home. Why had Jonah offered to drive them? Was he merely being kind—or did he want to know if Woody knew anything more?

Aunt Mary called her back to the present. "But you did convince them to treat it like murder, not suicide?"

"No, I convinced them to keep an open mind."

"They'll check the gun for fingerprints," Aunt Mary (an inveterate reader of mysteries) assured her. "They'll be able to tell immediately whether the gun was fired by Dean or merely pressed into his hand. Then when they trace the owner—"

"It's not that easy. Lieutenant Green says it's almost impossible these days to trace a gun, because people sell them so often. He's going to try to find prints on it, though, and when I left, the state crime lab was arriving to go over the room."

"I doubt they will find much in an office." Aunt Mary tapped one finger against her skirt. "So much in-and-out traffic."

"They are going to be looking for one set of prints that don't belong. Last Thursday, Dean was accosted by a man named Darius Dudwell. Not quite threatened, but almost."

"Darius Dudwell?" Aunt Mary spoke thoughtfully.

"Don't strain your memory banks—you don't know him. He's a mobster, I think, who's been in prison for sixteen years."

Aunt Mary nodded. "Prostitution, it used to be, and protection. Most recently he's run drug rackets, I believe."

"From prison, Aunt Mary?"

"He's very resourceful, I understand. Surely this lieutenant doesn't think Darius shot Dean Anderson in his office. A shot from a moving car or through an open window would be more Darius's style, I should think. Was the window open?"

Sheila felt as if she was being carried along on a stream before she'd quite gotten into the boat. "Yes, but Dean wasn't shot through it, unless . . ." She pictured the scene and shook her head. "No, he wasn't shot through the window. The angle is wrong."

Now she was ready to go back to the beginning. "How do *you* know Darius Dudwell, Aunt Mary?"

The old woman gave a genteel shrug. "I don't know him, Sheila, not socially. But when one lives in a city for many years . . ."

"I am sure there are *nice* old ladies who have lived here even longer without once hearing his name."

"Perhaps so." Aunt Mary wasn't interested in nice old ladies. She had a murder to solve. "Why should Darius want to kill Dean Anderson?"

"I don't know that he did. But Dean uncovered the evidence that sent Darius to jail in the first place, and his son, Neal—"

"Whose son—Dean Anderson's or Mr. Dudwell's?"

"Dean's. At the Galaxia reception Neal was terrified that Darius was going to come gunning for Dean as soon as he got out."

"Really, dear, your language! If you plan to remain in Atlanta, please strive to improve both your syntax and your choice of idiom. I presume you mean Neal feared Mr. Dudwell would shoot his father upon release."

"If you need a translation, yes. But when Darius showed up, he merely walked in with bodyguards and exchanged a few words."

"Walked in where? To the reception?"

"No, to Dailey's. While we were finishing dinner."

"You were there? And you never mentioned it?" Aunt Mary sounded as reproachful as if Sheila had neglected to mention lunch with the queen. Before she could think up a suitably scathing reply, Aunt Mary had gone on. "Surely he didn't threaten Mr. Anderson in public? Mr. Dudwell is usually so polite! He comes from a good family."

"He was polite," Sheila agreed. "His family could not have complained. He merely told Dean—and I quote, so you won't object to my language again—to 'stay out of my road.' Dean agreed, Darius exited—left."

"Then let us, for the moment, put Mr. Dudwell aside and consider other possibilities." Aunt Mary opened a drawer in the table beside the couch and produced a small pad and a pencil.

"Did you put those in there just for this conversation?" Sheila wondered aloud.

Aunt Mary did not deign to reply. In a businesslike manner she poised her pencil above the pad. "Please name our other suspects."

Sheila bit her lower lip and considered. "Well, first, as I keep reminding you, there is the enormous possibility that Dean killed himself. Darius Dudwell has by far the best motive for murder. But in addition, there are two sets of possibilities. One is Dean's family. Both children were giving Dean trouble on Thursday. Dean was upset because Neal prefers—or his mother prefers, I'm not sure—a small liberal arts college over the University of Georgia. His daughter Bayard was furious because she'd just found out she got her first job on her father's recommendation."

"In television?" When Sheila nodded, Aunt Mary sighed. "And I'll wager Dean didn't understand that whereas in any other field, his recommendation would have seemed merely fatherly to the young woman and unimportant to a prospective employer, in his own field it would carry weight and his daughter was bound to consider it interference." She wrote rapidly. "Thin motives, but they might be symptoms of something deeper. We'll put both children on our list. Now we need to know where the family spent the afternoon."

She slid her feet into her shoes and trotted out of the room. In only a few minutes she was back. "Laura says she and Neal were shopping downtown. He had the day off from school. Bayard was doing laundry and visiting by phone with friends until her cab arrived."

Sheila regarded her, astounded. "Did you just call a stranger and ask what she was doing when her ex-husband died?"

Now it was Aunt Mary who looked shocked—and a bit hurt. "Of course, not, Sheila! I have known Laura Anderson since she was a child—a homely, whining child, I recall. But she grew prettier in her teens, thank goodness."

She settled herself back on the couch, kicked off her shoes and sipped her tea before she continued. "I called to offer my condolences. In the conversation, I said how often it happens that death fixes in our minds what we were doing at the time—and mentioned that I can still remember, what I was doing when my dear mother died. Laura agreed, and told me what I just told you."

Sheila regarded her aunt with reluctant admiration. "I guess getting the information we wanted was worth the lie."

"What lie, dear?"

"That you remember exactly what you were doing when your mother died. Weren't you five years old?"

"Yes, dear. She died in the middle of the night. I was fast asleep." Aunt Mary picked up her pad and wrote a note, then raised her eyes. "You will notice that Laura and Neal were both downtown today. If I know anything about shopping with teenage sons—"

"Which you don't."

". . . they did not stay together the entire time." Aunt Mary finished as if the interruption had never occurred. "Laura also volunteered that Bayard heard of her father's death because the cab driver had a radio on and they announced it. She had him turn around and take her to the Webster Building, then called her mother from there."

Sheila shook her head. "Not unless she did it in the few minutes I was in Dean's office. She huddled in her chair the entire time I saw her."

Aunt Mary delicately licked the tip of her pencil. "That may be significant, dear. There! I've put both Dean's children on our list for the time being, and Laura, too, although that gives me pain."

"Looks to me like she's the one person who would have no motive at all," Sheila mused. "With Dean dead, won't her alimony end?"

"As I recall, the alimony stops anyway when the children become adults. How old is Neal?"

"Close to eighteen," Sheila calculated. "So you think—"

"I think Dean's will determines whether Laura had a motive or not. A woman about to lose her alimony but mentioned in a will might have a powerful motive for murder."

"And how do you propose to find out what's in Dean's will—call Laura back, or put on your furs and go charm his lawyer?"

Aunt Mary considered her with disdain. "How exhausting, Sheila! And it's far too early for furs. I think dear Charlie . . ."

Sheila groaned. "Not poor Charlie again."

Why Charles Davidson, one of Atlanta's leading financiers and Aunt Mary's business consultant (a man so formal that even his wife called him "Charles"), was willing to serve Aunt Mary for nefarious purposes, Sheila had never understood. Nor why he let his old friend call him "Charlie," or how he achieved the results he did. But whenever they needed evidence of a confidential nature, Aunt Mary called "Dear Charlie" and a brown envelope miraculously arrived. Thanks to Aunt Mary, dear Charlie must have cashed in most of his chips from a vast old-boy network by now. But if anyone could privately discover the contents of Dean Anderson's will, Charles Davidson certainly would.

"I have a recurring nightmare," she told her aunt. "I dream I've been called to the jail to post bail for you and Mr. Davidson, and I greet him with, 'Hi, Charlie!' "

Aunt Mary had put on her tortoiseshell half spectacles. Now she peered over them like a fluffy owl. "If you are having nightmares, Sheila, try warm milk before bed. To continue this list, did Dean Anderson have any other family?"

"Not unless you consider his girlfriend."

"I think we must, don't you?" The pencil poised for a name.

"Raven Hillis, the movie actress. Dean was hinting on Thursday that they were newly engaged. But I know nothing about her beyond that. I haven't seen a movie in years. Tyler . . ."

Aunt Mary had never been interested in Tyler Travis while he was alive. She feigned no interest now. She slid her feet into her black pumps again and crossed the living room. "Mildred?" she called through the kitchen door. "I need to ask you a question."

Mildred arrived, hands damp from the dishpan.

"We want to know about Raven Hillis. Where is she just now, for instance?"

Mildred had served Mary Beaufort for nearly thirty years. They had few secrets from one another. This was the first time, however, that Miss Beaufort had admitted to knowing about Mildred's vast acquaintance with the private lives of the stars. By mutual unspoken agreement, Mildred hid her film magazines and Miss Mary pretended not to know they existed. No wonder Mildred hesitated.

She knew the answer, however. "She's shooting a film in Hollywood until Christmas. She used to come to town, though, to see Dean Anderson—the one who killed himself today. I don't know why he'd do a thing like that. They were going to get married!" (So much for a secret engagement.)

"But she isn't in Atlanta today?"

Mildred shook her head. "Not that I know of, and I'd hear if she was coming. My friend Ginerva cleans for Mr. Anderson. She always lets me know when Miss Hillis is coming to town." She stopped, as if having a sudden thought. "She'll be sure to be coming for the funeral, and to get her stuff from his house. She put a lot of her own pictures and stuff like that in it."

"I wonder when she would be most likely to arrive?" Aunt Mary seemed to be speaking to herself, but Mildred wasn't fooled.

"She's superstitious about flying on odd days of the month, so she'll probably arrive here Wednesday unless she comes tonight."

"Thank you, Mildred. That will be all. You go on to bed."

As Aunt Mary resumed her seat on the couch, Sheila shook her head in fond amusement. "You know somebody with the answer to just about anything, don't you?"

Aunt Mary inclined her head like a tiny duchess. "Let us just say I believe in knowing where information may be obtained. Now, what is our second category of suspects?"

"If this turns out to be murder," Sheila reminded her. "Dean's co-workers, I suppose. And there could be several categories we won't think of—not knowing him very well." She said the last words with emphasis, thinking how fruitless this exercise probably was.

Her aunt merely said, "Tell me about these co-workers."

Sheila filled her in on Galaxia's tenth floor tensions and why they existed. As Aunt Mary added Jonah, Craig and Porter to her list, she finished, "And Wylene was in love with Dean, according to Elise."

Aunt Mary's brows rose again. "Killing a man to prevent his marriage to another is far more common in romance novels than real life, Sheila."

"I agree. But most people don't kill over arguments in business, either—or because they've quarreled with their father one more time. If you want my real opinion, none of these people had a motive sufficient for murder."

"Then we must look elsewhere," Aunt Mary said placidly. "Now Sally, for instance. Her leaving was certainly suspicious."

"Or she could have just decided she'd said all she had to

say. I'm sorry, Aunt Mary, because I know you like a good crime now and then, but I've been thinking it over while we were talking, and I really do think Dean must have killed himself. I don't know why—nor any good reason why you and I even *ought* to know why. But I think that's what must have happened. All these 'suspects' strike me as ordinary people trying to do their jobs."

"Ordinary people do murder, Sheila. But I'll agree that tonight we have very little to go on." She looked over her list. "I believe we can eliminate Elise. She's never angry, is she?"

Sheila considered. "Only once, that I've seen. But do you know, she swore worse than anybody else I ever heard."

Aunt Mary looked properly shocked. "I wouldn't have thought Elise would ever use foul language."

Sheila chuckled. "She didn't. All she said was 'Bad word! Bad word!' But I assure you it sounded worse than a Dutch sailor."

"I don't know any Dutch sailors. Now where were all these people when the crime was committed?"

Sheila listed the various alibis.

"Was there a break during the staff meeting?"

"Lieutenant Green"—Sheila emphasized the name and yawned to show how tired she was—"will interview everyone in the morning. I really don't think we need to do any more about this, Aunt Mary. You know I hate poking and prying into people's lives."

"But you know these people, dear."

"No, I do not!" Sheila rose and went to the window, gazed at Atlanta's lighted skyline to the south and west. "I knew Elise years ago, I met the others tonight. And don't try to tell me you know what they are like, either, because you don't. These aren't Southerners you've known all your life. They are practically strangers to each other, who have moved down from Minnesota, New York, and heaven knows where."

"That's always been the case in Atlanta, dear—it's never been a southern city, not really. Why, when General Sherman came to burn it down, it was Mr. Grant from Iowa, I believe, or Indiana, who was put in charge of fortifying the city for the

Confederacy. Unlike other southern cities, Atlanta has no old families—people move down from the North and get rich for a generation or two, then they slip into obscurity for a new generation. It hasn't changed all that much, Sheila. But we still don't like murder here."

Sheila closed the drapes and picked up her cup. "I never knew a city that did, Aunt Mary. But this case I believe we can leave to the very competent Lieutenant Green." She started toward the kitchen, and missed Aunt Mary's next question. "I beg your pardon?"

Aunt Mary replied in the tone of one who is determined to be patient in spite of her inclinations. "I asked, dear, whether this Woody knew Mr. Anderson well."

Sheila paused in the door. "On the theory that whoever finds the body could have committed the crime? I don't think so. Woody was all to pieces afterwards, but I think it was from shock. He admired Dean tremendously. He's also terrified of guns—the policemen nearly paralyzed him. If he did kill Dean, though, it will be tragic. Dean had just done a very special thing for him. I don't know if Woody even knows yet." She explained about *Visions of Vietnam*. Woody's part in it, and Dean's response.

She returned from the kitchen to find Aunt Mary turning the pages of a large book most people would put on their coffee table. (Aunt Mary's coffee table was covered with exquisite glass paperweights.) Her aunt patted the cushion beside her and Sheila joined her. Silently they examined the book together.

The photographer had depicted neither heroes nor enemies, but ordinary people carrying on the minutiae of living in a difficult time. Two soldiers shared a joke as they cleaned guns. A mother rested her cheek against her baby's hair while bombs exploded behind them. Three children peered from an empty box labeled EXPLOSIVES. It was that subtle juxtaposition of life and death that made this book such a powerful protest against war.

Between the pictures Dean had written a simple narrative, stories of people he had met and conversations he had had in Vietnam. In the front, beneath a dedication "To The Unknown Photographer," Dean had written:

The film for these pictures came to me as the result of action in Vietnam. I have not been successful in identifying or locating the one whose camera recorded these images. I must suppose the photographer is dead. I offer this book, therefore, in memory of one who saw and recorded for posterity the beauty of the human spirit amid the devastation of war.

Aunt Mary closed the book almost reverently. "Dean Anderson did a good job with those pictures. Probably the best work he ever did."

"The *last* work Woody ever did." Sheila's eyes smarted with tears. "It breaks my heart for him to be oiling hinges when he used to have this kind of talent."

Aunt Mary rose briskly and returned the book to its place on the shelf. "We can't do anything tonight about the dreadfulness of war, Sheila. We need to concentrate on the matter at hand."

"We can't do anything about that, either," her niece pointed out. "I've done my bit. I pointed them toward Darius Dudwell to make sure they didn't settle for suicide. If they don't find anything to incriminate him, I hope it was suicide."

The phone rang. Since Aunt Mary refused to have a telephone in her living room, Sheila rose with a sigh. "Unless you are expecting a call, that may be Mr. Dekker. I gave him both our numbers." She went back to the kitchen to answer it. It was, as she had expected, Elton Dekker. "I just got a call from Lieutenant Green. That gun has no fingerprints on it whatsoever. Green says it's been wiped clean. He's afraid —what he said was 'very much afraid'—you are right. Dean didn't kill himself. He was murdered."

He sounded baffled, as well he might. He ran a good company. This sort of thing was not supposed to happen there.

Sheila had few words of consolation to offer. "Thanks for calling. I think Mr. Hashimoto is going to expect me to be with you for a few days. Can you find a place to put me?"

"First thing in the morning," he promised, and hung up.

Sheila reported to Aunt Mary. "See?" she concluded. "Lieutenant Green is on top of everything. By now he's probably going over the room with the latest equipment, looking for Bayard's cab driver, and talking with all possible suspects. We can leave it up to him."

"Of course, dear. He can do the official investigation." Aunt Mary waved one hand as if making him a gift of it. "But there are people he may not think to talk with, nuances of conversation he may not catch. By being on the spot, you should be able to pick up a thing or two he won't."

"The last time you said that I got dumped in a deserted motel and nearly died," Sheila reminded her.

"Nonsense, dear. You are here, aren't you? Now I suggest that we don't discuss this anymore this evening, but wait to see what turns up."

On that, at least, Sheila reflected ruefully, they could agree.

12

"This has been a terrible loss, not only for Galaxia but for the nation. I appreciate all the cooperation you have given the police today." Elton Dekker's high forehead shone and he rubbed his hands together nervously. "I want to thank you, and also to ask a favor from each of you. Let us resume work as normally as possible. I'm sure that is what Dean would have wished. Yesterday threw us all off stride, but is there any hope you will have a script for the first film by Friday?"

"Sure." "I think so." Jonah and Craig spoke simultaneously, then looked at each other like dogs taking one another's measure.

They were gathered in the eleventh floor conference room—the tenth floor staff (except Sally, who had not come in), Dekker and Sheila. Sheila was not certain exactly why she had been included. From glances she was getting, the staff wasn't either.

Porter touched her arm to call attention to a pigeon looking in from the windowsill. Beyond the open window she could hear noises of traffic and construction. The others seemed to notice neither.

She had come to the office that morning resolved to do very little about Dean's death. She had full confidence in Lieutenant Green and his staff, and only one desire: to get back to Hosokawa as soon as decently possible.

She had not expected to be invited to sit in on Green's staff interviews, so she was not disappointed. She had been sorry, however, when Elton Dekker, full of apologies, suggested she use Dean's office as soon as the police finished with it. She had hoped he'd find her a quiet space near him on sixteen, preferably with a view, where she could read for a day or two and go back to Hosokawa having saved face for herself and Mr. Hashimoto.

Since the police were not quite finished with the office, and since she had absolutely nothing to do, she had readily agreed to Jonah's suggestion to ensconce herself in the film library with a television, video player, and a stack of Galaxia's best.

Wylene Fowler was not at her desk, so Jonah had selected the films himself. "I don't know where Wily's gone, but if she gives you any trouble, tell her to see me."

He had disappeared behind one of the shelves. "Are any of your films here?" she had called to him.

He put his head around the corner. "One. 'Please, Daddy.' "

So that's what Bayard had asked him at the reception. "What's it about?"

"Absent fathers who don't pay child support." He sighed.

"Are you sighing about the topic, or something else?"

He returned and deposited three videos on the table. "What happened after it was made. I filmed it here in in Atlanta, and just after it was aired, one of those fathers was killed. Shot. They never made an arrest."

"Did you have any suspicions?"

"His wife's brother was pretty upset because *he'd* had to help support his sister and her three kids. I wondered later if our show triggered something. But now I have another worry. Lieutenant Green talked this morning as if Dean's death might not be suicide. What if he decides I'm a gun-happy filmmaker?"

"Are you?"

He grinned. "I'm into wiping out evil, not people. In fact, I was working up my courage to ask Dean if he'd do a program on gun control with me. I wish we had," he added soberly. Then, as if to himself, "That gun just doesn't make any sense." Looking puzzled, he left.

He had chosen well, and she spent a peaceful morning watching films on varied subjects, from the life cycle of a butterfly ("no plot surprises," Jonah had said, "but excellent photography") to Jonah's own film. She was impressed, both by the quality of his work and by the way he got inside his characters. She could not imagine what made people open up to a camera that way. Jonah must surely have taken time to build a great deal of trust.

After lunch (which Elise wanted to eat at Macy's to commemorate high school shopping sprees), Elton Dekker had invited her to join the staff on the eleventh floor. Now, as he prepared to close the meeting, Wylene indicated with a quick movement of one skinny hand that she had something to add.

"I think we should all be very careful about what we say, and to whom," she simpered.

"We'll just tell the truth." Elise was as candid as a child.

Wylene shook her head, and her eyes circled the table. "We need to be very reticent. There are reporters who will stop at nothing to get a story. Security is trying to keep them contained, but if you meet one in the elevator—"

". . . or if, heaven forbid, one manages to creep up behind you on the tenth floor." Porter raised his hands, prepared to pounce.

Wylene shot him a look of pure venom, but it was Elton Dekker to whom she spoke. "I just think we need to be careful."

"I'm sure we will be." Mr. Dekker gathered up his papers and made his exit, Wylene following behind.

"Poor Mr. Dekker," Elise breathed when their elevator was heard to leave. "Wily must drive him absolutely crazy."

"He could fire her," Sheila replied practically.

Porter shook his head. "He can't, darling. Wylene is the daughter of the president of an encyclopedia that shall remain nameless. He agreed to the merger only"—he held up one hand to emphasize the point—"only, mind, on the condition that Wylene Fowler should retain the position of film librarian at Galaxia for as long as she desired. She also, I understand, owns a hunk of stock. Unfortunately, she shall reside in our little family—film librarian and official busybody—for eternity."

"We could make life hell for her until she quits." Craig took careful aim, but his toothpick missed the wastebasket.

Jonah sank an apple core and blew on his fingernails, buffing them on his chest. "Practice, Stofford. That's all it takes. Along with consummate skill, of course. And I agree. Elton ought to make life hard for Wylene. It's him she bugs the most."

"He wouldn't do that," Elise objected. "Mr. Dekker is a real gentleman."

"He's also stuck with Wily," Craig replied. "I wouldn't stand that woman for a minute. If I didn't fire her, I'd kill her."

"In case Dean turns out not to have killed himself, Craigie, may we consider that a confession?" Porter's voice was silky. "You weren't known to be very fond of him, either."

Craig glared at him. "I was in a meeting all day. Which is more than we can say about some people." His voice was full of sarcastic emphasis. "Where were you, I'd like to know?"

Sheila was surprised. She'd assumed when Elise said they were "all" upstairs, she was including Porter. Now she understood the silent agreement last evening.

Porter flicked an invisible speck of dust from his immaculate white cuff, fastened today with jet cufflinks. His black jacket hung, as usual, over the back of his chair. "Here and there," he said airily. "I've given a full report of my movements to the police, if you care to ask them for a copy."

"I'll bet you told them every little move," Craig sneered.

"Well, I didn't include my potty breaks. But then, I don't take as many as some people do."

Craig flushed to the roots of his hair. "I never left this floor! Even during the break Veronica and I were right here."

Veronica nodded. "That's right, we were. But why are we talking as if Dean were murdered? I thought he shot himself."

Elise's eyes widened. "Of course he did! Poor Dean, he should have waited until Thursday, so he could have had his date with Sheila first."

All eyes swiveled in Sheila's direction. She could feel her face growing warm. Porter patted her arm. "It must have slipped his mind, or he surely would have waited."

Before Sheila could reply, Jonah said mildly, "If we're giving our alibis, I'm afraid mine is rather thin. I went downstairs for a candy bar . . ."

"You were gone forever," Elise agreed, with the air of one helping out. Sheila met Jonah's rueful stare and gave him a smile of sympathy. With friends like Elise, nobody needed enemies.

"The machine took my money and I had to get a refund."

"Can you prove that?" Craig demanded, still flushed from the recent encounter.

"I would hope so, if Cheryl remembers giving me the refund. But if I can't, neither can I say where any of you were while I was gone." His eyes met Craig's squarely across the broad table, then he grinned and reached into his backpack. "Who wants an orange?"

"I do." Elise reached for one and began to peel it. "Oooh, sticky. Anybody got a tissue?"

"Here's my handkerchief." Craig handed it to her.

"Thanks, Craig. Here, take half the orange." She broke it into unequal pieces and handed him the smaller half.

"That's not half," he pointed out.

"That's so you'll get your heavenly reward."

Seeing his blank look, Sheila smiled. "Elise's third grade Sunday school teacher taught her that people who take smaller pieces always get a heavenly reward. She's been making sure her friends qualify ever since."

"Good girl." Porter patted her on the back, then caught Sheila's eye. "I would have said 'good woman,' but it doesn't have quite the same ring to it."

"It sure doesn't," she agreed.

Elise, meanwhile, had turned to Jonah. "While you were gone, I went for a cup of tea." She stuck a forefinger in one cheek as if that helped her think. "Then I came back and talked to Craig and Veronica." She stopped, stricken. "Do you reckon Dean was dead while I was down there getting my tea?"

"Did you see anybody?" Veronica asked.

Elise nodded. "Sally. And I heard Dean on the phone, so I guess he wasn't dead yet."

"Not likely," Porter agreed solemnly. "When did you all take this famous break?"

"About a quarter till three." Veronica spoke like one who knew for sure. "I called my husband, and he was still on *his* break."

"You went out for a while a little later." Craig turned to her with narrowed eyes. "Did you go down to your office?"

"No, I went to the bathroom, just like you did once or twice."

"You were gone a long time," he pressed.

Jonah held up one hand to cut the conversation short. "We were *all* gone a long time," he said wearily. "Me to the candy machine, Elise to get her tea, Veronica to the bathroom. You're the only one, in fact, who was never out of the room more than five minutes. Since you, Porter, were not with us, I trust you made a full confession to the police."

"Oh, I did, Father, I did." Porter started to sketch a quick cross on his chest, caught Sheila's eye and stopped with a smile of rueful apology.

Jonah pushed his chair away from the table. "Well, I for one have work to do, and I suspect most of you do, too. Let's call this quits for today."

They all rose in agreement, but before they could leave, Craig pointed at Sheila. "What's she doing here?"

Porter moved gracefully to stand behind her. "Why don't you rephrase that, Craigie, to 'What are *you* doing here?'? The lady is able to speak for herself."

Sheila gave them a wry smile and took a slight step away from Porter's protection. "But the lady can't answer the question, beyond saying I've been asked to stay on the tenth floor for a few days to make sure that the honor of Galaxia and Hosokawa are not tarnished by this crime. What precisely I am to be doing . . ." She shook her head. "Your guess is as good as mine."

"Well, my guess is you are supposed to be having a Coke with me in five minutes in the basement." Porter put a hand on her shoulder and steered her toward the elevators. "Let's make a getaway while the going's good," he murmured into her ear. "Craig in this mood is not pleasant to be around."

"Take the stairs," Elise hissed as they passed her.

Sheila thanked her with a wave, but led the way to the elevator. Unlike Elise, she had no worries about handling Porter in an elevator. Her diplomatic skills were probably equal to the task. If not, she had spent the summer renewing martial arts skills learned long ago in Japan.

"What are you grinning about?" Porter asked as the door closed behind them. "You look like the cat who ate the cream."

She had to come up quickly with a casual reply. It would never do to say she was picturing his face after he'd just been flipped in an elevator.

I s this a fountain Coke?" She pulled on her straw in delight. The drink had arrived in a tall, old-fashioned glass that bulged at the top above a narrow bottom.

"What else? Atlanta is Coca-Cola's interplanetary head-quarters."

They sat at a small marble table for two in the large oval lobby outside the coffeeshop. Across from them a man in gray was polishing the pink marble floor.

"I haven't seen Woody today," said Porter.

Sheila shook her head. "I heard Elton say he was home sick. I'm not surprised."

Porter nodded. "Poor guy was pretty shook up. He's not very strong. But I don't want to talk about Woody, I want to talk about you. Tell me about when you were a little girl."

She considered. "Well, I spent most of the time in Japan.

109

But once every four years we'd come home on furlough to my grandmama's in Montgomery, and I'd go to a drugstore with tables and chairs exactly like these—"

". . . where you'd eat strawberry ice cream cones." Porter licked his raspberry gelato with a wise look.

"How did you know?"

He wiggled his eyebrows at her. "You're a strawberry person, darling. You'd never like vanilla, because it's too, too ordinary, and chocolate would be everybody else's favorite. So you'd insist on strawberry. I'm right, aren't I?"

She nodded ruefully. "Probably even about my reasons. You really can be devilish, did you know that?"

"It's my specialty," he assured her solemnly. "Devilment on order. Craig, however, inspires me to my greatest heights. That man is a—" He stopped. "Fill in the blank as you will."

"What I'd really like to fill in is your own blank schedule for yesterday afternoon," she told him. "I had assumed that 'all of us' in staff meeting included you."

He shook his head. "Oh, no, I'm not one of the vulgar herd. At least not yesterday. I was down on four, looking at artwork for our next direct mail campaign. I don't really have anything to do with that, but they'd asked me to come give an opinion. So—as I'd run out of ways to say no to Craig's brainstorms for the television series—I decided to skip staff meeting." He bent toward her confidentially. "Actually, I couldn't stomach Craig bad-mouthing Dean when he wasn't there to defend himself. Jonah and Veronica handle it pretty well, and it goes over Elise's head, but I have had—or had had, I guess it should be—all I could take. Sorry to disappoint you, darling, for I'd like to maintain my reputation as a cad, but underneath this wicked exterior beats a heart of gold with an alibi cast in iron."

Back on the tenth floor Porter riffled through a small stack of pink slips from under a ceramic turtle on Sally's desk. "A call from on high," he murmured, handing one to Sheila. "Want to use my phone?"

All Elton Dekker wanted was to tell her the police were done and maintenance had cleaned her office. She could move in at once.

Dean's papers and videos still littered the desk, but they were neatly stacked and the Chinese vase had been set upright. Sheila opened drawers, seeking a place to stow his coffee mug and photographs of his children and Raven Hillis. The upper right drawer was almost empty except for a blue building directory with a number penciled on the front. Dean's memory for numbers had been legendary. Curious, she dialed it.

"Umber, Humphreys and Jacks," a woman answered. A very few questions informed Sheila she had reached an attorney who was supposed to have had his first appointment with Dean that very day.

That hadn't helped much. She took out Dean's pictures again.

Telling the temporary receptionist she would be gone a few minutes, she took the elevator to the first floor, where a wizened security guard watched Galaxia's visitors in and out from a stool behind a tall desk. He seldom spoke unless spoken to. Sheila wondered why he was there at all—and asked.

"I ansah questions." His neck was so skinny his Adam's apple looked like a golf ball in his throat, and his accent was pure South Georgia. "Tell folks 'bout the hist'ry of the buildin' if they want, or where t' find folks. People call me if there's trouble, too. Yestiddy, now, we had a shootin' up on ten. Dean Anderson, the television man. Shot hisself plumb through the heart. Leastwise, that's what we thought. Today the police're hintin' it may have been murdah." His voice dropped to a whisper on the last word, then rose again matter-of-factly. "I had to check it out, then call in the police. We don't handle shootin's and such."

"You were on duty all day yesterday?"

"Eight to five. The night men are on till eight, and people have to sign in if they come in early. After I get here, we just let anybody in." He shook his gray head in dismay. "Looks like we let in one too many yestiddy." He stopped and peered cautiously at her. "You ain't a reporter, are you?"

She shook her head. "I work for Elton Dekker."

"Oh. Mr. Dekkah. That's all right, then."

She held up the photographs she'd brought. "Did you ever see any of these people here before?"

He took the pictures and held them as far away as his arm would stretch, then fumbled in his shirt pocket and produced a pair of creaky black-framed glasses. Laboriously he unfolded them and put them on, then considered the pictures again. Finally he nodded. "Yep, these two younguns 'uz in here yestiddy. Not together, mind. First he come, about one-thirty, and then she did. They both left looking like thundah, I can tell you that. But I don't know who they came to see. They didn't ask for directions or nuthin'."

"Have you told that to the police?"

"Nope. They ain't axt me. If they do, I shore will."

S
he returned soberly to the office she shared with Dean's memory and began to read through his papers, hoping to find a clue to his death. When the others left, she had not yet finished. "Don't stay up here by yourself," Elise urged. "Somebody might get you!"

"Security checks everybody in after six," Sheila assured her, "and I doubt I'll be even that late."

"Have them walk you to your car," Elise commanded. She strolled toward Dean's bookshelf. "Where's the trophy Dean got for the Vietnam book? And the one he got for that series on the Middle East?"

"Aren't they there?" Sheila joined her.

Elise shook her head. "No, and two others are gone, too."

"When did you count them?"

Elise looked puzzled. "I never counted them. I just know them. They are all so different—" She stopped in midsentence and began to rearrange the shelf. Then she pointed to the four vacant places she had left. "The one for the Middle East programs was here, a darling little silver Arab holding one of those curved swords. The Vietnam one was here." She pointed to another gap on the shelf. "It was gold with a green marble base, and had a soldier carrying a child. Here there was another gold one with a world on top, and at the end here a silver football player carrying a ball that looked a lot like Dean must have used to."

If you want syntax, Aunt Mary, try Elise's, Sheila thought—trying not to picture Dean as a football. Still, Elise's artist eye had recorded those trophies in such detail that Sheila could probably pick them out of fifty. "I wonder if the police took them for any reason."

Elise's eyes grew wide. "Do you think maybe somebody hit Dean with them and then shot him? Or maybe—you don't think it was four men who did it, do you? One with each trophy?"

"I think that would have been a little excessive." Sheila turned so Elise couldn't see her expression.

"Maybe." Elise gave up her theory reluctantly.

"I think what we should do is report this to Mr. Dekker and let him tell the police," Sheila informed her. "If you are certain Dean hadn't taken the trophies home."

"They could look for them there," Elise replied with unexpected shrewdness.

They could indeed. Sheila moved to the desk and called the sixteenth floor.

13

Dean Anderson was buried on Thursday afternoon from North Avenue Presbyterian Church.

Sheila and Wylene rode with Elton Dekker, who apologized as he picked them up at the door, saying "Sorry, but my car's in the shop. I'm driving my son's." It was too late for Sheila to suggest her Maxima instead of the tiny red compact.

Wylene managed to lose the inevitable mannered jousting for the nonexistent back seat. As Sheila folded her limbs in awkward places and smoothed her navy skirt to keep it from wadding, she fervently damned car designers to several eons of purgatory riding in their own back seats.

North Avenue Presbyterian, she reflected as they approached the large granite edifice, was Dean's kind of church—perched on a conspicuous corner, attended by prestigious people with political clout and conservative theology. And big hearts, she mentally added, noting inner city children and their mothers clustered around the back door.

There is no graceful way to unfold oneself from a small back seat. Sheila was grateful that today, at least, news-hungry reporters lurking in the church parking lot were more interested in national noteworthies climbing from limousines than in dignitaries from Encyclopedia Galaxia.

It was another glorious day. She would have preferred to

take a long walk or bask in the sun somewhere out of the breeze. She was there, however, not merely out of duty. She had been genuinely fond of Dean.

As soon as they entered the door an exceedingly thin young man in black asked their names. "Dekker?" he murmured. "You are to sit in the fifth row." He wore an expression that could only be that of a mortician. Surely they must pass exams in the Somber Look before being allowed to wear it in public.

As she followed Wylene's chic back up the long aisle, she tried to see who else had come. Most of Atlanta, it seemed, and half the world besides. She saw several faces she'd only previously seen on national television and some she had met in her days as an embassy wife. The mayor was there, and the governor. Probably a White House representative, too, although she didn't immediately recognize one. Strange how easily she had gotten out of the habit of knowing the entire cabinet and junior staff by sight.

Elise sat with Veronica and Jonah near the back on one side. Porter was directly in front of Lieutenant Green on the other. (Had Green deliberately sat where he could keep them all in view?)

Only as Sheila turned to enter her pew, however, did she glimpse, far in the back corner, a familiar silver head under a saucy black hat. It gave Sheila a slight, well-bred nod.

Sheila settled onto rose plush cushions deep in thought. What had lured Aunt Mary from her comfortable apartment to attend the funeral of a man she had never met? Did she—like the police—think someone should be watching the congregation from the back? Obviously she did not consider Lieutenant Green sufficient. But what was she watching for? Or expecting to happen?

The scent of flowers intruded into Sheila's speculations. This close to the front the aroma was almost dizzying, for the entire width of the sanctuary was banked with wreaths of carnations, roses, lilies, and some flowers Sheila didn't try to identify.

Wylene gave her arm a slight pinch to make Sheila turn

her way. "Ours." She nodded toward a purple and yellow gladiola wreath.

Not mine, Sheila wanted to protest. I loathe glads, and I'd never have chosen those colors. Only years of habit molded her mouth into an appropriate smile before she turned her attention to the steel-gray casket beneath its blanket of white roses.

Incongruously, a larger blanket of red ones was draped across a florist's stand on the other side from where the family would sit. She wondered fleetingly why there were two, then decided she didn't really care. She was far more interested in the organist's excellent rendition of a Bach fugue and in the sun, streaming through the stained-glass windows to gently caress the creamy walls with rainbows.

She was engaged in studying the front windows—John Knox, exclaiming "Give me Scotland or I die!" and Martin Luther, "Here I stand, I can do no other"—when she heard the rustle of people turning in their seats. The family had arrived.

Not only the family. They had scarcely entered their three pews—a stony-faced Laura and her children, a stocky man who must be Dean's brother with his wife and four children, a small weeping woman who must be his mother, a shrunken red-faced man with a square jaw who could only be his dad, and a plethora of other southern-style relations—when Wylene (who had turned to look back down the aisle) drew in a long breath between her teeth.

"Look! There's Raven!" someone exclaimed softly behind them.

Raven Hillis was as shapely (Sheila supposed some would even say "ravishing") offscreen as on. But her primary splendor was not her body or even her equally beautiful face. Her trademark was her astounding hair. Born Katie Hillis, her film name was inspired by the blue-black waterfall that swung to her hips. Raven Hillis films always had one scene where she whisked out a pin and let her hair cascade down her back. It was a scene some fans panted for.

Today, however, it was pinned soberly in a bun at her

neck, above a suit as dark as her hair, black spike heels and stockings (studded, regrettably, with tiny black hearts). From the tilt of her chin, the shininess of her perfect nose and the redness of her hazel eyes, it was obvious that Raven was determined on one thing: to play the role of Dean Anderson's chief mourner.

She went to the very front pew, cast a look at the side reserved for "Family," and took her place alone in the opposite pew, directly in front of the blanket of red roses. Now Sheila understood the two blankets, and pitied the funeral director who had had to choose which to place on the casket.

During the entire service Raven wept, dabbing at her eyes with a white handkerchief bordered in black lace. Sheila wondered where she had gotten one on such short notice. A prop room? She chided herself. If Raven was theatrical, it was only to be expected. It was how she made her living, after all. She could also be genuinely mourning Dean.

Laura Anderson's reaction—and those of her children—were blocked from Sheila's view, but she could see that Raven's presence distressed Dean's mother very much. She ached for the sweet-faced woman dragged into such limelight by the loss of a famous son.

After the service Sheila cast a wistful look across the parking lot at the International House of Pancakes. She could do with a cup of coffee right now. Elton didn't suggest coffee, but at least her pause was long enough for Wylene to climb into the back of the car.

The procession wound through some of Atlanta's poorest streets to Oakland City Cemetery, the city's historical burying place. As she surveyed its decayed neighborhood pitted with factories and vacant lots, Sheila recalled James Dickey's poem about buying a plot high in a mountain churchyard to avoid an urban burial. Had Dean wanted to be buried here? She also wondered how his parents felt about his being buried beside Ada and William Bayard, Laura's grandparents, in his ex-wife's family plot.

After the graveside service, as Sheila and her party turned to go, their path was suddenly blocked. "Oh, Mr. Dekker, I am so glad to meet you." The curvaceous brunette took no notice of his female companions, but zeroed in on Elton. Onlookers might wonder if Raven Hillis only attended her lover's funeral to meet his employer.

Traces of tears still lingered on her cheeks and the hazel eyes were still dewy. But now Raven had other things on her mind. With apparent disregard for clustering reporters and popping flashbulbs she laid one hand urgently on Elton's arm.

"I have a little problem. You see, I left some things at Dean's when I came through town—he was keeping them for me."

How innocent it all sounded!

"I don't know whom to see about getting them back."

"Have you tried the police?" Wylene asked bluntly.

Raven dismissed her with a glance. "I wondered if perhaps you could take me over there, Mr. Dekker, help me . . ."

"You are taking nothing from that house." The voice— well modulated and as deep as Aunt Mary's—spoke behind them. They turned to see Laura Anderson confronting them, to the dismay of her children.

Laura's face was heavy in the jowls, her chin beginning to double. But she drew her still-trim figure to its full five feet and confronted the other woman with icy politeness. "What is in Dean's house belongs to his children. If you want to discuss it further, have your lawyer call Dean's lawyer."

With her bosom thrust high, she resembled a bantam hen fighting for her chicks. These particular chicks, however, resented her protection. Bayard, eyes puffy and hair in its usual disarray, was carefully looking across the old cemetery toward a nearby MARTA station. Neal scuffed the ground with one toe.

"Come on, Mom," he said in a low, urgent tone.

"I certainly will not." Laura spoke with emphasis.

Reporters jostled closer. Mikes appeared from nowhere. Laura spoke directly into them. "I will not let Dean's children be deprived of their inheritance. Nothing leaves his house without our lawyer's express permission. Now if you will leave us to our grief . . ." She pressed a tissue to her eyes and

119

turned from the reporters toward a waiting limousine with such poise that Sheila was momentarily surprised—until she reflected that as Dean's wife, Laura had often appeared with him in family specials.

"You see what she's like," Raven told Elton. "I will never get my things unless you help me. Will you?"

"What seems to be the problem here?" Lieutenant Green's voice was calm, even consoling. Raven turned to him with eyes suddenly full of tears. Sheila missed what she said, wondering how the woman had conjured the tears that quickly—and how reporters knew to zoom in on them at once. She only caught Lieutenant Green's reply.

"Well, now, ma'am, perhaps Mrs. Travis here would accompany you to the house. She's helping with this investigation, you see."

Sheila looked at him in astonishment—and indignation. On Monday he had accused her of forcing him to make a thorough investigation. Tuesday he had pointedly informed her that staff interviews were private, and later, when she had called about the trophies, he'd complained that she was giving him too much work to do and informed her that his men had the case well in hand. She had not heard from him since. She would love to see Dean's house, but not to be sent in this off-handed way.

"I beg your pardon . . ." she began.

His gloomy voice went on as if she were not there. "I've got two people at the house right now, and I'll give them word you are to be let in. You may not remove property, but list what you claim is yours. Then you can arrange to have it removed after the lawyers are finished." He gave her a mournful smile.

"I'm sorry," Sheila informed him, "I'm with Mr. Dekker . . ."

She was talking to air. Lieutenant Green was already moving along the path.

"You can ride in my car." Raven started down the walk, certain that Sheila would follow.

"Thank God Dean didn't live to marry that woman," said Wylene with a sniff.

Sheila turned to Elton Dekker for help. She met a shrug and a rueful smile. "We've been bamboozled. But better you than me. My wife would never believe I went with Raven Hillis only under police orders." He and Wylene headed toward his car.

Sheila hurried after Raven, muttering all the way. "Bad word! Bad word! Bad word!"

14

A thin woman with permed gray hair and a nervous habit of clearing her throat was sitting in the limousine when Sheila got there. She did not seem surprised that Raven did not bother with introductions. "Hi, I'm Zena." She thrust out one hand. "Miss Hillis's companion. Where to now, honey?"

"Dean's." Raven did not speak again. Zena gave the driver instructions, then perched on the edge of her seat taking in the grubby children and sagging houses of Cabbagetown and the gradual improvement as the silver limousine purred up Boulevard. Raven closed her eyes, and Sheila was glad. She had nothing to say to anyone—except Lieutenant Green, Mr. Hashimoto and Aunt Mary.

Sheila was pleased to see that Morningside had remained almost unchanged since she was a girl. It was still a neighborhood of gracious homes, well-kept small lots, and an atmosphere of peace and prosperity.

They stopped in front of a Tudor house, perched on a hill with an enormous live oak filling most of the front yard. Roses lined the drive, ivy covered the bank and azaleas grew almost as tall as the first-floor windows. Sheila could see why Dean, after a lifetime of junketing around the world, would want to settle into this charming old house. It exuded permanence and comfort.

"We're here, honey," Zena piped.

The chauffeur spoke over his shoulder. "I'm sorry, ma'am, that we can't go up the drive. Someone's already there."

Swearing, Raven tugged open the door and jumped out to look. Sheila could see the drive from her window, and the blue Buick that claimed the flat space at the top. A squad car was parked across the street, presumably Owen Green's men.

With another swear word and strides as long as her heels would permit (and with no thought for her companions), Raven climbed the drive. Zena followed as fast as her short legs would carry her.

Sheila ambled, in no hurry. While her view of the stoop was still obscured by azaleas she heard Laura Anderson's command—"You are *not* to come in here!"—followed by the thump of someone being shoved against a door. A small sheltie dashed down the walk as if running for its life.

Sheila bent and caught the dog by its collar. "Oh no, you don't. Back to the house with you."

She half dragged, half carried the dog up four steps in time to see Raven and Zena disappearing inside and Laura rubbing one hip.

"May I help you?" Sheila stuck her purse under her elbow and offered Laura her free hand.

Laura set her lips in a tight line. "I'm bruised, and if she tries to take one thing from the house I'll sue for assault *and* theft!"

Excited by the woman's fury, the small dog began to struggle and bark. Laura dissolved into a sneezing fit and Sheila felt as if she were being torn in half between them. She dropped Laura's arm, opened the screened door and pushed the dog inside.

"Raven won't take anything out," she assured Laura once the dog was safely stowed. "Lieutenant Green asked her to list everything that is hers, but he explicitly said nothing can go out of the house at this time."

She guarded against the dog getting out while Laura went in, then slipped in herself, only to trip over a large pile of books, pictures and dishes stacked in the front hall. Rubbing her knee, she gave Laura a reproachful look. "*Nothing*," she emphasized, "is to leave this house. Lieutenant Green was quite clear. Make a list of anything you feel is rightfully yours, not part of the estate. But put everything back where you found it."

"That's what I told them." The redheaded officer she had seen Monday came from beside the newel post and stuck out his hand. "Frank McGehee, ma'am." His eyes held the welcome of a besieged fort finally sighting the cavalry. The little dog danced around him, yipping as if her life depended on it.

Without speaking, Laura went to a desk in the living room and began pawing through the drawers. Raven, nearby, was pointing out an oil painting while Zena wrote rapidly on a pad.

The small dog, perhaps remembering a familiar smell, dashed to Raven's heels, still barking. "Hush, Lady," Raven said, without conviction. The dog continued to bark.

"Lady!" Sheila spoke in the tone Aunt Mary used to quell recalcitrant children. It worked. The dog looked around, ceased her yips and came tentatively toward the one who spoke with such authority. Sheila rubbed her behind the ears. "Has she been fed?"

The officer nodded. "A neighbor's had her since Monday. They just brought her back when we arrived this afternoon."

She wanted to ask where the dog would go now, but Laura had important issues on her mind. "Have you seen any pearls around here? They belong to Bayard. Miss Hillis is *not* to have them." Her breath was ragged, her eyes glared.

Raven looked over her shoulder. "Today I am only listing what is mine. I'll wait to see what Dean has left me in his will." She gave Laura a pitying smile. "Probably more than he left you."

"Good luck." Neal spoke bitterly from the couch. He was so hunched in the cushions that Sheila hadn't noticed he was there.

Raven hadn't either. "Oh, hello, Neal. I don't think I'll need luck. Dean told me last week he was revising his will."

"Talk!" Neal's lip curled with disdain. Sheila thought it a

shame he didn't smile occasionally. His weak face was pink and pimpled enough without his increasing its homeliness. His conversation, too, left much to be desired in his father's home on the day of his father's funeral.

He was already in the middle of his next sentence. ". . . big on talk. Getting him to *do* something was harder."

Zena, who until now had been only a silent partner, turned angrily. "That's no way to speak of your father, young man."

"But true." Bayard came down the steps and lounged in the living room archway. "Daddy was famous for promising to rewrite his will. He said he would several times. But did he? Your guess is as good as ours." She shrugged. "Unless he saw his lawyer Monday morning, we may all be in for a shock."

She turned and swept back upstairs, head high. An exit, Sheila thought, worthy of Raven herself. Sheila was surprised to see Jonah Baker waiting for Bayard at the top of the stairs.

"Hello, Sheila," he called. "I'm helping Bay out."

So it was "Bay" already. It had been Crystal and Woody Robles on Monday. Was Jonah really only the errant knight he seemed?

Laura had been through every drawer of the secretary. Now she began to pull books off the shelves and look behind them.

"Could I help you?" Sheila asked.

"No, if they're here, I'll find them." Laura abandoned the bookshelves and headed toward the dining room. "Watch her, Neal," she ordered with a jerk of her head toward Raven, who was stroking a small brass sculpture on the mantelpiece.

Raven turned to Sheila with tears in her eyes. "How can she be so horrible? No wonder Dean left her. All she thinks about is his *stuff*." She said it as if it were an obscenity. (And as if she hadn't been the first to bring up the will.) "When Dean—poor Dean . . ." She dropped onto a chair, sobbing.

"This has been so hard on her," Zena told Sheila. "I'll get you some water, honey." She headed for the kitchen.

"Hey, it's okay." Neal rose and went to stand beside the

126

star, patting her shoulder awkwardly. When Raven gave him a damp but dazzling smile, his face turned scarlet.

"I'll be okay. It's just being here without him." Her voice trembled again. "I will be fine," she said resolutely, rising and taking a deep breath. "Let me just get on with my list. After all, Mr. McGehee"—she flashed him a smile, too, but Sheila noticed he did not blush—"said we only have an hour. I need to finish downstairs, then see what I left in the bedroom."

Neal's own blush deepened and he stumbled on his way back to the couch. Sheila decided to overcome her natural distaste and join him. Lady circled three times and lay on her feet.

"I'm Sheila Travis. We met last week at the Galaxia reception. You were warning your father about Darius—"

"Fat lot of good it did me." Neal looked very young and miserable. "Why wouldn't he listen to me just once?"

"Do you think Darius killed him?" she asked.

He shrugged. "Sure. Who else? If the police would just get off their fat—"

She knew what he was about to say, and didn't want to hear it. "What if it wasn't Darius? Can you think of anybody else who would want to kill your father?"

Neal's laugh was decidedly unfilial. "Only those who knew him well. Good old dad—the world's best friend. But don't expect him to be around when you need him." He gave another short, high laugh. "You want to know who might have killed him? Whoever it was, they did us all a favor!"

He leapt to his feet and rushed down the hall.

Sheila's eyes followed him thoughtfully. But for now, her task was not Neal, but two women circling Dean Anderson's house, coveting his possessions. Heavens, was Laura looking inside the humidifier?

Sheila leaned her head against the high cushions of the couch and watched through her lashes. Sure enough, the woman had thrust her arm into the humidifier and come up wet to the elbow, but still dissatisfied. She headed for the kitchen, full of purpose.

Raven, meanwhile, was drifting through the small den

behind the living room, picking up first one of Dean's souvenirs and then another. Officer McGehee was keeping an eye on both of them.

Alone in the living room except for the dog, Sheila was glad to sit for just a while and do nothing.

It was a peaceful room, but what personality it had came not from its decor but from Dean's own personality impressed on it through mementos from his travels. Mentally Sheila repainted the walls a soft rose, tossed out the brown suede sofa and matching chair, the leather recliner and Scandinavian rug. She placed an overstuffed sofa before the bay window and deep, soft chairs to flank the fireplace—near the built-in bookshelf so she wouldn't have to get up for a book. She hung a watercolor over the carved mantel and replaced the tan miniblinds with floral draperies to match the sofa. On the polished wood floor she spread a creamy Oriental bordered in shades of rose and blue.

With a start she realized what she was doing—putting her own furniture into Dean's house. "I'm as bad as the rest of them." She'd water the plants—they could use it, and it would give her a perfectly good reason for following everybody around the house. She went in search of the kitchen, Lady tapping at her heels.

She located a pitcher and filled it, glancing out the window over the sink as she did so. Neal was in the small fenced backyard, kicking at leaves.

Lady trotted to the back door and whined pitifully. "Out you go," Sheila said, holding the door. The dog went down one step then turned, waiting. When Sheila started back in, she came back up the step, dragging her tail. "You're a pest," Sheila told her. But when a glance over her shoulder showed the young policeman keeping an eye on both Laura and Raven, she followed the dog down the steps.

She picked up a stick and tossed it across the yard for Lady to fetch. The dog retrieved the stick and returned it not to Sheila, but to Neal. He looked at it without expression. "Throw it," Sheila suggested. He did, listlessly. Lady retrieved it. He threw it again. She returned it to Sheila.

"Three-way catch."

"Yeah." He didn't smile, but seemed more relaxed.

They played for several minutes, with Lady choosing whose turn it was. Although Neal never spoke, his face lost some of its haunted look.

Finally Sheila decided perhaps she could ask one question. "Somebody said you visited your dad the day he died. Would you mind telling me why?" She watched as she asked the question, and saw his startled look. Immediately he lowered his gaze.

"Wasn't me. Must have been somebody else. I was shopping with Mom until three." He tossed Lady's stick across the yard.

His last word gave him away, of course. If he hadn't been there, why alibi only the early afternoon? He turned on one heel and headed toward the house. "Guess I'd better see if I left anything around the house—the *two* times I was here."

Before Sheila could whistle for Lady and follow him, Bayard came down the steps. "Who are you?" she demanded without preamble. "And what do you want with Neal? When I met you last week at the party, Daddy said you were his friend. At Galaxia on Monday, they treated you like a VIP. You came to the funeral with Mr. Dekker but now you show up as a friend of Raven's. What's your game?"

Sheila gave her a rueful smile. "Patsy, I think. I work for Hosokawa International, Galaxia's parent company. They sent me to the press reception on Thursday, where I saw your dad for the first time in ten years. They also sent me over on Monday as a way of showing honor to your father. Japanese are very sensitive to honor and protocol. That's why I went to the funeral with Elton Dekker. But I would have gone anyway. I liked your father very much."

"Yeah." Bayard scuffed a few leaves with one toe. "So what are you doing here now?"

"Walking the dog." Sheila pointed to Lady, snuffling in the boxwoods. "Will you take her home with you today?"

"Mom's allergic to dogs. Why did you come with Raven?"

If she was this single-minded about all her stories, Bayard would make a good reporter. Sheila answered carefully.

"Raven asked Mr. Dekker to come, and he and Lieutenant Green sent me with her instead. Mr. Dekker had work he needed to do."

"So you're not her friend?" Bayard watched her closely.

Sheila shook her head. "I'd never met her until today, after the funeral. Mr. Dekker asked me to come with her. Once she drops me off at Galaxia, I never expect to see her again."

"She's not a bad sort," Bayard said unexpectedly. "I think Daddy really did love her, in his way. He liked having her around. Maybe they could have been good together. But Mama doesn't bring out the best in her." She paused, then muttered, "Mama doesn't bring out the best in anybody."

Sheila, caught between being polite and being honest, chose not to reply. Instead, she wandered over to where Lady was sniffing down an animal hole in a small bed of well-tended roses. Bayard wandered to the other side of the yard and pulled leaves off a spindly pyracantha. Sheila almost didn't hear her when she muttered, "Damn it all to hell!"

The women's eyes met across the small yard. Bayard chewed her lower lip defiantly. "He didn't need to leave us like this."

Sheila tried a frontal attack. "You're worried about the will?"

Bayard nodded.

"Well, if you're short of money and need an advance, I think your lawyer could . . ."

The vehemence of Bayard's reply startled her. "Advance? Advance on what?" Her scorn overcame any reticence about discussing personal matters with a stranger. "God only knows what Daddy did with his money. Probably left every penny to some good cause."

Sheila didn't know if she was more disturbed by the idea that Dean would neglect his family, or Bayard's sullen acceptance of that. "Surely he will have left you and Neal something. He loved you very much!"

"I know." Bayard didn't doubt that. "But he was pretty upset with us both about five years ago, and he talked about making a new will then. Said he'd leave everything to Save the Children, since his own children were beyond saving. Of course, he could have made it later, during his 'Say No to Drugs' period, or earlier, in his world hunger period."

Seeing Sheila's surprise, she gave a low, sad laugh. "He didn't do charity spots or anything, but Daddy always gave away a lot of money. One of my earliest memories is a fight he and Mama had one night when I was in bed. Neal wasn't even born. Mama said, 'Dean, we could be rich if you'd stop giving everything away.' And he said, 'But honey, they need it so much worse than we do.' I was proud of him—proud of him!" She turned her head and wiped at her eyes with one hand.

Jonah appeared on the kitchen steps. "You all right out here?" Bayard turned her back so he couldn't see her tear-stained face. He joined her and pulled her around gently. "What's this about?" he asked, tilting her chin with one finger.

Tenderness was one thing against which Bayard had no defenses. Great sobs shook her. He held her until she could speak. "I sound so greedy," she said in deep, gasping phrases. "I'm not. It's not me—it's Neal. I'm scared Daddy hasn't left him anything, and without money, he'll be tied to Mama all his life!" She ended in a wail.

Sheila pulled a tissue from her jacket pocket and offered it. "If Dean meant to make a new will, maybe this time he did."

Bayard collapsed onto a bench with a groan. (Aimed, Sheila suspected, at the denseness of older people.) "My daddy," she said in the tone of one explaining the obvious to an imbecile, "had an in-box stuffed with good intentions. He was going to do this, and going to do that. But then something else—or somebody else—would come along and he'd forget." She scuffed the ground with one toe. "He wasn't bad—he just wanted to love everybody all the time. You can't do it. Even *he* couldn't do it. And now this will thing—it's making us all crazy. The lawyer won't tell us a thing until we meet with him tomorrow, so we don't know whether we'll get anything, or whether he's left it all to Raven or a good cause."

Jonah dropped to the bench beside her. "I suppose your mother could contest—"

Her face flushed with fury. "Don't you understand anything? That's exactly what Neal and I do *not* want to happen. Another round of her on television dragging Daddy's memory—and us—through the mud and courts. We've done that, thanks." She fished in her pocket (today she had on a black baggy jacket and a black skirt) for the soggy tissue she'd stuffed there a few moments before. With a loud snort she blew her nose, wadded the tissue and returned it to her pocket. Then she sat with tear-damp eyes, defying either of them to come up with a solution.

Jonah stood and, shoving his hands deep in his pockets, went to join the dog. "What have you found, Lady, a rabbit hole?"

Sheila wondered if the time was ripe to ask a question. "Bayard, you went to see your dad on Monday, didn't you? Why?"

The girl stood and spoke as if she had not heard. "I need to get back in. I've got some clothes in an upstairs bedroom." Without another look at Sheila, she went up the stairs.

"Did she really?" Jonah strolled back to where Sheila still stood, watching the door.

"Yes, and she's the second Anderson to discover an urgent need to go inside when asked about that."

"Probably doesn't mean a thing. She's pretty cut up." He patted Sheila on the shoulder in a comforting way, making her feel ancient. As he followed Bayard, Lady at his heels, Sheila was tempted to plop down on the bench for the rest of Raven's stay. Only curiosity and a sense of duty (to whom? she wondered) lured her back to the kitchen.

McGehee was standing at the sink, drinking a glass of water and giving the full pitcher a bemused look. She lifted the pitcher from beneath his gaze. "I was going to water the plants, but the dog had to go out."

"They're going through the bedrooms now," he said, lowering his voice confidentially. "Lucky it's Walters upstairs and not me. That wife is looking for something she can't find, and she isn't going to give up a thing without a fight, is she?"

"A woman of strong character," Sheila murmured, departing with her pitcher.

"I'm going out for some air," he called, slamming the door.

Dean either loved plants or couldn't turn down a nursery. It took nine pitchers of water to do just the downstairs. Like McGehee, Sheila decided to abandon the upstairs to poor Walters, whoever he or she might be.

As she moved about with her pitcher, the others came and went. Laura clumped down the basement stairs. Raven called a greeting from the top of the stairs. She thought she heard Jonah and Bayard in the kitchen and Neal in a front bedroom.

She was finishing up in the front hall, wondering if she'd overwatered the rubber plant, when she heard a loud whisper coming from the small butler's pantry that separated the dining room from the kitchen. The door was cracked, or she would never have heard. As it was, she could not tell who was whispering, and whether he or she was speaking to another person. But she recognized the tone of voice. Someone was very frightened.

"I've got to get it back—I just have to! Otherwise, I could be in a lot of trouble."

15

Sheila crossed the dining room to the pantry and shoved open the swinging door. The room was empty. Behind her, the doorbell rang. Annoyed, she went to the door accompanied by Lady, barking.

The chauffeur stood there, head cocked deferentially. "Pardon me, ma'am, but how much longer will we be? I have another client at five, and will either need to leave soon, or will need to call someone else to take that run."

As Sheila bent to shush the dog, Raven spoke from behind her. "You'd better call someone else. I may be a while yet."

"You can leave now." Laura was at the foot of the stairs.

"Oh, Mother." Bayard came down the staircase followed by Jonah.

Neal, from the living room arch, pleaded, "Can't we go soon?"

They had all gathered. But where had they come from?

"Were you upstairs?" Sheila asked Raven.

"Of course, where else? I had to get some things out of the bedroom." Her emphasis on the last word could only be for Laura's benefit. To illustrate, she held up rose satin pajamas.

"Were you with her?" Sheila asked Laura.

The ex-wife raised one eyebrow. Her tan eyes beneath

135

penciled brows regarded Sheila curiously. "I don't believe we were introduced. Things were so hectic. Are you with the police?"

"Oh, no," Sheila assured her. "It's just that I wouldn't have answered the door if I'd realized anybody was nearby."

If she had hoped that her tone of embarrassed apology would bring forth a spate of explanations, she was wrong. Officer McGehee, however, surprised her by backing up her request.

"I'd like to know where everyone was, too."

"I was upstairs," Bayard volunteered.

"And I was with her," Jonah added quickly. Neal threw him a look of surprise.

"I was in the sitting room." Neal jerked his head in that direction. He, at least, was lying. Sheila had just watered the plants in that room, and it had been empty.

Laura pulled herself to her full height. "And I have no idea where I was—I've been wandering about. I am through upstairs," she said, turning to her children. "Do you have lists ready?"

Bayard shrugged. "I don't have anything except clothes and a couple of books."

"I don't have anything," Neal muttered. "I only came twice."

"By your own choice," Bayard snarled. "Daddy invited you."

"Children, children," Laura cautioned them. "Very well, I think we can be going as soon as Miss Hillis is ready." She stood in the hall, arms akimbo.

"You go on," Raven said graciously. "I may be a while."

"The officer said an hour," Laura reminded her sharply. "It's been almost that, and I'm certain he wants to close the house."

"He can tell me when he's ready." Raven smiled at him and walked up the stairs as only a film star can.

Laura bent to pick up a picture from the floor. "This was a gift to both of us years ago," she informed McGehee, "and it's quite valuable. I don't want to leave it here."

He put out one hand. "I'm sorry, but my orders are that *nothing* of Mr. Anderson's is to leave the house. Just put it on your list." With obvious reluctance and smoldering fury, Laura handed it to him and started for the door. "You just make sure that *she*,"—she jerked her head toward the stairs—"doesn't take anything either. If she takes a single thing out of this house, I shall hold you personally—"

Bayard grabbed her by the arm. "Listen to me. That woman loved Daddy, and she lived here with him. You've got to accept that as fact. Those were her pajamas and it's her pink toothbrush in his bathroom. If you try to make a scene about her taking those things, you're going to look like a fool. Now why don't you cool it, and let Mrs.—uh—" She paused, had the grace to look embarrassed.

"Travis," Sheila supplied.

"Yeah, let Mrs. Travis take care of Raven. She's from Galaxia, and was a friend of Daddy's. She won't let Raven take anything that isn't obviously hers, will you?" She turned to Sheila to complete the sentence.

Sheila shook her head. "Lieutenant Green said nothing was to be taken. I personally think you'd save trouble in the long run if he let her remove very personal items."

Laura considered, lips tightly compressed. At last she gave a short nod. "Very well. I will count on you," she said to Sheila formally, "to look after my children's interests."

Considering that she had not yet formed a very high opinion of either child, Sheila thought Laura might have chosen the wrong champion. Laura, however, was already on her way out the door. "Come, Neal. Bayard."

"I'm going with Jonah." Bayard moved closer to him as she spoke. "We're going to get some dinner, then I'll come home."

Laura's face became an unpleasant, mottled red. "Tonight? Of all nights? When your father is barely in his grave? What will people think? You can't just go to a restaurant like nothing has happened! There will be reporters swarming all over town."

"I am a reporter," Bayard reminded her. "They don't scare

me. We'll be home about eight." She took Jonah's hand and more pulled than led him down the steps and toward a car parked in front of the next house. Laura, mindful of her audience, contented herself with a sorrowful sigh until she was beyond the small stoop, but she had not reached the car when she began to rant again. They could still hear her voice as the car backed down the drive.

"Poor Neal," Sheila said to McGehee.

He nodded. "Like you said, a woman of character. Why did you want to know where she was when the doorbell rang?"

"I'd just overheard something when the bell rang." Sheila told him about the voice and what it had said.

He propped one elbow on the newel post and pursed his lips in a silent whistle. "And you don't know who was talking or who to?"

She smiled briefly. He'd just proved that not everybody in Atlanta spoke Aunt Mary's perfect grammar. But because her smile puzzled him, she shook her head. "It could have been any of them."

He scratched one cheek. "Do you think I ought to report this to Lieutenant Green?"

"Probably."

"I'll tell him," he said magnanimously, "it was you who overheard them."

"Do that," she said. "It will make his day. And ask if Raven can take her own clothes, while you're at it."

She waited in the living room while he called. He returned and jerked his head toward the upper floor. "Think you can hurry her along a bit? Tell her she can take her toothbrush, clothes, personal things like that."

Sheila mounted the stairs, Lady trotting behind. "Mr. Hashimoto," she muttered as she climbed, "you and I are going to have a very long talk one day."

Zena found two grocery sacks and began filling them with lacy underwear and satin pajamas, under the eye of a ruddy-faced young policeman who must have been Walters. He leaned against one window frame, ostensibly watching each item as Zena shoved it into her bag. Actually his eyes were more often on Raven, who was drifting around the room smoothing the spread, touching the draperies, or examining her flawless skin in Dean's mirror. Being a policeman's a tough job, Sheila thought, but somebody's got to do it.

"Give me a hand, will you?" Zena asked her.

Her voice was husky with unshed tears, and Sheila looked at her with surprise. Was Zena one of millions of women who would cry themselves to sleep tonight having buried Dean Anderson as they had loved him—via television?

Surrounded by Dean's most personal things, she could have wept herself. His robust charm smiled down from photographs that covered one whole wall—shots of Dean with most of the important people the world had known in the past thirty years. Because they were here, and not publicly displayed, Sheila suspected Dean hung them not because of his own face in each, but because of the memories the other faces evoked. She was glad she wouldn't have the sad task of packing away these pictures and his clothes.

Sheila picked up the second sack and began to empty a drawer of sweaters. Lady looked inquiringly from one woman to the other, then trotted into the bathroom and back out again.

"She's looking for Dean," Raven said to the room at large. "How do you tell a dog her master has died?"

"If they've been together long, I think they sense it," Walters said, "but this dog, now, she doesn't seem to be grieving."

Raven threw him a dazzling smile as if he'd made a brilliant deduction. "Dean had only had her a few weeks." She picked up a photo from the dresser. "He must have just framed this." She held it out to Sheila. The policeman moved closer, too, to have a look. He stood near enough to Raven to inhale the musky perfume she wore. As he examined the picture, he clenched and unclenched his fists and Sheila wondered if it was her chaperonage or his rigid training that kept him from pulling the pins from that famous hair and watching it fall down Raven's back. Maybe she had been wrong. Perhaps for Officer Walters this was a *very* difficult assignment!

She turned her attention to the picture. It showed Raven and Dean, Lady between them, on top of a mountain.

"Look, baby, it's you and Daddy and me at Fort Mountain." Raven bent to show the photo to the dog. Lady sniffed it, licked her hand, then trotted back toward the bathroom. Raven touched the photo gently. "We went there just a few weeks ago, right after he got Lady." Tears formed in her eyes and she clasped it to her breast. She moved to the window and stood there, struggling to regain her composure. "I do think this is mine, don't you?"

Officer Walters had to clear his throat twice before he could reply. "Sure," he croaked. "Nobody else would want it." Then, aware that could sound rude, he slipped in the mud and wallowed in it. "I mean, of course, a lot of people would want it, because it's of you and Mr. Anderson, but, I mean, nobody would want it like . . ." He came to a full stop, his face beet red.

"Thank you." Raven slipped the photo into her enormous purse. Sheila wondered for a moment what else might be in that purse, but decided she didn't really care. With a sad little smile Raven looked around the room once more. "That's it, I think. We can go." Every ounce the movie star, she swept through the hall and down the stairs, leaving Zena to bring the sacks.

Not until they were out of earshot of her devoted admirer did she hand Sheila a list and say in a spiteful voice, "Here's my list of what else is mine in the house. Mrs. *Anderson* will probably fight for every picture and stick of furniture, but she won't get them. I'll give them all to charity first!"

She led the way toward the limousine. Zena followed, staggering under the weight of two heavy bags.

Sheila went to give McGehee the list, accompanied by Lady. He was at the sink again, having another drink. His head must have gotten hot, too, for he had removed his hat and was fanning himself with it. "I don't know what it is about

140

old houses," he said with a sheepish grin, "but they make me thirsty."

"It's the weather, I think," she nodded. "I've been yearning for coffee for hours." She informed him that Raven was done, and what Officer Walters had let her take. "Here's her list."

He put out his hand and scanned the handwriting. "Nope, this doesn't match either. Look at this, will you? I found it in the wastebasket by his desk before you all arrived."

He held out a letter. It was written in green ink, in a large, sloping hand, on a small notecard. The message was brief, and to the point:

I do not know how you can cause me so much pain. Please do not let this go on, for both our sakes. I am growing desperate.

"Any idea who that might be from?" he asked. "It's not Mrs. Anderson or the girl, either. The handwriting doesn't match." He held out the lists Laura and Bayard had just written. Laura's writing was small and careful, Bayard's an almost illegible scrawl.

Sheila examined the note again. "It could be any one of a thousand besotted women who loved him from afar."

He nodded, tapped his thigh with his hat. "I'll turn it in and see what the lab can make of it."

He walked her to the door and bent to scratch Lady behind the ears. "I don't know what to do about this dog. The family doesn't want her, and without the lawyer's permission I can't offer her to that young lady out there." (One man at least, Sheila noted, was not smitten by Raven's charms.) "I don't suppose you could take her home with you for a few days, could you?"

"Sorry, no. I live in an apartment, and I'm not sure they take dogs. Since I don't have one, I never asked. Besides, we aren't supposed to remove Dean's property, remember?"

141

He shook his head. "But I can't just leave her here, and the neighbors who were keeping her go on vacation tomorrow."

Sheila looked at Lady and Lady looked at Sheila.

With a sigh of self-disgust, Sheila bent and scooped the small dog into her arms. "Only for a day or two," she warned both her companions.

"Sure," the policeman agreed easily. After all, it wouldn't be his problem after today.

As Sheila slid into the limousine, Raven raised one eyebrow. "I thought *you* came to make sure nobody took anything."

Sheila had learned some things from Aunt Mary. She did not deign to reply.

16

Lady lived up to her name. When she saw Aunt Mary's Alfred snoozing on his blue pillow by the window, her tail wagged as if she would love to trot closer and begin a friendship, but she never left Sheila's side. The white Persian yawned and winked.

Aunt Mary, on the other hand, positively bristled. "What is that creature doing here? Dogs aren't permitted in this building!"

"Tell the owner," Sheila replied. "You invited me to dinner, so I had to bring her along." She ushered Lady to the kitchen door. Mildred readily agreed to give her a dish of meat scraps, and by the time Sheila left them together they were fast becoming bosom buddies.

Sheila returned to the living room, flung herself down into her chair and sipped the coffee Mildred had handed her. "Oh, but that's good! I've been wanting a cup of coffee since we left the church."

"Where have you been, dear? Surely you haven't been at the graveside this long. The funeral was over three hours ago."

Sheila countered with a question of her own. "Why were you there in the first place?" She stretched her legs to their full length on the soft old ottoman and settled in for a bit of pleasant bickering before dinner.

"I went to pay my respects." Aunt Mary smoothed her

wool dress over her knees. She had changed funeral black for a soft pink that exactly matched her living room, and she made a charming picture.

Sheila was familiar both with that charm and the devious mind it concealed. "Respects to whom? Laura Anderson?"

"Of course, dear." Aunt Mary appeared hurt. "And her mother. We're on several boards together. I forget which—"

"Because you never attend the meetings," Sheila hazarded.

Aunt Mary shrugged delicately. "It exhausts me so to sit through long meetings, making trivial decisions. I have to take care of myself." She laid one hand on a heart as strong as Sheila's own. "But I do what I can."

She did, Sheila admitted. Aunt Mary was a most generous patron of Atlanta's cultural scene, and if she failed to attend board meetings, she could be counted on to work behind the scenes—a powerful ally for those to whom that sort of politics mattered.

"And Dean Anderson and I occasionally had business together."

"What kind of business?"

"Oh, this and that." She waved her little hands to show it was of no importance. Sheila amused herself in the silence that followed by picturing Aunt Mary in fatigues, filming a revolution—or perhaps financing a revolution so Dean would have one to report.

"Now before you rest a bit, tell me where you got that dog. If I'd known you wanted a pet, I could have found you a lovely cat."

"I don't want a lovely cat. I didn't even want a dog." Sheila described her afternoon. Because Aunt Mary thrived on details, she painted as colorfully as she could the picture of two women squabbling over Dean's possessions, his two unhappy children, Jonah's unexpected presence and the whisper she had overheard.

"I've got to get it back, or I could be in a lot of trouble," Aunt Mary repeated when Sheila finished. "What could he or she have been talking about, dear? And is it possible someone

144

is looking for a way to return, rather than retrieve, whatever it is?"

Sheila considered. "That hadn't occurred to me, but four trophies are missing from Dean's office shelves." She explained.

Aunt Mary sipped from her never-empty glass of iced tea. "All we can conclude, I think, is that one of five people— Laura, her children, Mr. Baker or Raven Hillis—either has something or has lost something which might incriminate him or her. If you'd spent less time watering flowers and playing with the dog, dear . . ."

"I didn't play with the dog," Sheila replied, stung. "Except for a short time, with Neal. I'd hoped to find out why he was at his father's office Monday, but he went into the house without answering my question."

"You are so blunt, Sheila. You should try a little tact." Before Sheila could respond, she continued, "It looks as if the only thing you actually got out of this afternoon was a dog." She sighed the sigh of a woman who could think of a hundred things Sheila might have done in the same time. "I suppose it can't be helped. Well"—she fished down between her cushion and the arm of the sofa—"I'd planned to wait until after we ate, but perhaps, if you aren't too weary . . ." She reached down between the side of the sofa and her cushion and brought out a brown envelope. "Charlie brought this over at noon."

Sheila's eyes twinkled. "I hope the condemned man ate well. One of these little lunches with you is going to be his last before jail." She opened the envelope and read the contents, then her eyes met Aunt Mary's. "Several people are going to be very surprised."

Aunt Mary nodded. "And one is going to be very pleased. We have certainly found one motive for murder."

Sheila's cup was empty. She rose to refill it. "Do you want more tea while I'm up?" She walked just quickly enough not to hear the end of Aunt Mary's predictable "You drink too much coffee, dear."

When she returned, Aunt Mary was reading a book. The

New York Times was on her own footstool. She settled into her chair and picked up the first section without a word.

The light in the penthouse mellowed as the sun set over the Coca-Cola building to the southwest. Aunt Mary moved about the room switching on lamps, but she did not draw the drapes. "I live high so I don't have to shut myself in," she had been heard to say. What would she do when high buildings rose close enough to be neighbors? Probably buy them and make certain nobody lived this high up!

Mildred came quietly into the room, bearing a tureen. "Dinner's ready." She moved efficiently into the dining room.

Sheila checked her watch in surprise. "Are we eating early?"

"We are going out, dear." Aunt Mary went with dignity to the head of the table and waited for Sheila to join her for grace. But Sheila scarcely heard the prayer. She was too busy wondering what could be important enough to lure Aunt Mary out for the second time in one day.

T hey had just finished their peach pie and coffee when the bell sounded indicating someone was in the lobby. "That will be Jason. Let's go, dear." Aunt Mary trotted toward the door. Sheila followed, tired and more than a little wary.

Jason was an enigma to the family. He had been with Aunt Mary for ten years now, having come as a muscular young man of twenty-one. Until then, Aunt Mary had cadged rides from friends or used cabs. Suddenly, without explaining to her family, she had purchased a sleek silver Cadillac and hired Jason. (Or, Sheila sometimes suspected, hired Jason and bought the Cadillac to match the handsome gray and maroon uniform one of them had chosen for him.)

Sheila often wondered where Aunt Mary had found him, and why he stayed. Chauffeurs were a vanishing breed among Aunt Mary's friends, and Jason was obviously well educated. He spoke in a deep, cultured voice, with a vocabulary far bigger than that of the average man—as if he read the dictionary for pleasure. His interests were catholic—auto mechanics, politics, what Mildred put into her famous cakes, the latest stock reports. He was also clever. What made him continue to earn his livelihood driving a wealthy old woman?

Yet Jason stayed, year after year. Perhaps he liked the salary, or the hours to himself between Aunt Mary's trips. (Getting her to leave the apartment was a feat in itself.) But what did he do in all his free time besides a daily workout? Sheila's father, Mary's knowing brother, suspected his sister relied on Jason to keep her au courant with Atlanta's black community and to gather information she could use in business. In any case, in public Jason was as deferential as Mr. Hudson on "Upstairs, Downstairs." In private, Sheila had heard them swap jokes and tales that made her (and should have made Aunt Mary) blush.

He drove them this evening to a modest brick ranch on a tree-lined street. Middle-class blacks had lived in this part of Atlanta long before the civil rights movement got underway. Now, as prosperity had enabled former residents to move into larger homes, the community had fallen on hard times. Porch screens hung torn, paint peeled, discarded furniture littered front yards. Bushes once meticulously trimmed now grew higher than first-story windows and flopped over cracking driveways. It was a strange place for a woman as fastidious as Sally Webster to be staying.

She answered the bell, however, wearing an exotic silk robe patterned like leopard skin and fuzzy slippers with high heels. She stood in the doorway, framed in the light from the living room behind her, and spoke to Jason from behind a locked screened door. "How you find me?"

With Jason, Sheila noted, Sally used the familiar black idiom and intonation that had been absent on Galaxia's tenth floor. She did not so much address as challenge him.

Sheila could not see Jason's face, but could hear the easy smile in his "Sugar, I keep my eyes on you all the time. I knew when you at your father's establishment, and when you transferred to Junior's here."

"Cops know where I am?"

147

"Not from the portals of these lips."

"What you want?" she asked him bluntly.

"They require your assistance." With a grand wave of one hand, Jason indicated Aunt Mary and Sheila behind him.

Sally seemed to notice them for the first time. She started to shut the door. "That woman works for the police."

"Wait! We're not police." Aunt Mary looked like a midget three steps down from Jason, but her husky voice was reassuring. "I am Jason's employer."

"I saw *her* with the police at the office."

"Not with the police, with Mr. Dekker," Sheila said quickly. "I work for Hosokawa, Galaxia's parent company. My boss sent me to see what was going on."

"She's my niece," Aunt Mary added. Sally looked to Jason, who nodded. Aunt Mary mounted the cracked concrete steps. "May we come in?"

Sally hesitated, then unlocked the screen. "Might as well. I don't want the neighbors seeing me." As they followed her, she muttered audibly to Jason, "You didn't need to bring them *here*! I could have seen them somewhere else. How do I know they won't squeal on me?"

"Because, sugar, they are as desirous as you are of avoiding the police at this point in time."

Sheila certainly was. If Owen Green knew they were conversing with a fugitive, they could beat Charles Davidson to jail.

The inside of the house belied its exterior. The furniture looked new and costly, and sat on a deep plush carpet. A stereo system filled one whole wall of the living room, a wide-screen television another. In the other front room, through an arch, Sheila noticed a keyboard, a steel guitar case, amplifiers and parts of a drum set. "Her brother has a band," Jason explained. "Plays in a club. He's working tonight."

Sally waved them to the orange velvet sofa, where they sat in a row. She took a matching chair, crossing one bare leg over the other and lighting a cigarette with hands that were none too steady. But here, on her own turf, she was no longer a receptionist at others' beck and call. Every line of her body proclaimed that this was her kingdom, where she made the rules. "What do you want to know?" She blew smoke into the air above her with fine disdain.

Aunt Mary bent forward and spoke in the tone of one woman asking another for gossip, "I want to know what really happened at Galaxia last Monday. The media are so vague."

"Why?" Sally demanded bluntly. "If you aren't police, why do you care?"

"Mr. Anderson was an acquaintance of theirs," Jason told her. "Mrs. Travis knew him when she was living with her husband Tyler Travis, the famous diplomat, out in Japan. She is extremely distressed by his demise, and wants to learn the pertinent facts."

Sally considered, rubbing a pattern into the velvet of the chair beside her. Finally she lifted her head. "I don't know anything." She blew smoke up above one shoulder. It floated and circled her head like an aura. Sheila was reminded of film scenes where an exotic young priestess stands before the smoke of sacrificial fires. Was that how Sally was feeling about this visit?

"Just tell them what you *do* know, sugar." It was the first sentence of one-syllable words Sheila had ever heard Jason utter.

"Why should I? What's in it for me?"

Aunt Mary and her driver exchanged looks. She nodded. "Miss Beaufort is aware of your, ah, extracurricular activities at your place of employment." He spoke casually, pulling one sleeve down over his cuff with the air of a man more concerned with his appearance than with what he was saying.

Sally sprang to her feet. "Did you rat on me?"

"Not me, sugar. I didn't know until Miss Beaufort here told me about it. It never occurred to me your daddy would involve his own sugarplum in his rackets. And *so far* the police don't know either. I suggest you tell Miss Mary what she wants to know."

Sally sat down, her mouth sullen. "My business is my business. Daddy's got nothing to do with it." She sat back down and recrossed her legs. "What do you want to know?"

149

Aunt Mary began. "Where were you when Dean Anderson was killed?"

She shook her head. "I don't know *when* he was killed. I wasn't there. I was downstairs, and I didn't see a thing." *That's my story and I'm going to stick to it.* She didn't say it, but it was conveyed by the toss of her glossy curls and the swing of her very long beaded earrings.

"Tell us about the afternoon, after lunch," Sheila suggested.

While Sally tried to remember, she swung one leg so the slipper dangled from her toe. "Well, I did some typing for Mr. Anderson right after lunch, then I had some letters for Porter—I work for *all* of them, you see. Then Mr. Anderson had that express letter he wanted to send—I mentioned it to the police. To Raven Hillis." She waited until Sheila nodded before she went on. "So I ran it down to the mailroom. That's in the basement." She raised her eyes and looked Sheila straight in the eye. "On the way back I stopped to visit a friend, and we, uh"—she slewed her eyes toward Aunt Mary—"we had a little break." Her slender hands twisted in her lap. "When I got back—" She shook her head as if she couldn't believe what she was remembering. "When I got back," she repeated, "the others were all crowding Mr. Anderson's door making a lot of noise. Before I could get to the door, they came out and said Mr. Anderson had killed himself, and not to go in. So I didn't. I watched his funeral today on TV, and they said somebody else killed him. Is that right?"

Sheila nodded. "It looks that way. Did anybody come up to see Dean that day—say, after lunch?"

A sneer touched Sally's lips briefly. "Not Darius Dudwell, but Mr. Anderson's whole family. His ex was there right after lunch and they had a hell of a row. Something to do with the lawyer, because he buzzed and told me to set up an appointment for the next day. I called Mr. Umber and made the appointment. When I went in to tell him, Mr. Anderson said to his wife, 'You satisfied now?' "

"Did he give you the number?" Sheila asked.

Sally shook her head. "I had to look it up, then I gave it

to him. He wrote it down on the front of his building directory."

"Who else came by?" Aunt Mary asked.

"His son was there for a few minutes. At least, I think it's his son. Kid with more pimples than face." Sheila nodded and Sally went on. "He stormed in and stormed back out, calling over his shoulder something about not being finished with the conversation."

"Was that before or after his mother came?"

"Barely after. I'm surprised they didn't meet in the lobby."

"But you didn't hear these conversations?" Sheila asked.

Sally flared her lovely nostrils, indignant. "I had my *own* work to do! I type for everybody on that floor. I don't have time to listen to other people's conversations!"

"Of course not," Aunt Mary said soothingly. "I don't suppose you saw his daughter come in, too?"

"I saw her, but she didn't see me," Sally admitted, slightly mollified. "I'd gone to the storeroom for Porter's letterhead, and from there you can see anybody get off the elevator. She went into his office happy as you please. I went back to my desk, and in a few minutes I heard him shout something at her—'Where the hell did you get that?' or something like that. I had forgotten to get envelopes, so I went back to the storeroom. While I was in there, she ran out of his office madder than . . ." She paused to let each complete the sentence in his or her own way. "I thought it might upset her to see me, so I waited in there until she got an elevator." Sally drew on her cigarette and exhaled through her nostrils. "It wasn't the way I'd want to leave my daddy for the very last time."

Her words sobered them all into a moment's silence.

Aunt Mary was the first to speak. "What time was Miss Anderson there, do you remember?"

Sally considered. "I went to the mailroom at five past three. I remember because express mail has to get down by half past if it's to get out that day, and I was cutting it close. She must have come in about quarter till, I guess, and left twenty minutes later."

"And you are certain Dean Anderson was alive when she left?"

Sally shook her head. "Like I told you, I heard him shouting at her earlier. But I didn't hear him again, and after she left I didn't go back in his office. I had to hurry to finish my envelope and get Mr. Anderson's express letter down. I should have taken it before I started Porter's typing, but I never thought it would take me so long."

Aunt Mary's eyes held Sally's. "Do you think that young woman killed her father?"

Sally shook her head. "She didn't look shook enough, I don't think. More mad than scared, I thought."

Sheila's eyes met Aunt Mary's. "One who killed in anger might still look angry minutes later," Aunt Mary suggested.

Sally shook her head. "I don't think she did it."

"Was that why you didn't tell the police she was there?" Sheila asked.

Sally shook her head. "If she doesn't want them to know she was there . . ." She concluded with a shrug.

Jason leaned forward. "Tell them about the vase, sugar."

"Oh, yeah! Now that *might* have something to do with the killing." Sally rearranged her curves on the chair and crossed the other leg over, stubbing out her cigarette to give the story her full attention. "Happening on the same day and all. Mr. Anderson keeps a vase on his desk—a sort of Chinese thing."

It was sixteenth century, Sheila believed. Dean's good-luck talisman—a talisman, she thought sadly, that failed. She tuned Sally back in.

". . . real mad. 'Somebody's robbed me,' he said. 'I had forty dollars in that vase when I left here last week, and today when I reached in to get it, it was gone.' I was afraid he was accusing me, but he patted me on the shoulder and told me he wasn't. What he wanted was for me to call Security and have them check out the vase. Maybe for fingerprints, I don't know."

"And did you?" Aunt Mary asked.

Sally shook her head. "I forgot. I had to do some quick

typing for Craig for the afternoon meeting, then I went to lunch. When I got back, I forgot all about it until the next day. You might ask the police to check that vase," she added to Sheila, who nodded.

"Is that all?" Aunt Mary asked.

Sally nodded. "You know all I know." She uncrossed her legs and stood, clearly dismissing unwanted guests.

As they all stood, Sheila asked, "But why did you leave so suddenly last Monday?"

If Sally intended to answer, she never had the chance. Instead, there was a shout of "Freeze!" and suddenly the room was full of large black men, all brandishing weapons.

"Oh, Billy," Sally said in a tone of utter disgust.

"Not my idea, baby," said one of the men. "Boss's orders." He turned to Sally's visitors. "You folks come with us."

The guns never touched their backs as he herded them down the steps and into a waiting limousine, but Sheila felt prodded just the same.

The windows of the limousine were covered, so she had no idea where they were being driven. She had started to ask at one point, but Aunt Mary patted her lap. "Just wait, dear." The old woman seemed completely unperturbed. Jason looked as frightened as Sheila felt.

"Okay, we're here." The limousine had come to a stop. Billy gestured with his gun. "You," he told Jason, "stay right here. You ladies come with me."

It was too dark to see much of the house, other than that it looked far too modest to be connected with this limousine. Like the one they had just left, however, it was more luxurious within than without. They found themselves in a large living room carpeted in red and full of deep black leather sofas and ebony chairs. In one chair, which resembled a throne, sat a man as ebony as the chair.

"Hello, Mr. Dudwell," Sheila said, surprised that her voice still worked.

He inclined his head and waved them to the sofa. When they were settled, he reached for a glass of amber liquid at his elbow, held it up and considered it with satisfaction.

"Sweet tea with lemon and mint. You don't get that where I've been. Would you ladies like something to drink?"

"Thank you." Aunt Mary accepted a glass of tea as if this party were the kind she was accustomed to. Sheila followed her lead. "May I ask why we have been brought here?" Aunt Mary asked when she had taken a fortifying sip.

The man rested his fingertips together and considered them for a full minute before he replied. "I wonder that a bit myself. I'd given the boys instructions to keep tabs on anybody who showed up at Sally's, and bring in anybody who looked suspicious and stayed more than five minutes. Let us say they got a little overzealous. But perhaps you would not mind telling me what you were there for?"

"We had gone to find out what she knew about Dean Anderson's death," Aunt Mary replied.

"And why she ran away last Monday," Sheila added. She was beginning to be lulled into a sense of safety. She jerked herself back into watchfulness.

To her astonishment, Darius Dudwell threw back his head and laughed, a deep belly-shaking laugh that showed not one but three gold crowns and countless fillings. When he'd recovered himself, he wiped his mouth. "Why she ran away? You don't know?"

Sheila shook her head.

"Because *you* sicced the cops on me. It was you, wasn't it?"

"I told them you'd come to see Dean in the restaurant," she admitted.

"Well, that was enough." His tone reminded her of Lieutenant Green's. Neither of these black men appreciated her interference, it seemed. "Sally flew out of the building and came to warn me."

"Why?" Sheila asked.

"Because," Aunt Mary said gently, "she's his daughter, dear."

Now Sheila could see a resemblance—primarily in the long fingers and shape of the head, although Sally was much

154

lighter and her features finer. "She looks like her mother," Darius said, as if reading her mind. "And uses her mother's maiden name. It made things easier in school, and all."

"As long as we are here, would you mind telling us where you were when Dean Anderson was shot?" Aunt Mary said it like she was asking where Mr. Dudwell spent his last vacation.

He drained the glass and set it down, then looked back at Aunt Mary. "Now why should I tell you that, ma'am?"

"Because," she said, meeting his gaze, "I knew your mother."

He hesitated, then chuckled again. "It's as good a reason as any, I suppose. Well, I was with my lawyer all afternoon that day. Both he and his secretary can corroborate that fact. And listen, I had no plans to get rid of Mr. Anderson. I even liked the guy, in a strange way. Can you believe that?" He waited for them to nod, then shook his head in dismay. "Looks like Sally ran for nothing, doesn't it?"

He had leaned back in his chair, relaxed, but Aunt Mary's next words brought him upright again. "That's not the only reason she ran. She's been dealing drugs at Galaxia."

He leaned forward and jutted his chin toward her. "Watch what you say, ma'am. That's my daughter you're talking about!"

Aunt Mary nodded. "That's why I thought you'd want to know."

He cocked his head to one side. "You sure of that?"
She nodded again.

His eyes narrowed and he considered his fingertips again. His lower lip jutted out, and Sheila expected it to start working like Lieutenant Green's. Instead, he stood. "I'll deal with that. And I'll have my boys return you ladies to the place they found you. No hard feelings?" He put out an enormous hand and Aunt Mary twinkled as she took it.

"None at all, Mr. Dudwell. I knew your mother's son would never do me harm."

He smiled. "That's right, ma'am. I never harm a lady."

As the Cadillac purred back to the penthouse, Jason spoke to his passengers. "I don't know about you ladies, but that's closer than I want to get to that particular man again."

Sheila heartily agreed, but Aunt Mary said, with a pensive look in her eye, "I don't know . . . with a little attention paid to him . . ."

Sheila had no idea what plot she was hatching, but for the first and only time in her life, she pitied Darius Dudwell.

17

The next day the temporary receptionist did not show up. The office was hectic enough before Wylene came. She arrived wearing a false smile and followed by a maintenance man carrying folded boxes. "We're to pack up Dean's things," she informed the staff.

"Not us—we've got a deadline." Porter spoke for the art department.

"And we're working on that television series," Jonah told her. "Dekker wants something by four P.M." Craig hadn't even bothered to come out of his office to answer her summons.

"Ms. Travis, are you going to desert me, too?" Wylene asked playfully. When Sheila began to shake her head (intending to say she had no intention of packing Dean's things), she continued, "Why don't you start by wrapping and packing his lovely trophies?" Her voice trembled slightly, and she pressed a fist beneath her nose as if that would keep back incipient tears.

Reminding herself that she might uncover a clue in the process, Sheila reached for a box—reflecting that Wylene wouldn't have shot Dean. She would have skewered him on one of those long, strong nails instead. Perhaps she painted them that particular shade of blood red so nobody would notice when she'd just claimed a victim.

Wylene's use of the word "we" was overstatement. She

157

appeared once, to suggest that Sheila pack books separately from papers. Otherwise she was at her own desk or perched on Porter's, one thin calf swinging, making what he called "non-conversation."

Sheila found only one thing of value as far as the crime was concerned—a pink memo slip with two words scrawled on it: "See me?" She thought the handwriting matched that on the letter found at Dean's, but could not be sure until she checked with Lieutenant Green. She put the pink sheet into an envelope with a memo of her own and slipped it into her pocket, intending to mail it later.

She hoped, as she boxed up the last of the correspondence, that someone (Bayard?) would have the sense to use these letters from worldwide figures as part of Dean Anderson's biography—and the further sense to write it before the public found a new hero.

Her packing was frequently interrupted by Porter, escaping Wylene by popping in and out of Sheila's office to urge her to join him for coffee.

"That's what you get for encouraging him," Jonah warned as he passed her door on his way for hot chocolate.

He was having trouble of his own. Craig, having decided he was Dean's logical successor as executive producer, was writing a script. Occasionally he prowled into Jonah's or Veronica's office to bark suggestions that sounded more like orders. When Jonah rejected several of his ideas as impractical, the noise of battle finally drove Sheila, Elise and Veronica to the basement for gelato.

"They're worse than my children." Elise took a thoughtful bite. "I wonder if either of their mothers ever spanked them? Oh!" she exclaimed. "That reminds me! I was going to tell you, Sheila. It's about Neal—Dean's son? He's in Robby's class. A real mama's boy, Robby says, but anyway, last year he got into some kind of trouble. Threatened to kill somebody, I think. Something like that."

Veronica looked baffled, as well she might. Sheila, aware of Elise's tendency to get things wrong, remained unperturbed. "Someone should check it out. I'll tell Mr. Dekker."

"Or do it yourself," Elise agreed, licking her cone.

To change the subject, Sheila pointed to a man in gray mopping the floor. "Has Woody ever come back? I haven't seen him since Monday."

"He's got the flu that's going around," Veronica told her. "Wylene is fit to be tied. Half the mailroom staff is out, too, so mail was an hour late today."

"I suggested that she could help them deliver it, but she wouldn't." Elise sounded so earnest that the others had to smile.

Sheila turned to Veronica. "You work with Jonah and Craig. What are the chances they will pull off this television series together?"

Veronica shrugged her heavy shoulders. "Together, probably not a chance. But Jonah and I already have specs and a script for a pilot ready to give Mr. Dekker. Just don't tell Craig."

Sheila was astounded. "You mean you have written something without his knowledge?"

Veronica nodded, swallowing the last bites of her cone. "We decided last week the best thing to do was work at home evenings and come up with a pilot that doesn't depend on an overall theme for a series. So we did. Jonah's lined up interviews, and I've found footage to illustrate it and written some connecting stuff. We think Mr. Dekker will like it. But," she predicted, "if you think this morning's been bad, wait until Craig finds out. He's going to be *really* mad."

"I'm glad I don't work for him," Elise told her. "How did you get the nerve to work with Jonah behind Craig's back?"

Veronica rubbed both cheeks with her palms. "It was my idea." Both women regarded her with new respect. Any woman who could decide to defy Craig was worth knowing. Veronica went on. "I realized if somebody didn't come up with something, we could argue for months. Except I probably wouldn't be around to hear it. Unless the series gets started soon, they aren't going to need two full-time writers on staff. And CNN has about four thousand applicants for my old job.

159

Besides, I want to work on this series—make sure it's not too male or too white, begging your pardon."

"You don't have to beg my pardon," Sheila assured her. "I'm with you. How about Jonah?"

"Jonah's with me, too. Now all we've got to do is convince Dekker. *And* live with Craig."

Sheila considered taking the afternoon off. Craig in a foul mood was hard enough to put up with. Craig "really mad" she had no desire to see.

"He's a mean man," Elise said as if she had been considering the matter and had just finally reached a decision. "Craig, I mean. He . . ."—she sought the right word—"he needles people."

"He sure does," Veronica agreed. "When Dean was here, Craig kept telling Jonah he was too good to work for Dean. Now he acts like Jonah isn't good enough to work with *him*."

"He drives me crazy," Elise continued. "He comes into my office and leans over my shoulder to see what I'm drawing, and he says 'not bad, not bad.' " Her high breathless voice sounded nothing like Craig's, but her intonation was flawless. "But there's something about him that makes me want to tear everything up and start over."

Sheila smiled. "Not a pleasant man, we all agree."

Elise was never one, however, to speak more ill than good of another. Bending to pick up her orange purse off the floor, she suggested, "Maybe his father left before he was born, and Craig's been mad ever since."

As they returned to the tenth floor, Sheila entertained herself with a picture of Craig as an angry fetus.

At noon, Jonah and Veronica grabbed coats and headed for the elevator. Sheila was surprised Craig hadn't caught on that something was up—every time the conspirators' eyes met they danced with excitement, then looked away.

"Today you are going to eat with me if I have to drag Elise along as a chaperone." Porter stood in Sheila's door, shoulder on one side and legs on the other, effectively blocking her exit.

"Very well," she nodded. "If you'll ask Elise, too, I'll lunch with you."

"For you, darling, see how I am willing to suffer? Like MacArthur, I shall return." He stood upright and left. In a minute he was back. "She says yes, and can we eat in the park? She needs to look at a pigeon."

Sheila shuddered. "Why would anyone want to look at a pigeon?"

"Because I have to draw one," Elise said matter-of-factly, coming up behind her boss and peering around him. She was shorter than usual, having replaced her orange heels with yellow running shoes. "There are pigeons in the story I'm illustrating, and I can't remember what they look like."

"Fat, bossy and waddly," Sheila replied with loathing.

"You have a special animus against pigeons, darling?" When Porter raised one eyebrow like that, he looked remarkably like a drawing of Machiavelli in Aunt Mary's old encyclopedia.

"She got scared by some as a little girl," Elise answered for her. "I remember on prom night, she wouldn't even eat Cornish hen because it looked like dead pigeons. Do you eat them now?"

Sheila shook her head. "Not Cornish hen, or dove, or even small chickens," she said firmly. "But I'll go to the park and ignore the pigeons. How's that?"

Porter put an arm around each woman, then smiled wryly when they both pulled away. "Okay, my beauties, we'll have a platonic lunch ignoring pigeons. And I was going to invite you out for squabs on Saturday," he lamented.

"You can invite," Sheila assured him, "but I won't come."

They maintained their lighthearted banter for four blocks, inspired by the weather. "I'd forgotten October was so gorgeous here," Sheila told them. "Is it always going to be soft and warm, with no clouds in the sky?"

"You bring the sunshine," Porter replied.

From Peachtree Street's shadowy canyon they strolled

161

into the sunny oasis of Woodruff Park, where escaped office prisoners and homeless people were welcomed equally by pigeon maître d's.

"Is a hot dog good enough for you?" Porter asked.

Sheila nodded. "Get me two. I love hot dogs. When we used to come home on furlough, I wanted them twice a day."

"You all claim a bench and I'll get the food." Porter started to turn away, then stopped, his face a picture of horror. "Did you hear what I said? I said you-all. I've only been down here four months! What *will* I be like by Christmas?" He moved, gloomy but graceful, to take his place in line.

Sheila and Elise sat on one of the benches thoughtfully planted around small oaks and watched him approach a little wagon that advertised hot dogs "cooked over real charcoal." Sheila was wondering what artificial charcoal might be when Elise bent down and cooed, "Come here, darling, let me look at you!"

A sleek purple and black pigeon, resembling an elderly dowager dressed for lunch with the queen, tapped its way toward them and pecked at Sheila's feet.

"This is too much!" she exclaimed, drawing them back

"You scared her!" Elise gave her a reproachful look. "And just when I was about to really get the line of her back." She regarded her pencil and pad sadly. The likeness to that particular pigeon was remarkable, even without a back.

"There are plenty of others, and they don't need to peck my feet," Sheila informed her. "Stick out your own."

Elise reached down and rubbed her fingers, hoping to attract another pigeon. When it saw she had no food (pigeons, Elise explained, are quick to notice such things) it gave her a disdainful look and waddled away.

"Poor Elise, won't they come to you?" Porter handed her a hot dog. "See how they respond to genuine charm." Before he was seated between the women, pigeons had begun to stream toward them from all directions. "Good luck ignoring these," he teased Sheila.

She groaned. "What we endure for the sake of art."

"May I join you?" Craig stood above them, his back to

the sun so his face was shadowed. He held a bag of fast-food chicken.

Porter and Sheila hesitated, but Elise moved away from Porter. "Sure. But don't scare the birds. I'm trying to draw them."

Craig settled into the space provided and leaned across Porter to offer Sheila a package of fries. "Want some?"

"Thanks." As she reached for the package, their hands failed to connect. It fell to the ground at Porter's feet and was surrounded by pigeons.

"That's great!" Elise's pencil glided over her paper. "Look at the action!"

"Just great," Craig said sourly. Sheila suspected her apology fell on deaf ears.

After that, nobody spoke until the food was gone and the drinks reduced to watery dregs in the bottoms of cups. Elise was the last to finish, of course, for she kept interrupting her meal to snatch up her pencil and quickly sketch a bird as it plodded past. "If only I could remember the colors," she sighed.

"Gray, gray, gray, purple and gray," said Craig.

"Honestly, you are as bad as Sheila! Just look at that one." Elise pointed to a particularly fat specimen hovering near a man (equally fat) who was devouring his third hot dog and throwing crumbs liberally around him. "He's blue and light gray and rose and silver and green and charcoal and purple—how can I ever get that purple?" she wailed. As several people looked their way, Sheila and Porter exchanged glances.

"We could move to another bench and hold hands," he suggested.

"Or walk briskly around the block to settle our lunch."

"Is that a challenge? Come on, I'll race you."

Elise threw down her tablet. "Oh, goody. Are we going to run? I got up too late this morning."

Porter drew down his mouth. "*We* were going to walk, darling, just Sheila and me. I wasn't proposing a communal event."

"Why don't you two run?" Sheila suggested. She hoped nobody had told him Elise was once the third-fastest woman runner in the state. She also hoped Elise could still run.

Porter looked from one, eager, to the other, still sitting. "Very well," he told Elise with a grimace, "I'll lope along beside you if I must."

Sheila counted down. When she said "Go!" Elise took off like a shot. Porter lost a few seconds to amazement.

Craig watched them circle the park, saying without interest, "Show-offs. Just because the rest of us weren't on our college track teams."

"What were your interests?" This might be the best chance she would get to know Craig better, if she could repress that picture of an angry fetus and keep a straight face.

"Oh, I liked living dangerously, pitting myself against nature. Canoeing the boundary waters, rappelling, spelunking, cross-country skiing. Now I get the same thrills from real estate. This town is wide open, did you know that?"

He was picking his teeth. They were large, square, and very white. To keep from saying, "Why, grandmother, what big teeth you have!" she acknowledged, "I don't know much about it. Are you buying or selling?"

"Both, eventually. I'm buying now, of course—I've got one town house and am working on getting another. I'll hold on to them until the price is right, then sell. I met a guy named Jack Kay in Underground Atlanta last week who knows everything there is to know. If you are interested . . ." It was the most enthusiastic she'd ever seen him, but she wasn't interested in real estate.

"Is Underground Atlanta fun? I haven't been there."

He shrugged. "I suppose, if you're with somebody who enjoys it. I went with Bayard, Dean's daughter, and—" He stopped, as if struck by a sudden thought. "I wonder if it was her gun."

"Her gun?"

He tossed his toothpick at a passing pigeon. "She showed me a pistol she had bought to carry around New York. Or so she said. I hope that wasn't the gun that killed Dean."

"Are you suggesting his daughter shot him?" That frantic whisper yesterday. Was it Bayard, desperate to retrieve her gun?

Craig shook his head. "I don't know. I hope not. It wouldn't do my reputation any good if it were known I'd dated a murderess."

"Nor hers, either," she replied tartly, turning her attention back to the runners.

They were on the last lap. Sheila watched them, amused. Porter had gotten a slow start, and Elise was hampered by a deeply instilled belief that no woman should beat a man. But besides being a southern lady, Elise was a competitive runner. At last she put on a spurt and beat him by a hair. They collapsed onto the bench, breathing hard, to a smattering of applause from bystanders.

"Next time, darling," Porter reproached Sheila, "I'll race *you!*"

"Hey, that was great!" Jonah and Veronica breezed up.

"Thanks." Porter panted a few times, then cocked his head to one side. "Why do you guys look like a couple of cats who have swallowed a couple of canaries?"

Sheila knew why they looked so pleased with themselves, and also knew it would be better not to air Galaxia's dirty linen in public—as Craig would do if the subject of the television series were brought up.

"I sure am glad to see you people," she said with enthusiasm. "I'm in all-round disgrace. First I scared Elise's pigeons, then I dropped Craig's fries, and finally I tricked Porter into racing Elise. I'll never be asked again."

"Go with Elton Dekker." Craig heaved himself to his feet. "He'll take you to the top of the Westin Peachtree and let you watch the city go 'round and 'round."

"She's been there." Elise, busy with her pencil again, spoke without looking up. "Last week before our reception. How long are you going to have to stay here?" she asked Sheila, changing the line of a wing. "Until you finish detecting?"

Sheila heard someone catch a quick breath. Both Jonah's

165

and Veronica's eyes widened, while Craig's narrowed. Only Porter spoke, in a drawl. "Are you detecting, Sheila? How fascinating."

She shrugged. "Not exactly. I was sent—"

Elise's navy eyes fixed on her reproachfully. "You are. You know you are." She put away her pencil and started to gather up their trash, addressing the others like a child boasting of her big sister's skills. "Sheila has this fabulous aunt, and together, they figure things out. They do it all the time! Before we know it, they'll have figured out who killed Dean. Then"—she smiled happily—"we can all get back to work and stop worrying."

She stood and started back to Galaxia, blissfully unaware that no one else in the group shared her delight.

18

Sheila returned to find Wylene in Dean's office, slapping a letter against her palm. "It came for Dean, marked 'Personal,' and I don't know what to do with it."

"Do you know who it's from?"

"A publisher." Wylene started to leave, taking the letter.

"Mr. Dekker will know what to do with it. I need to see him anyway. Shall I take it up?"

Wylene handed her the letter with obvious reluctance.

Elton Dekker opened it with equal reluctance, scanned it and handed it back to Sheila, puzzled. "I don't know what they are talking about."

She read it. "I do. Elise and Dean were talking about this at dinner last week. Apparently one of your maintenance staff, Woody—the one who found Dean's body, sadly enough—was the 'unknown photographer' of Dean's *Visions of Vietnam*. Jonah discovered it, I believe. When he told Dean, Dean called the publisher to arrange for future printings to carry a corrected title page, giving Woody credit. The publisher is asking for a picture."

Elton reread it and nodded. "I see." He reached into his desk and pulled out his blue building directory.

"If you are about to call Woody, he's out with flu."

Elton wiped one hand across his head. "You really do know everything, don't you?"

167

"Everything but the important things."

"Will this help? They're Lieutenant Green's notes about their progress so far. You might want to look them over this weekend."

"Thanks. I'd also like to talk with Woody. May I leave early and go by his house to see if he has a picture? I'll call the publisher, too."

Of course he agreed. What top executive isn't glad to get a volunteer for a nitpicking piece of work?

"One more thing." She fished in her skirt pocket. "Do you recognize this handwriting?"

He looked at it, then looked up with no expression on his face. "Is it important?"

"It could be. A letter was found at Dean's, and I think the writing matches. Lieutenant Green has that letter."

He drummed on his desk with one hand. "Let me check around. At this time I wouldn't like to say until I'm sure." He picked up a sheet of paper. She was dismissed.

It was fine to detect, she thought wryly as she went down in the elevator, so long as one did not detect too close to home. Which of his staff (for it was obviously staff) was Elton Dekker protecting?

S heila was alone on the tenth floor. Most of the staff had gone upstairs to wrangle about the television series. Wylene had gone to the mailroom. "If you take any calls, put the messages under the turtle on Sally's desk. Porter and Craig keep asking for a message center with pigeonholes, but this is what Dean preferred. People know to look for them there."

Sheila had spread the police notes on her desk to read when she heard the elevator doors open and someone cross the foyer. Bayard Anderson appeared at her father's door, wearing slacks and a pullover for a welcome change. Her hair had been pulled back into a French braid with a small red bow at the end. It looked lovely.

Her face, however, was pale, and she gave a start when

she saw Sheila in her father's chair. "What are you doing here?"

"I've been assigned this office for a few days." Sheila folded her papers and put them in a drawer. "What are *you* doing here?"

"I came to get some things. Daddy's mug, stuff like that. Is all that his? I can't carry so much—I'm parked blocks away."

"Did someone call you about picking up Dean's things?" The girl's pause was enough. "I'm sorry, Bayard, but we can't release his things until we know exactly who gets what. I think everything will be sent to his house for his lawyer to distribute."

Bayard's short laugh held no mirth. "Distribute? Distribute to whom? We got the glad tidings this morning. Good old Daddy—Mr. Do It Tomorrow—only wrote one will in his life. The one he wrote when he and Mama got married. I think Granddaddy Bayard probably made him write that one—he always likes things done 'decently and in order.' "

Sheila smiled. "A Presbyterian?"

"How did you know?"

"My aunt is one. She lives by that phrase." She already knew the answer, but said anyway, "So your mother gets everything?"

"Every penny and stamp in the drawer. That's why I came for the mug. I gave it to him, and I'll be—"

Sheila opened a box and handed it to her. "Take it. Nobody need know but us."

"Thanks." Bayard sneezed. "Excuse me. Must be a lot of dust in here."

Sheila was impressed. This was the first time she'd heard Bayard use the manners she was sure Dean and Laura had taught her. "There's a box of tissues on the receptionist's desk."

"Thanks." The girl went and brought back a wad, talking as she blew her nose. "I can't believe Daddy didn't bother to make a will when he had children." She sounded more bitter than she had yesterday. Or was it more hurt?

"People put things like that off." Sheila said, hoping to soothe her. She was making a mental note to find a lawyer herself as soon as possible. Since Tyler's death, her own will left everything to an organization *he* had been enthusiastic about in their first years of marriage. It hadn't occurred to her back then that she could choose her own beneficiaries. It occurred to her now. She'd leave instructions to buy a dog and give it to Mildred. That would give Aunt Mary a conniption.

Bayard reached for the vase on Dean's desk.

"Don't touch that yet," Sheila requested. "It was lying on its side the day your dad was killed, remember?" Bayard nodded, wary. "Well, the receptionist has said that the day he was killed, Dean reported some money missing from that vase. I want to be sure the police fingerprinted it when they were here."

"You don't think that had anything to do with"—Bayard gulped—"with whoever killed Daddy, do you?"

"I don't know. But I think the police need to know about it."

"Oh." Bayard stood for a moment, apparently lost in thought. Then she turned her attention to some videos on the desk.

Sheila wondered about giving Bayard Dean's photographs. Would they be needed for a trial? No, she decided, the police could make their own pictures. She handed them to the girl. "I think you can take these, too. It might save some trouble later on."

Bayard considered the one of Raven. "You're not kidding." Sheila was glad to see her finally smile. It definitely improved her appearance.

"What's in here?" Bayard moved casually toward the bookshelves and touched one sealed box.

"Some of his trophies. Four seem to be missing. You don't know anything about that, do you?"

She wrinkled her forehead. "I think one of them . . ."

"When you were here that afternoon?"

Bayard took a step back. "I wasn't here."

170

"You were, Bayard. Someone will swear you were here from two forty-five until five past three. Your father shouted at you and you left very angry."

Bayard clenched her fists, then rubbed one finger against her nose. Just like her dad when he had something he didn't really want to say.

"Sit down," Sheila suggested.

Bayard flopped onto the sofa and Sheila took a chair across from her—and nearer the door. She'd had one experience already of how fast Bayard could run when she was steamed up. But she had other experience as well. She knew that waiting silently brought more confessions than questions. She waited.

When Bayard raised her blue eyes to Sheila's, they were wet with tears. "I didn't know I wouldn't ever see him again." It wasn't, Sheila thought with unexpected relief, how one would begin a confession of murder. Bayard swallowed hard, and went on. "Daddy and I shouted a lot at each other. But we didn't really mean it. It was the way we let off steam. Mama holds grudges. Neal seethes. Daddy and I just explode . . ." She stopped, aware that the present tense was not accurate but unable to use another. Her gaze fell to her hands, clenched in her lap.

"I can understand that. But what made your father so angry that day? Were you still furious about his part in getting your job?"

"Oh, no!" Bayard's eyes widened, surprised. "We talked about that Sunday. Daddy told me about people who helped him in his career, and said I should use any contacts I have. It's the way to do it, he said." She squeezed her lids together, but tears still escaped. "We had the *nicest* time on Sunday. And then . . ."

She looked around the room, suddenly crouched with her head in her lap. "I can't stand this room. I can't!"

"What did you argue about?" Sheila had a sudden inspiration. "Was it the gun?"

Bayard sat up slowly, her lips quivering and her face wet with tears. "What . . . what gun?"

171

"Your gun. I know you have one. Is that the one . . ."

Before she could finish, Bayard had begun to moan. "Don't! Oh, don't. I can't stand it! I can't stand it!" She was becoming hysterical.

Sheila moved to sit beside her and clasped her tightly around the shoulders. "Bayard, you have got to tell me. You didn't kill him, did you?"

The question restored the girl as nothing else could have. "Of course not!" Her whole body stiffened with indignation, then she collapsed against the sofa and her voice was a hoarse whisper. "But somebody used my gun." She swiped her nose with the back of one hand. Sheila stood up, went out to Sally's desk and brought the whole box of tissues. Bayard blew loudly and was finally ready to talk.

"Begin at the beginning," Sheila suggested. "You told the police you took a cab to the airport. Did you stop here on the way?"

Bayard nodded. "Then when I'd seen Daddy, I took MARTA on to the airport. I lied before because I thought it wouldn't make any difference—I didn't kill him!"

No wonder the police were having trouble tracing that cab!

"But when I was here, there was nobody around."

"Someone was getting typing paper from the storeroom."

Bayard considered. "Oh. Well, I came in to say goodbye, and to give him something." Her voice had dropped almost to a mutter, then she flung back her head and said defiantly, "Oh, you might as well know. I took his money. That first Tuesday I was in town. I dropped by to see Daddy, but he was away, so Craig asked me to dinner. We went to Underground Atlanta afterwards and it . . . it was pretty awful. He spent most of the evening trying to impress some wheeler dealer named Jack with how smart he is in real estate. Then he got drunk, and we had a quarrel. Finally I'd had enough. I stormed out, then discovered I didn't have enough money to pay for a cab home. I remembered that Daddy keeps . . . kept"—her voice faltered—"money in that vase. I had the cab bring me here and told the security guard I'd forgotten my umbrella. He knew me—he'd let me in earlier and we'd talked a bit—so he brought me up. While he was looking for an umbrella, I took the money." She waited for Sheila to say something, but Sheila had nothing to say.

Bayard went on. "I got cash on my last day of vacation to repay it. That's why I came up. And to give him one more hug." She smiled, but it trembled, then toppled entirely. Her eyes filled with tears. "He didn't want me to give him back the money, but I insisted. Oh, if only I hadn't!"

Before Sheila could ask why, Bayard told her. "If I hadn't opened my purse, he wouldn't have seen the gun. I'd bought it while I was here, from a friend—thought it would make me feel more secure in New York living alone."

Sheila's brows rose. "Had you planned what you were going to do with it at the airport?"

Bayard obviously had not. "I thought I'd just check it . . ."

Sheila shook her head. "It's a lot more complicated than that. But go ahead. What happened here?"

"Daddy was livid! I don't know if you know how he felt about guns," Sheila nodded, "well, he couldn't believe I'd bought one. He acted like I'd betrayed him personally—ranted and raved 'No daughter of mine,' 'You'll end up killing yourself'—all sorts of things. Finally he grabbed it and shoved it in a drawer. I stomped out." She stopped, unable to say the rest.

"How did you find out he was dead?"

"At the airport. I'd checked my bags and gone for a Coke. They had a television. An announcer broke into the program and said Daddy had shot himself. I got the next train back."

"Not a cab?"

"At five in the afternoon? MARTA's a lot faster."

The mayor should interview Bayard as part of his campaign to expand rail service. But the police were not going to be pleased.

Sheila considered what she had discovered. "And you saw nobody around when you left?"

Bayard shook her head. "Not even that lovely black

woman. Was she the one who saw me?" Sheila nodded. "I didn't see her."

"And you think one trophy was gone when you were here?"

"Yes. There was a sort of gap in the front row. But I don't know what it was."

"There's no reason why you should." Sheila noted Bayard's trembling hands and suggested, "How about some coffee?"

She fetched coffee for two. Her own hands were shaking, not so much from Bayard's story as from what must have been its sequel. As she put sugar and creamer packs on a tray, she couldn't help wishing with Dean's daughter: If only she hadn't opened her purse to get out the money. Would Dean be still alive? Or was there someone who would have found another way to remove him if that gun had not happened along so handily?

Bayard had stood and was looking around the room, examining a video. Almost absentmindedly she held it up. "This is Daddy's. I'd like to take it, too."

Sheila shook her head. "The videos belong to Galaxia. Your dad just had them in here for reference, I guess. But he had some letters that would be terrific material for a biography. Have you thought about doing one?"

"No, but it's a good idea."

Bayard put the video on Dean's desk and carried her coffee to the window. Sheila joined her, wondering if she dared ask another question. "If it's not too personal, Bayard, what did you and Craig quarrel about? Was it anything to do with Galaxia?"

Bayard's laugh was more like a snort.

"Well, then, was it about how you got your own job?"

"No, that was earlier. He said I only got my job because of Daddy, and I said that wasn't true. So he offered to call somebody he knows in network personnel to see if Daddy's name appears in my file. It does, of course. But how did you know about that?"

"I was in Dailey's when you left," Sheila replied with a twinkle.

Bayard's eyes narrowed, then she grinned. "A real exit, wasn't it?"

"Sure was. I also saw Craig give you something at the reception. The proof?"

Bayard nodded. "I was livid, of course, but"—she swiped at her eyes with one hand—"that all seems so silly, now."

Sheila nodded. Dared she ask again about the quarrel? Bayard remembered, instead. "At the end, we quarreled about whether I'd go home with him after we left Underground Atlanta. I know sex on a first date is cool for his generation" (Sheila, in the same generation, winced), "but I don't happen to think that way. He tried to convince me I was naive, so when he went to the john—for the tenth or fifteenth time— I skipped. But it was pretty late for a bus and I didn't have money for a cab, so . . ." She shrugged. "I already told you the rest." She turned back to the window. "They're coming along with that building, aren't they? Daddy really loved this view. Look at those men up on top. They look tiny."

Bayard pointed. Sheila had to bend and crane her neck to see. "It looks like rain later today," she noticed.

"Yeah." While Sheila was still examining the clouds and enjoying the view, Bayard backed away. "Well, I must be going. I'll see you later."

By the time Sheila had turned, Bayard was already at the door. "Thanks." She waved, and Sheila heard the fire door to the stairwell click behind her.

Not until five minutes later, as she was gathering up her purse and jacket, did Sheila realize that Bayard had taken more than a magazine and her father's pictures. The video had also been taken from the desk.

S heila went in search of Wylene. "Dean's things are boxed. Please arrange for someone to remove them from the office."

Wylene fluttered her lashes. "All you have to do is just call maintenance."

Sheila had had as much as she planned to take this afternoon. "*You* call maintenance. I'm leaving for the day." She added what was, for Wylene, the magic word. "I have to do an errand for Mr. Dekker."

19

Woody lived in a small brick bungalow in Virginia Highlands, a family neighborhood that had suffered in the sixties. Since Sheila was last in Atlanta, the neighborhood had been discovered by young professionals. Most houses now had shining paint and screened porches—or scaffoldings indicating imminent repair. Woody's own paint was peeling, his front porch screen hanging in ribbons.

Perhaps in spring the huge old azaleas would blaze in glory to attract attention from passersby. Today even they looked unkempt. The whole house wore the look of a place where somebody tried very hard, but couldn't do enough.

Sheila made her way up four cracked cement steps to a gray porch floor that sagged a little in a perpetual pout. Someone had set a sad-looking purple chrysanthemum in a green plastic pot on the top step beside the screened door, but had failed to water it.

Woody shuffled to the door to meet her, dressed in a red plaid bathrobe and scuffed slippers. He was going to talk to her at the door, but Sheila exerted her charm until he invited her in.

Immediately, she wished they had stayed on the porch. The room was hot, and smelled like Woody had spent the week smoking rather than bathing. Stale cooking odors did nothing to improve the air.

"How are you feeling?" She sat down on a big red vinyl chair, wondering why Woody had bought it. It was neither attractive nor comfortable.

"Not good," he grunted, peering nearsightedly through his thick glasses. His hands, she saw, shook when he held them out.

"I'm sorry to hear that. They miss you at Galaxia."

"Galaxia?" He had turned back to a television show, but at that word he swung his head in her direction. "You aren't from Galaxia!" His tiny eyes peered at her suspiciously.

"I met you there. Remember? I stumbled over you in the hall on my way to the reception last week." (It seemed like last year.)

"Oh." He nodded. "Yeah. I remember." He returned to his show with no curiosity at all.

She brought out the letter. "Woody, did you know Dean Anderson—" She stopped. What should she ask? Did you know Dean Anderson was about to give you credit for *Visions of Vietnam*? Perhaps Woody didn't even know about the book. Should she ask?

Her pause took less than three seconds, but long enough for Woody to become thoroughly angry.

"Of course I knew Dean Anderson! Don't talk to me about that man! Don't mention his name!" His eyes rolled behind his glasses. She'd forgotten for a minute that he'd found the body.

"It's okay, Woody, I didn't come to talk about Dean. I want to talk about a book—a book Dean did with your pictures. He—"

Woody thumped the cushion beside him. "He stole my book! That's what you ought to say. You ought to say he took my pictures and made himself rich on my book. I took those pictures. Me!" He bounced frantically on the sofa.

His daughter hurried into the room. "Hush your ranting," she said harshly. Woody subsided. She looked at Sheila with a pair of lovely green eyes that were as cold as a winter sea.

"What do you want?" Her speech was not as pretty as her eyes, but Sheila sensed she was being abrupt, not rude.

Sheila had forgotten how thin Crystal was, and today she looked exhausted. Dark circles under her eyes indicated she was not sleeping well. In one hand she carried a large spoon, which she tucked behind her back with an apologetic "I was getting supper."

"Hello, Crystal." Sheila introduced herself and reminded the girl that she had been at Galaxia on Monday. Woody interrupted.

"This lady was talking about my book." Woody muttered. "My book. The one Dean Anderson stole."

"Hush!" Crystal turned back to their guest. "Is that right?" She sounded willing to be impartial. Almost uninterested.

Sheila nodded. "I don't know if you know the story or not. Your father and Dean Anderson were together in Vietnam."

She nodded. "I know. Somebody told me last week. Daddy was hurt and Dean Anderson wasn't. So Dean Anderson took Daddy's pictures and published a book under his own name."

"Dean didn't know who your father was. He tried very hard to find out who took those pictures, and finally concluded the photographer was dead. That's why he dedicated the book to 'The Unknown Photographer.' He found out only last week that Woody took the pictures, when Jonah saw other pictures and told him."

Crystal puckered her forehead, puzzled. "Is that right? I thought . . ." She broke off and nodded. "Well, I did show Jonah Daddy's other pictures, one night last week." She gestured toward a bookshelf in a dim corner. One shelf was filled with albums.

"I'm glad you did. When Jonah told Dean, Dean called the publisher to try to make amends. I have a letter here." Sheila fumbled in her purse and produced it, handing it to Crystal. "It says they want to put your father's name on future printings. They want a picture and a few paragraphs about why Dean couldn't locate Woody when the book was first published, and how he finally discovered who the photographer was. I came to see if you have a picture."

Crystal read it twice. "Do you think this is on the level?"

"I'm sure it is. Dean told me about it at dinner last Thursday night. He was thrilled to finally locate that photographer."

"So he didn't steal the pictures?"

"Heavens no." She told the story as Dean had told it.

Crystal looked very relieved. "I wondered why Mr. Anderson would have stolen Daddy's book. He always seemed so nice, on TV."

Woody was still watching television. The new program featured Donald Duck's wealthy uncle. Sheila would have sworn he was not listening to their conversation, but suddenly he bounced up and down and pointed at the screen. "I could be rich as that duck if Dean Anderson hadn't stolen my book. Rich as that duck!"

"Hush," Crystal said automatically. But she turned to Sheila with the same question in her eyes. "*Did* he . . ." She swallowed. "*Did* he make a lot of money from the book?"

"I don't know what royalties run on a book like that, but he may have," Sheila admitted.

"Do you think a lawyer . . ." This was more than she could ask.

Sheila, understanding what she had been about to say, was doubtful. Especially if Laura Anderson inherited royalties with everything else. But Woody's claim deserved a chance. "I don't know, but I will check. It might be possible to get royalties transferred to your father, especially since Dean had already talked with the publisher. Do you have a picture of Woody?"

"Like he used to be?" At Sheila's nod, she went to a bookshelf and took down one of the albums. "There's one in here."

Sheila considered the shelves in amazement. "Do those albums all contain your father's pictures?"

Crystal nodded. "From Vietnam. That's when he sent pictures to Mama, you see. So she could see what it was like."

"I'm not going to work." Woody spoke suddenly, his voice gruff. "I may never go to work again. I'm a sick man. I can't be expected to stand on my feet all day, mopping and carrying and stooping. Bring us a beer, Crystal. Bring us all a beer." His voice had become petulant.

"You're going to work as soon as you get better," his daughter informed him in the tone a parent uses with a recalcitrant child. She handed Sheila an album and asked, "Would you like a beer? Or a Coke?"

"A Coke would be nice," Sheila agreed. The room was very warm.

Crystal disappeared into the kitchen, and Sheila carried the album to a sagging rocker. She began to turn the pages idly, then with mounting excitement. No wonder Jonah had been thrilled. These were good! No, better than good—great. Gently the camera had captured an old man's tears mingling with rain while the ruins of his burned home steamed behind him. A pig rooted for food in the ravaged garden. By the time Crystal returned with their drinks, she was staring at a picture tucked in front. Woody, as he had been.

Even if the faces had been the same, twenty years had blurred most resemblance between the young man in khaki about to swing aboard an army jeep and the middle-aged man in a red bathrobe slumped on his sagging couch. But it was the eyes that pierced Sheila with a sorrow that stopped her breath for a moment—eyes that stared at the world keen and full of curiosity.

"Does he have to work?" Sheila asked in a low voice. "Doesn't he get veteran's benefits?"

Crystal bit her lip and shook her head. "He isn't a veteran, he was a free-lance photographer. He got some insurance, but it's been gone a long time now." She passed one thin hand over her mouth.

"And your mother?"

"She died when I was eight. Working and looking after

both of us—it wore her out. He's easier to handle than he used to be. Or maybe I'm just used to it. I never knew him like that." She nodded toward the picture Sheila still held.

Woody looked up from his beer and beamed at his daughter. "She's smart, Crystal is. Goes to college." He swigged deeply, returned to his program.

"What are you studying?"

Crystal's laugh had little mirth. "Special education. I've got so much experience, you see. But I can only take a course now and then. I have to work, too, when I can. Sometimes he needs me . . ." She turned, unable to say more.

Sheila stood and went to give her a hug that surprised them both. The girl stood rigid, as if hugs were an unaccustomed experience in her life. Then she relaxed against the older woman. "You're very brave, Crystal. I'll go now and let you get back to cooking dinner. If I may, I'll take this picture and have it copied. I'll send the publisher the copy and return this one."

On the television, Scrooge cavorted atop his money pile. Woody shouted in the anger that seemed always just beneath his surface. "I could be as rich as that duck, if Dean hadn't stole my book! And if I hadn't gotten blown up. Rich as that blasted duck."

The girl gave him a smile. "Yeah, Daddy. Now you just watch your show." She replaced the album on its shelf. "I think you'd better go," she said in a low voice to Sheila. "His temper has been worse this week. It must be the flu. And visitors upset him."

Sheila turned toward the door and saw, on a small table in a dim corner, Dean Anderson's trophy for *Visions of Vietnam*. It looked exactly as Elise had described it.

"Where did you get this?" She hoped she sounded admiring.

Crystal took a step forward, but it was Woody who answered. "Dean gave it to me. Good thing he did. It shoulda been mine. Even Dean said so. Said it oughta be mine." Doubt had crept into his voice at the end, as if he was wondering what he was talking about. He turned back to his program.

"We should have put it in the back room," Crystal said. "When Craig was here last weekend, he thought Daddy had stolen it. Daddy doesn't steal!" Her cheeks were pink with indignation.

"Of course not." Sheila hoped that was truth, and not just soothing noises. She had another question. "Why did Craig come?"

"He wants to buy our house." She looked around her. "Daddy says he'd give us lots of money, but I don't know where we'd go. It's not much"—her lips curved in a valiant grin—"but it's all we've got."

Sheila had one last question. "Did Dean give your father any other trophies?"

"I don't think so. Daddy? Daddy!"

He glared at her. "You are interrupting my show."

"Just for a minute. Did Mr. Anderson give you other trophies?"

Woody glared at her without answering.

Sheila sat beside him. Since credits were appearing on the screen, she suggested, "Could we turn the television off for a few minutes, Woody? I need to ask you one or two things. It won't take long." It certainly wouldn't. Sitting this near Woody she was nearly asphyxiated by fumes of beer, tobacco and unwashed flesh.

"It's time for—" he began.

Crystal pushed the button. "Talk a few minutes, Daddy."

Woody looked from his daughter to his guest. "What do you want to talk about?"

"How many trophies did Dean Anderson give you?"

"One. I told you. Mine."

"When did he give it to you? The afternoon he died?"

Woody shook his head. "The day after the reception. Friday. I was polishing the floor. He called and said come right up, he wanted to give me something. He sure did!" He clapped his hands in sudden delight. "I showed it to all my buddies.

They couldn't hardly believe that Mr. Anderson would do that!" As abruptly as he had gotten excited, Woody got mad. "But he stole my book. I got nothing but a trophy. Good thing he's dead!"

"Tell me again about finding Mr. Anderson. Do you remember what time it was?"

"I don't want to talk about it."

Crystal spoke sharply. "Talk to her, Daddy. Tell her what you know."

Woody rested his pudgy hands on his knees. The robe swung open at the bottom to reveal hairy calves. One contained a deep red scar. "It was half past three," he said. "Usually I take my break at half past, but Mr. Anderson's light was bothering him. I went up there first."

"You fixed the light?"

"No, I found him dead. I couldn't have fixed it anyway. It's the ballast. That's what's wrong. I can't work on that. I would have reported it. But they might not have fixed it. I reported the toilet. They didn't fix *it*." He shook his head sadly.

Sheila wasn't interested in toilets. "And you found him dead."

"I don't want to talk about it!" Woody roared, as suddenly angry as he had been sad. "He was a bad man! He stole my book!"

Sheila shook her head. "He didn't steal your book, Woody. He tried very hard to find you after your accident, but you were in the hospital. And you didn't have a name inside your camera bag. When Dean found out those were your pictures, he ordered new copies of the book printed, with your name on them."

Woody looked as if he were trying very hard to understand. "My name on them."

Sheila nodded. "On the first page, with your picture. Everybody in the world will know that you took those pictures. Dean did that the week before he died. It was going to be a surprise for you."

"A surprise? For me?" Woody picked at the skirt of his robe. "Dean Anderson made a surprise for me?"

"Yes, Woody. And the books will still be printed, even though he's dead. I promise. Dean Anderson did some things wrong, but he was a good man. Do you understand that? He was a good man."

Woody's face crumpled like a child's. Then he began to moan like an animal in pain, swaying back and forth.

Crystal touched Sheila on the shoulder. "You'd better go now. He takes these spells sometimes." They tiptoed across the room.

Once on the porch, Crystal began to talk as if reluctant to let a visitor go. "I'm glad you told him. He always admired Dean, and I think it nearly killed him thinking Dean swindled him." She smiled briefly. "Me too." When Sheila started toward the steps, she continued, "Both Craig and Jonah said they'd help us publish another book. Do you think they really will?"

Sheila considered how to answer that both honestly and reassuringly. If Woody's other pictures were as good as the ones Dean had published, they could very well make not one, but several excellent books. But Craig and Jonah were professionals. Could either of them help publish a book of the magnitude Woody's was likely to be, and not take a big chunk of the profits for himself?

She decided to answer the question with another suggestion. "I have to call the publisher on Monday, to tell them I've got Woody's picture. Let me see what they advise."

"Would you?"

"Yes, I'll get back to you on Monday," she promised.

Crystal smiled. "I haven't known what to do. What if Daddy takes a notion to give the albums to Craig or Jonah before then?"

"I don't know. Let's hope he won't."

Crystal shook her head. "If he did, I wouldn't be able to stop him. Wait!" She turned and hurried into the house, and returned in a moment with all the albums. "I heard him going to the kitchen for another beer. You take them, please? Keep them for me until you find something to do with them. Lately I've been afraid . . ." She broke off, thrusting the albums into Sheila's unwilling arms.

The trust and admiration in Crystal's voice startled Sheila. Was this child so desperate for advice that she would latch on to any adult woman who came through her front door—without even checking her credentials?

She wanted to shake the girl for her naïveté, but you can't shake somebody just because they admire you.

Sheila staggered under the weight of the albums, and their dust was tickling her nose. "Just for a few days," she agreed. "Only until I've talked with the publisher."

Crystal followed her to the car, held the passenger door for her to stow the albums, then held out one hand. "I'm so glad you came. I forgot to ask your name."

Yet you trusted me with what may well be a fortune in pictures. Sheila wanted to say it, but she didn't. "You asked at the beginning. I just forgot to give it to you." Solemnly, feeling a bit foolish, she introduced herself and found one of her cards. "I'll be at Galaxia until this murder is cleared up."

"I thought you were with the police." Crystal studied the card, puzzled.

Sheila shook her head. "No, I'm working on this for Hosokawa, Galaxia's parent company." She really ought, she thought, to get some cards printed up that said that. "But I'm in touch with the police from time to time."

"Oh." A shadow flitted across the green eyes before Crystal shook her head. "I hope you won't have to ask Daddy more questions. He gets terribly upset whenever he hears anything about it on television or the radio. He keeps saying he's not going back. But he has to. He just has to!"

Sheila nodded. "Give him a couple more days, then I'll send one of his co-workers to drive him in one day. Maybe he's just afraid of being on the tenth floor. He could work other floors for a while, until he gets used to it."

"Great." Crystal smiled as if all her burdens had rolled away.

Sheila started her motor. "If you need me, call—will you?"

"Okay." She waved gaily as Sheila drove away.

Sheila was glad to be heading to her bright new apartment and even her excitable new dog. She also felt as guilty as could be for abandoning Crystal Robles to the drabness of her daily life.

20

She had scarcely gotten back from walking Lady when the phone rang. "You left without saying goodbye," a voice reproached her.

"Porter?" she hazarded.

"Of course. I was all set to ask you to dinner when Wylene said you'd skipped out early. You missed the tantrum!"

"Tantrum? What tantrum?" She was pretty sure she knew.

"I won't tell you, unless you promise to have dinner with me. May I pick you up at seven?"

Sheila, remembering Bayard's story and Elise's dire warnings, and considering the probable cost of a cab from Atlanta to Peachtree Corners, suggested, "Why don't I meet you somewhere instead? I live pretty far out, and I may want to go by my aunt's afterwards."

He chuckled again. "What *has* Elise been telling you? But very well. How about the Krispy Kreme on Ponce de Leon?"

"For dinner?"

"No, silly woman, for a place to park your car. Seven o'clock?"

They agreed. Sheila was in the shower before she realized he had not called her "darling" once. She found it a great improvement.

189

She was almost on the interstate when she began to notice the strange behavior of the green car behind her. When she slowed, it slowed. When she sped up, it followed not far behind. As an experiment she turned into the parking lot of a large industrial complex and drove around three sets of buildings. When she arrived back at Jimmy Carter Boulevard, the car was pulling around a nearby corner.

She was not particularly alarmed. What could anyone hope to do to her in six o'clock traffic and broad daylight? But when the car proceeded behind her toward the interstate and followed her to the fast lane, she found herself annoyed.

She watched for a break in the lane to her right and nipped in, crossed into another lane, and slowed. Sure enough, the green car passed her, but the sun was at an angle to prevent her seeing who was driving. Now she was behind, and determined to have some fun.

As soon as possible she pulled back into the fast lane and came close enough to her pursuer to almost read the tag. The car sped up. She followed, but when her speedometer hit 85 she eased up. She had no intention of getting arrested, no matter who this might be.

The green car sped to the next exit, made a quick dash across several lanes, and hurried up the exit ramp. She was not surprised to look in her mirror five minutes later and see it behind her again.

By now she was getting angry. She had planned to exit soon and wind down narrow streets toward Ponce de Leon, but this creature was just strange enough to convince her to take the broad North Avenue exit at Georgia Tech and follow that well-lit street to her destination.

She was perplexed about what to do at Krispy Kreme. The wise thing, of course, would be to cruise by several times until she saw Porter was there, but she did not know his car. "This is silly," she told herself sternly. "You'll be perfectly safe in that parking lot." This doughnut shop was a favorite for all of Atlanta, and usually busy.

190

Her problem was solved when she drove slowly through the lot and saw Porter himself, nose against the plate glass window at the end, no doubt watching hundreds of doughnuts swimming through hot grease and sliding under sheets of melted sugar. Sheila had always enjoyed the sight herself. Tonight she enjoyed the sight of Porter more. She slowed and rolled down her window. "Can I give you a lift, sir?"

He turned, and she beckoned urgently. The green car had paused just at the corner of the parking lot.

Porter sauntered over and she waved him to the passenger seat. "Hurry, please!"

He slid in without a word, then raised one eyebrow as she headed west on Ponce de Leon. "Are you in the habit of picking up men in parking lots this way?"

"No, but neither am I in the habit of being followed for twenty miles. Look behind us. Do you recognize that car?"

"What car?"

She looked in her mirror. The green car had vanished. And when she returned to the Krispy Kreme parking lot, it was nowhere to be found.

"It was there," she insisted. "I know it was."

"Some poor guy got a doughnut craving just as you left home," Porter told her. "He was probably worried stiff that you thought he was following you, until you picked me up. That probably shocked him so much he went home without a single glazed."

Porter was a delightful dinner companion. He suggested that they walk the few blocks to the Abbey, in what used to be a church, and took pains to be sure she got exactly what she wanted to eat and drink. After a while she couldn't help commenting on the difference between this Porter and the one she knew at Galaxia.

He smiled. "It's an act, of course, darling." He drawled the last word. "To keep me from getting too close to people, I guess."

"You don't like people?"

"Oh, I like people fine. But . . ." He stopped and took a sip of red wine. "I won't bore you with the story of my life, but I lost a wife and daughter several years ago in an automobile accident, two people I cared very much about. I haven't wanted to get too close to people since. Does that seem silly to you?"

She shook her head. "It's probably a natural reaction. But why not merely act standoffish? Why the flamboyant come-ons?"

He grinned. "Because that particular kind of come-on is the fastest way I know to turn women off. Men aren't fooled—at least not many of them. The ones who come on to me, I can handle. Besides, I'm a naturally flamboyant person. That part isn't fake, just the emotion."

"I hope you don't plan to live that way forever."

"No, I'm beginning to stir a bit. Tonight, for instance." He paused, then raised one eyebrow. "What about you? Elise said you lost your husband last year."

She nodded. "But it's entirely different." She stopped, wondering how to explain years of living with an enormous male ego fed by media lionization and professional success— and the relief when it was over. She decided not to try. "I've found it pleasant to be on my own for the first time in my life," she finished lamely. "Tell me about the office tantrum."

His grin brought back the Porter she knew. "Oh, darling, you wouldn't have believed it! We got into staff meeting and Elton Dekker asked, 'Have you come up with an idea for that first television program?' At the same time—and I mean the exact same time—both Jonah and Craig said, 'Yessir.' I thought I was back in the army for a minute."

"Were you ever in the army?" She was astonished. She could not picture Porter Phillips in boot camp.

He shrugged. "For about a minute. In our day they drafted almost everybody, you know. But anyway, poor old Elton thought they were talking about the same thing, and so did I. It seems that everybody but me knew what was going on—even Elise."

She nodded. "Veronica told us in the coffee shop this morning."

"What? You too?" He signaled the waiter. "I need a stiff drink, sir. How about black coffee for two?" When the waiter had decided he really meant it, Porter said, "Let me gather up the shreds of my dignity and I'll try to continue. But I have never felt so left out in my life."

"When could we have told you?" she asked. "We'd have said something at lunch, but Craig came up. Then you went straight to the meeting."

"Not until Elise dropped her bomb. Are you really a detective?"

She hesitated, then nodded. "Yes, of sorts. Strictly amateur, of course. But that's the reason I was sent back to Galaxia. I would have been glad to leave things to the police, but I have an aunt—"

His look was sudden and sharp. "Do you really?"

"Sure. Why?"

"Nothing. I just wondered . . . Oh, here's our coffee. Thank you, kind sir. You have just saved a life." He raised his cup in a toast. "To aunts, where'er they be."

Sheila obediently raised her cup, with no idea what the toast was about. "Tell me about the tantrum. You never did."

"Oh, well, it was just that Craigie had his own script and Jonah and Veronica had theirs. Elton played eenie, meenie, miney, mo and chose the latter. Told Craig they could use his at a later date.

"Craig smiled very nicely in front of the boss, but when we got downstairs he said some very nasty things to Jonah. He isn't speaking to Veronica at all, lucky woman. Elise tried to make peace, of course, and got so chewed up for her pains she left in tears. She really is a dear softy, isn't she?"

Sheila chuckled. "Yes. You should have been there the night we tried to teach her to play hearts. You know that game, where the point is not to take any hearts or the queen of spades?" He nodded. "Well, the first three games we played with Elise, she won every time. Finally, the fourth time, she took a heart. With the saddest look on her face she assured us, 'I didn't mean to. I was trying to let you have them all.' The funny thing is, she'd missed the whole point of the game. She won, thinking she was helping *us* win!"

Porter drained his cup and signaled for a refill. "When I first hired her, I thought Elise couldn't be real. But the more I work with her, the more I wish everybody else was a little bit that crazy."

Sheila nodded. "Spacy, but special. That's what they said about her in our yearbook, and she still is. I wish she could find someone to appreciate her. Sounds like she's made some pretty poor choices marriagewise."

Porter held up his hands in mock horror. "Don't look at me when you say that. Working with Elise is one thing. Living with her would be something entirely different."

"But never dull," she pointed out. "You could do worse."

"Poor, poor, poor," he told her. "I was thinking maybe I could do infinitely better. Maybe we ought to discuss a nice, neutral topic like your aunt."

"Want to meet her?" It had just occurred to her that Porter and Aunt Mary might enjoy each other very much.

T hey found her curled in a corner of her couch, reading a mystery. The mystery to the family was when she ever did the vast amounts of work that must be required to manage her fortune. Never in the presence of others, certainly.

She offered sherry and chattered to Porter as though she'd known him all his life. When Sheila excused herself for a few minutes, she returned to find them deep in a very southern discussion of family, seeking common ancestors.

"I thought you were a New Yorker," she chided Porter as they prepared to leave. "That's what you said."

"I never," he returned. "I said I came to Atlanta from New York. I was born in South Carolina not far from Miss Mary here."

"And only a few decades later," Aunt Mary twinkled.

"A very few, ma'am. Now I see where your niece gets her charm."

"And I see why she wanted me to meet you. It's been a delightful evening. Come again."

P orter insisted on showing Sheila Underground Atlanta. She did not arrive home until very late, and she looked forward to sleeping late in the morning. As she was getting ready for bed, her phone rang.

"Aunt Mary? What are you doing up so late?"

"I wouldn't be, dear, if you had come home earlier. I was worried about your safety. Do you know who that man is?"

Sheila was surprised. Her aunt hadn't worried for her safety when she'd been in some situations that warranted it. "You're worrying unnecessarily, Aunt Mary. Porter is art director at Galaxia's film division and a charming companion."

"He's more than that. His mother's sister was Maria Graziano. Dean Anderson was engaged to Maria at Georgia, but when he came home from Korea with a television contract, he broke it off. She jumped off a building that same evening. I woke Mildred up after you left and checked to be sure I was right. Her magazines dredged up the story when Dean started dating Raven Hillis. Mildred says Maria's father threatened to kill Dean. He didn't, of course, but it's possible that his grandson got revenge."

"Aunt Mary, not all Italians are Borgias. And Porter is highly unlikely to have committed murder for something that happened when he was a child."

So why did a picture flitter into her mind: Porter, lifting his coffee cup with a toast: "To aunts, where'er they be"?

21

She woke the following morning to a gentle cold touch. She pushed herself up onto her elbow, startled, and her face was gently licked by a soft tongue. "Oh, Lady," she groaned. "Not yet. What time is it?"

It was just past seven. Besides, it was a dim gray morning beyond her open curtains, one on which she would ordinarily have stayed in bed and read for a couple of hours before getting up.

Alas, dogs keep the same schedule every day of the week. By the time Sheila had dragged herself to her feet, rolled up her pajama bottoms, put on a raincoat and slid her feet into loafers without socks, Lady was prancing at the front door. "Just let me comb my hair, and pray we don't meet anybody," Sheila told her.

They got back from their walk at half past seven. Lady stretched out for a snooze by the heating vent. Sheila, now thoroughly awake, made coffee and, still wearing her raincoat, carried a mug onto her deck.

The deck was one of the things that had attracted Sheila to her third-floor apartment. Accessible only from her living room and facing east, it was very private. Decks on lower apartments were around the corner, so the wall beneath it was blank. She had furnished it with cushioned wicker rockers and a table to hold her new trident maple bonsai tree, which she watered daily just before propping her feet on the railing to enjoy her first cup of coffee and welcome the rising sun.

This morning there would be no sun. The sky, which had only begun to lighten, was a low, flat white, already turning gray. The air was heavy with approaching rain. Sheila hugged her coat around her and was glad her coffee was hot and her deck sheltered from the rising wind. She wouldn't be able to stay out long, it was too chilly. But for a few minutes she wanted to take deep breaths of outside air and finally read through the police reports.

They didn't tell her much that she didn't already know. Dean had been shot at close range, then the gun had been wiped clean. There was no evidence to link Darius Dudwell to the crime. Furthermore, he had a difficult alibi to break—he'd been with his lawyer all afternoon.

Many different fingerprints and footprints had been lifted. It was probable they would match with staff at Galaxia. The vase contained fingerprints that did not appear elsewhere in the room. Sheila made a note: "probably Bayard's." She read down a list of assorted hairs found on the premises, and wondered how often hair proved a valuable clue to a crime. In this case, it primarily eliminated Darius Dudwell again.

She sipped her coffee and scanned the list of what the vacuum cleaner had turned up. A paper clip. Empty scraps of paper. One small gold-colored bead, pierced through.

She considered that bead. Had it come from a woman's jewelry? Laura's when she was there? Bayard's? Even one of Dean's co-workers could have dropped it and never noticed. But since Sheila had never seen Bayard wear anything but wood jewelry, the bead drew her attention back to Laura Anderson. Neal said he and his mother had been shopping together that day, but each of them had managed to see Dean alone. Had one of them come back? She noted the question in her margin. Of all the persons who might have wanted to kill Dean Anderson, Laura's motive was by far the strongest—if (and Sheila knew this was a big if) she had known about that will.

The wind had died down a bit, so she fetched another cup of coffee and returned to her deck to watch, across a small yard, brown ducks bobbing for breakfast on a drainage pond (part of the "natural surroundings" that upped her rent). Soon she would be wanting her own breakfast. But not until she finished her coffee.

She mulled over whether to fix an American breakfast or a Japanese one. She had just decided to fry an egg and bacon, make hot buttered toast, spread it liberally with strawberry jam and indulge in a third cup of coffee when she heard her phone. She hurried inside. She was not expecting any calls, but in a new place, each call is a possible adventure.

This was not the kind of adventure she'd had in mind. She listened, hung up, and sagged against the wall, feeling like she'd been kicked in the stomach.

The voice had been a hoarse whisper, impossible to recognize. It spoke sentences rich with sexual imagery. Its message, however, had been practical in the extreme: "Get out of Galaxia—or die."

The Whisperer called twice again. When Sheila asked the phone company to trace the calls, she was told those calls could not be traced, but she could purchase that service for "a few dollars a month." Explaining in no uncertain terms why she thought call tracing ought to be provided to all customers as part of the regular service, she took the phone off the hook and went for a walk. Perhaps she ought to invest in one of those impersonal answering machines after all.

The rain had finally come, hard and drenching rain that streamed off roofs and hurtled down concrete drives. She plodded up and down hills enjoying each crisp indrawn breath and the small din of raindrops on the hood of her long coat— and trying not to wonder if the caller knew not only her number, but where she lived as well. If so, could he (or she) be somewhere nearby?

Sheila had what she knew to be an irrational fear of the dark, but she was not normally nervous out of doors in broad daylight. Today she found herself avoiding large bushes and lonely lanes.

Finally she returned to the apartment, wet, cold, and longing for company.

"Want to go see Mildred?" Lady rose with alacrity, as if the trip were one she'd taken every day of her life. "Not until

I get dry and have some more coffee," Sheila told her. Lady lay down again, but right by the front door.

As she rubbed her hair with a towel and put on dry slacks and a large cotton sweater, Sheila was glad she wouldn't have the smell of wet dog all the way into Atlanta. Did dogs find the smell of wet humans equally offensive? If so, Lady was too well bred to show it.

Aunt Mary was sitting as usual, feet tucked beneath her, working the morning crossword. In ink. "Your phone is out of order," she informed Sheila, peering over the top of her half glasses like an inquisitive sparrow. "And why did you bring that dog?"

"I wanted to see you," Sheila told her, "and Lady wanted to see Mildred." She pushed the dog through the door to the kitchen.

"Mildred doesn't like dogs, dear," Aunt Mary replied, ignoring the sounds of joyful reunion they could both hear.

"Right." Sheila followed the dog.

"Want some coffee? I can make it in a minute." Mildred turned toward the coffee canister, but Sheila shook her head. "What I'd really like is a glass of milk and some of that coffee cake."

Mildred handed her a plate. "Cut as much as you want. You're looking kind of peaky. And you may as well sit down to eat it. Miss Beaufort isn't going to take any notice of you until she's finished her puzzle."

It was nearly half an hour before Sheila carried coffee to the living room, where Aunt Mary was now placidly reading the mystery she'd laid aside the evening before.

Sheila flopped into her usual chair and swung her feet onto the ottoman. "My phone's not out of order," she said directly, "I was getting obscene calls."

Aunt Mary removed her small glasses and laid the book beside her on the couch. "Oh, Sheila! Surely not!" She couldn't have sounded more rebuking if Sheila had confessed to making them.

"Afraid so. I answered three, then took the phone off the

hook and went for a walk." She sipped her coffee to steady her nerves.

"Was that wise, dear?"

Sheila was touched. "I'll admit that idea crossed my own mind. Anyone who knows my number may be able to watch me, as well. Somebody—and it could well be the same person—followed me from my apartment all the way to where I met Porter last evening."

"I meant to take the phone off the hook, dear. Someone important might need to reach you. I tried myself."

"I don't know anybody important," Sheila replied, nettled.

Aunt Mary tapped her book with one nail. "Is it a man?"

Sheila shrugged. "I can't tell. The voice is a loud whisper. But it's someone connected with Dean's death. The gist of the messages, stripped of their colorful trappings, is that I am to get off the case immediately."

"Wonderful!" Aunt Mary slid her feet from beneath her and sat erect on the couch, short legs almost reaching the floor. Her eyes sparkled with excitement. "We've got someone scared, Sheila! Perhaps the next move will give him away!"

"You read too many of those books. He's not scared—if it is a he. He's scaring *me*. The next move he *describes* concerns me rather personally. Whether it gives him away or not won't matter to me much if I'm dead."

"You're not going to be dead." Aunt Mary dismissed the notion with a wave of her hand. "Tell me what he said—and how he knew to call you in the first place. I expected you to be more discreet than that, dear."

Sheila shoved her fingers through her thick, curly hair and tugged it firmly. Aunt Mary often had that effect on her.

"I was discretion itself, Aunt Mary. But my good friend Elise informed the entire office yesterday at lunchtime that I've been sent to Galaxia to 'find things out.' Bayard is seeing Jonah, so if he told her, she's probably told her family." She sighed. "And yesterday afternoon I felt so sorry for Crystal Robles that I told her I'm working on the case, to call if they need anything." She sipped her coffee and set the empty cup carefully in its saucer. "I shouldn't be surprised I've gotten calls from one person—I ought to be astounded I haven't gotten them from several."

"All of that is unfortunate, dear, but it cannot be helped. Tell me what you learned yesterday." Aunt Mary reached for her pad and pencil again. "I didn't like to talk in front of Porter."

"Have you been watching Perry Mason again? You look nothing at all like Della Street, you know."

"Tell me what you learned." Aunt Mary remained unperturbed.

Sheila reported on what Elise had said about Neal, and her own visit to Woody. She saved the best for last: Bayard's theft.

"A video. How strange." Aunt Mary sat and tapped shell-pink nails on her pad. She seemed to be thinking what to do next. At last she heaved a deep sigh. "I deeply regret this wasted time, Sheila. It never occurred to me you'd be out playing last evening if you had discovered anything important."

"It was nothing that wouldn't keep," Sheila protested. "At least while you were toasting your toes and reading mysteries, I was asking questions and taking nasty phone calls!"

She could not sit still any longer. Maybe Aunt Mary was right. Maybe she was drinking too much coffee. Her hands were shaking, and she felt as if her bones would jump out of her skin any minute now. She got to her feet and began to pace in front of the enormous south window. "What does any of it lead to, really, anyway? For all we know, a stranger walked into Dean's office and gunned him down."

She indicated the skyline of Atlanta. "This city isn't what it was when you first came here, Aunt Mary, or when I was living here before, for that matter. Look at the eleven o'clock news! One murder after another. That's all they ever talk about."

Aunt Mary nodded placidly. "I often wish Atlanta had more newscasters and fewer crime reporters. That's why I usually go to bed at ten with a good book. But I'm not convinced the city is more evil than it used to be, Sheila. Evil takes over a city the same way good does, one person at a time. Our job is not to condemn the city, but to help the good by letting it use us whenever it can. All any of us has to do is fight the battles we are given."

Sheila stared at her. "The battles we are *given*? We weren't given this battle! You insisted that we be let in on the case!"

Aunt Mary cocked her head to one side and seemed to consider the matter. "What if I did, dear? Would you back down now?"

"You can bet your bottom dollar I would! You and I can't solve a case about which we know almost nothing. The Atlanta police are perfectly capable of solving it themselves. I am ready to go back to Hosokawa and forget all about it."

Aunt Mary's voice was cold and distant. "Very well, dear, go."

Sheila shook her head. "It's not that easy. Mr. Hashimoto venerates age. He's not going to release me from Galaxia until you call and say you are satisfied."

Now it was the silver curls that shook. "But I'm not, dear."

"Tell him anyway!" Even Sheila was surprised at the force of her reply.

Aunt Mary's gaze pierced her. "Those calls affected you more than I think you know, Sheila. Sit down."

Embarrassed, Sheila obeyed, trembling all over. Aunt Mary trotted to her walnut secretary, and returned with a small snifter of brandy. "Drink this."

Sheila gulped it down and sat clutching the glass, still shaking.

"One feels so violated after obscene calls." Aunt Mary spoke softly, as if to herself. "You can tell yourself it was nothing. A few seconds of pressure on the eardrum. You may even laugh a bit. But you feel bruised and dirty all over." She rested one small hand on Sheila's shoulder. "We should have dealt with that, Sheila, before going on with our conversation. Let me get you more brandy."

It was as close to an apology as Sheila was going to get, but she still wasn't satisfied. "It's not just an obscene call, Aunt Mary. It was a death threat."

"Nonsense, dear. You are well able to take care of yourself. Besides, I am here." She refilled Sheila's snifter with more brandy than she usually considered appropriate for a lady to drink.

"Do you plan to stand guard at my apartment?" Sheila retorted before raising the snifter to her lips.

Aunt Mary seemed to be thinking that over, but just as Sheila was beginning to feel a warm glow all over, Aunt Mary gloated, "Just think, Sheila, we have your caller, and the police don't. And you know the people involved. We are getting very close to the murderer!"

"That's a lot of comfort," Sheila assured her.

Sarcasm was wasted on Aunt Mary. With the air of one who has just made a very difficult decision, she rose and headed for her telephone. "I think we must make a little trip," she said—with obvious reluctance.

23

"Brookwood Hills is one of my favorite neighborhoods." Aunt Mary peered in contentment at the brick homes and tall hardwoods they were driving past. "You'd never know you were right off Peachtree, would you? I understand that they have an active community association. Perhaps because it's so well contained."

Contained was the word, Sheila thought. Only three streets provided access to the neighborhood, and they were scarcely noticeable. Most people's attention would be on the bulk of Piedmont Hospital across Peachtree Street.

They went down a hill, past tennis courts and a pool under repair. One or two houses also sported scaffolding, as owners chose to double the size of existing houses rather than leave this stable in-town community.

"Here we are." The house was a modest two-story with an uninteresting lawn. "Dean and Laura moved here twenty years ago, if I remember correctly, and she remained when he left. She's never had a green thumb, poor Laura."

"Like two other people we know," Sheila pointed out. "The only difference is, we live in apartments. And you need to remember before tears start to flow that poor Laura kicked Dean out."

"I suppose that is technically correct," Aunt Mary agreed, "although he was doing a great deal of traveling by then. During this visit, Sheila, please restrain any animosity you may feel for this unfortunate woman."

"This unfortunate woman, who just inherited a small fortune, didn't restrain the animosity she felt for me on Thursday."

"Never mind that, dear. We are paying a call to a house of mourning. Keep that in mind, please."

"Does she know we are coming?"

"Of course! I don't drop in on people without calling first. You never know what you might find."

Privately, Sheila thought that could be more helpful when investigating murder. Aunt Mary, however, was unlikely to let murder interfere with her social code.

Laura opened the door herself, wearing a gray tweed skirt, soft blue blouse, and pearls at her throat. When Aunt Mary introduced Sheila formally as "my niece, the widow of Tyler Travis," Laura Anderson was more cordial to her than she had been Thursday. Money not only talks, Sheila reflected as she followed their hostess, it changes how people talk to you. Laura led them into a living room tastefully furnished in mahogany. An Oriental rug Sheila wouldn't have minded owning herself covered the polished floor.

Laura offered tea and went into the kitchen to put on a kettle. Aunt Mary perched on the sofa and patted the cushion beside her as if Sheila were three and accompanying her on a social visit.

Sheila took her seat, understanding the gesture. If Aunt Mary had stood hesitantly in the room, waiting for Sheila to take a seat so she could totter over and perch beside her, the situation would have been very different. She had one instruction for her aunt, however. "Find out about those pearls."

When Laura returned with the tea, she also brought a plate of pound cake and four cups and saucers. They chatted about the latest blossoms at the botanical gardens, the High Museum's latest art exhibit. Sheila wondered how Aunt Mary knew so much when she never went out. At one point the elderly woman deplored that someone had murdered Dean

Anderson. If Laura realized that Dean's will gave her the best motive, she gave no sign.

Only when they were drinking their second cups of tea did Aunt Mary say in an admiring voice, "Your pearls are lovely, Laura. I don't remember seeing them before."

Laura touched them briefly. "Dean brought them back from Japan several years ago."

"Are they the ones you were looking for Thursday?" Sheila asked casually.

Laura nodded. "They were in Dean's safety deposit box at the bank. The lawyer gave them to me yesterday."

"Oh. I thought you said they were Bayard's."

"No. They are mine." Laura touched them possessively.

Sheila sipped her tea to hide her expression. She had helped Dean choose those pearls before he left Tokyo. He had arrived home to find Laura already on the news proclaiming to the world her plans for divorce. He must have chucked the necklace into the bank and waited for someone else to give them to. Poor Dean, once again he had procrastinated too long. Bayard would get those pearls only over her mother's dead body.

Aunt Mary now said, hesitantly, "How are you sleeping, dear? You look plumb worn out with all of this!"

"I've been needing something most nights," Laura admitted.

Aunt Mary sipped her tea and nodded. "The death of a spouse is so difficult."

Laura leaned forward as if inhaling the sympathy radiating from the wrinkled face. "So few people understand that, Miss Mary. They think when you're divorced, you don't care if the other person dies, but it's still like a piece of yourself is gone. I can't believe Dean is really dead." She dabbed her eyes with a handkerchief she produced from a pocket. Sheila noticed it was perfectly dry when she finished.

"He was one of our generation's great men," Aunt Mary mused.

Sheila took a sliver of pound cake and watched Laura out of the corner of her eye.

Dean's ex-wife nodded. "He was, Miss Mary. He truly was. This last week I've wondered if I did the right thing ten years ago. I thought I couldn't stand any more of his being gone all the time, but now that he's truly gone, I wish I had had just a bit of him those last ten years. And no matter what he was, he was the father of my children." She dabbed her eyes again and stuffed the handkerchief back into her pocket.

"Your children must be a comfort to you." Aunt Mary's voice was huskier than usual, as if she, too, held back tears. "How long will your lovely daughter be with you?"

Laura sniffed. "She leaves tomorrow. I was so glad they'd given her another week off. She is a tower of strength to me. Neal, too, of course. I don't know if I can stand for him to leave next year. I'm trying to convince him to stay in town for his first two years of college."

Aunt Mary leaned forward and patted Laura's hand. "Has he fully recovered from that trouble last year, dear? Or has this time been especially hard on him?"

Laura looked into her teacup, out the window, anywhere but into those brown eyes so near her own. "He's fine. Neal has never given me any trouble. And he and his father were never close. It's Bayard who has taken this hard." She rose and called up the stairs, "Bay? Bay? Come down. We have guests."

Now Sheila understood the extra cup on the tray. It was for when Laura needed to call in reinforcements.

Bayard clomped down the steps, looking younger than usual in jeans and a sweatshirt, a French braid, and no makeup. When she saw Sheila, she stopped on the bottom step until her mother called, "Come on in." It was more command than request.

She approached the table with her chin at a defiant angle, but there was something in her gait that reminded Sheila of a child expecting to be whipped.

"I don't believe you have met my friend Miss Mary Beaufort. Miss Mary, this is my daughter Bayard. Miss Mary, Bay, is Mrs. Travis's aunt."

"I see. Glad to meet you." Bayard took a piece of pound

cake and waved away the tea. "I'll get myself some coffee." She padded to the kitchen and returned with, of all things, her father's mug, which she proceeded to cradle in both hands as if for warmth. Sheila eyed the mug enviously and refused a second cup of tea.

If Laura had hoped that Bayard would contribute to the conversation, she was disappointed. But her mere presence enlivened her mother. She chattered about Bay's good job with the network as if the young woman were not there, then boasted of her college accomplishments and even her prowess as a high school gymnast. "Honestly, I think she'd have been a trapeze artist if we hadn't steered her in other directions." Laura tapped Bayard playfully and Bay glared back.

At last the phone rang. Laura rose with obvious relief, leaving Bayard staring after her with narrowed eyes.

"So why have you come?" she said to Sheila as soon as her mother was out of earshot, totally ignoring Aunt Mary.

"I came with my aunt. But since you asked, I've wondered why you took that video off my desk yesterday."

Bayard met her gaze, decided not to deny it. "It was Daddy's. I told you."

"Really?" Two pairs of brown eyes urged her to tell the truth.

In the silence that followed, they could all hear Laura saying to someone on the telephone, "Oh, yes. It only mentions me by name, not as 'my wife, Laura Anderson.' That's what made the difference!"

Bayard ducked her head in embarrassment. "Sorry about the family linen. Mom doesn't know how to wash it except in public."

Sheila smiled back. "That's okay. So what about that video? I went through all of them myself, and none of them was personal. They were—" She stopped, remembering one unusual subject. "It was Neal's, wasn't it? From the college he wants to attend."

Bayard knew when she was beaten. "Yeah. He'd taken it to Daddy to watch. I don't know if he did or not, but I didn't like the idea of it lying around the office. I mean, I don't know when Neal gave it to him, but if somebody found it, they'd be sure to think he'd been up there that day, wouldn't they?"

"So you tricked me, picked up the tape and left." Sheila nodded. "I see. Did you tell Neal what you were going to do?"

Bayard shook her head. "But he was freaking out about it."

"At your dad's house on Thursday, was that you two whispering in the butler's pantry just before the doorbell rang?"

Bayard looked at her with new respect. "You really do get around, don't you?"

"I try." Sheila was remembering that Jonah had lied. Why?

Another doorbell rang. Bayard started to rise, but Neal called, "I've got it" and clattered down the stairs.

When he had passed the living room, Sheila said softly, "You don't have to worry about Neal, Bayard. The security guard saw him come in and go out long before you were there. Since someone heard Dean talking with you, Neal won't be in any trouble."

"Whoosh." Bayard let her head fall against the back of her chair. "You mean I did my snatch-and-grab act for nothing?" Sheila nodded. Bayard tugged at her hair. "God, how I hate taking care of other people!"

"If that's a prayer," Aunt Mary said crisply, "there's an easy answer. Just stop. Let people take care of themselves."

Sheila made a mental note to suggest, at the earliest possible moment, that the elderly woman follow her own advice.

Laura's voice rose, and Bayard uttered a blunt expletive.

"Atta girl." Jonah Baker stood in the archway, applauding. "Meet your problems with profanity. Solves nothing, but makes you feel so much better."

Bayard looked at him suspiciously. "Are you laughing at me?"

"Heavens, no. I'm weeping for you. A writer who has to resort to profanity needs a larger vocabulary." He came into the room and stopped. "Oh, hi, Sheila. I didn't see you. Are you here in your role as public person or private eye?"

"Private person," she replied. "But maybe you'd like to tell us why you said Bayard was with you last Thursday at her father's house when she was with Neal, instead."

Neal came up behind Jonah. "Yeah—I wondered about that, too."

Jonah rubbed one ear. "Misplaced gallantry, I guess."

Aunt Mary rose. "I don't believe I've met you, young man. I am Mary Beaufort, Sheila's aunt and a longtime friend of Laura Anderson's family. We came to offer our condolences."

He was not in the least quelled. "Glad to meet you, Ms. Beaufort. I'm Jonah Baker. As I understand it, congratulations would be more in order."

"And why are you here, young man?"

He was old enough to enjoy being called young. "I came to take Miss Foulmouth here to Underground Atlanta for lunch. She had a bad time there once, and I wanted to let her know it can be fun."

"We're just going," Aunt Mary assured him. "Neal?" She addressed the young man who was kicking the rug in the hall. "Would you give me your arm to my car? I am a bit shaky on the steps."

If it occurred to Neal to wonder why Aunt Mary didn't call for Sheila's arm instead, he was either too polite to say so or (and Sheila suspected this was the case) too eager to get out of the house and have something to do. He stuck out one elbow at an awkward angle and Aunt Mary took it with the air of departing royalty.

"I am sorry not to wait for your mother," she told him as she made her very tottery way down the stone steps. "Please tell her I will give her a call another day. I tried yesterday, but the phone seemed to be out of order."

"Oh, no, ma'am, it's not out of order. She was probably talking. She's been on it a lot since Dad died. Clearing things up."

Sheila eyed him suspiciously. He sounded merely charming and sincere. Was he being sarcastic as well? She could not decide. But she also listened with amazement. Who would have guessed that the sullen young man of Thursday had this many manners? Since he attended the same school where Sheila had first met Elise, she had already accepted that part of her prejudice was disgust at the school's current quality of students. For the first time she saw that Neal might, away from his mother, be a credit to their mutual alma mater.

"Are you bearing up well?" Aunt Mary asked him.

"Oh, yes, ma'am. We didn't see much of him anyway."

"When you took him the video the afternoon he died, was he much as usual?"

Neal was young, but he was a good liar. He only paused a fraction of a second before replying, "I don't know what you mean, ma'am. I gave him a video about my college several weeks ago. I didn't see him that day at all."

"Oh. I understood that you and your mother . . ."

"Mama took me to town but we split up. I had some CDs to check out and she was trying on clothes. We met at Muse's at three."

"You keep up with those CDs." She gave him a little pat.

Sheila wondered if Aunt Mary would be so approving if she knew Neal referred to compact discs, not certificates of deposit.

He gently helped the old woman into her seat while Jason held open the door. "You-all drive carefully, now."

She reached out and took his hand. "Neal, you aren't having any more trouble after last year, are you?"

He paused, then shook his head. "No, ma'am. I'm fine now. The doctor says that was definitely a phase. I'm looking forward to college next year, and everything."

"But you were very angry then, weren't you? I heard you threatened somebody."

His tan eyes were puzzled. "Oh no, ma'am. I wasn't mad at anybody else. It was myself I tried to kill."

24

It was early Sunday afternoon. Sheila was lying on her sofa, drowsily reading a Japanese novel, when the telephone rang again. Steeling herself for another obscene call (since surely Aunt Mary was snoozing away the afternoon), she was thrown off balance by desperate sobs on the other end.

"I can't understand a word you are saying," she finally said.

The person on the other end pulled herself together. "You said call if I needed you. I don't know who else I can call. Oh, Mrs. Travis, I don't know what to do!"

She identified the caller. "What's the matter, Crystal? Is your father ill?"

"No, not ill." Crystal gulped and took a deep, ragged breath. "Oh, Mrs. Travis, it's worse than that. Far worse. He turned himself in. He killed Dean Anderson!"

Sheila reached the small house in Virginia Highlands in record time. Crystal met her on the porch. Today her hair was clean and curled, and she wore a dress and lipstick. For the first time Sheila realized how pretty she was, even with her nose bright pink and her eyes still wet with tears.

She started into the stuffy little living room. Sheila put a hand on her arm. "Couldn't we just talk out here? It's lovely out."

Crystal nodded and sank into a webbed aluminum chair as if her legs would no longer hold her.

"Now tell me what happened." Sheila took the other chair.

"Well, I went to church, like always, and left Daddy here." Her voice wavered at this betrayal by her regular schedule. "When I got home, he wasn't here. I thought he'd gone up to the intersection to buy a paper or something. He does that sometimes, so I wasn't worried. But then Mrs. Williams came over, from next door." She pointed to a cheerful green house with geraniums on the porch. "She said . . . she said she saw a police car come and take Daddy away!" Tears streamed down her cheeks. She wiped them on her sleeve, until Sheila produced a tissue. (As distressed as Crystal was, Sheila still couldn't help reflecting that if this case went on much longer, she ought to buy stock in a tissue company.)

When Crystal's weeping had lessened, Sheila asked, "What makes you think he turned himself in?"

"I called them. They said he called and said he killed Dean Anderson. He asked them to come pick him up because he didn't have a car." She broke down again and sobbed.

Sheila was puzzled. "Had he said anything to indicate he was planning to do this, Crystal?"

Crystal gave a soggy shrug. "All day yesterday Daddy kept asking, 'Crystal, was Mr. Anderson a good man?' I didn't pay him any attention—I was studying for an exam Monday." She swallowed hard. "What should I do, Sheila? We don't have a lawyer, and I don't know how we could pay one if we did."

Sheila stood. "Let's go down to the police station. You can make decisions better after you've talked with your father."

A h, my able assistant." Lieutenant Green rose from his desk and showed Sheila and Crystal to a chair. "I hope you have heard that we have a signed confession for the murder."

216

She nodded. "You remember Crystal Robles, Woody's daughter. May we see him?"

"I'm afraid not, just now. If you will check with the desk on your way out, they can tell you about visiting hours. Mr. Robles has been assigned a lawyer," he told Crystal. His voice was as deep and mournful as the bay of a hound.

"But he couldn't have done it!" she insisted, twisting her hands in her lap. "Daddy couldn't shoot somebody. He's terrified of guns!"

"That was his problem." Lieutenant Green pulled a sheet from a stack of papers before him. "Normally I would not let you see this, but seeing that you are accompanied by my assistant . . ." He handed it to Crystal and bent his head to his desk, but not before Sheila had seen the compassion in his eyes for the girl before him. "I believe his lawyer will want to plead self-defense. He thought Mr. Anderson was going to shoot him, as you will see."

Sheila pulled her chair over so they could read together.

I went to see Dean Anderson to ask for money for my book. I thought he had stolen my book, but the lady said he didn't. He tried to find me, but couldn't. I did not know that at the time. I knew he got money for my book, so I went to ask him for some. He said "We'll have to see what we can do." He opened his drawer and took out a gun. I do not like guns.

I thought he was going to shoot me. I grabbed the gun. It went off. Mr. Anderson was killed. He fell. I ran out of the room. I was afraid my fingerprints were on the gun, so I wiped the gun with lots of Kleenex. Then I ran down the stairs.

"I was very afraid. I could not think what to do. I remembered a toilet on five that I needed to check, so I went down there. So I could think some more what to do. I decided to go get Ms. Fowler and tell her I had found Mr. Anderson. She was in the mail-

room. *That's where I found her. She told me to go get the other people up on eleven while she went to see if Mr. Anderson was really dead or just hurt. He was dead. I knew. I saw him fall.*

I got the other people and then I went to Jonah's office and waited for the police, like he told me to. I did not go back to Dean Anderson's office, because I was scared. When the police came, I said I had found Mr. Anderson dead. I was glad he was dead, because I thought he had stolen my book. But the lady said he did not steal my book, he was making books with my name in them and I might even get some money. I cannot take money from Mr. Anderson, because I killed him.

The confession was signed in a large scrawl: *Woodrow Wilson Robles.*

Crystal grew very pale. "He did it," she whispered. "He really did it! Oh, Sheila, what are we going to do?"

T he first thing we have to do," Aunt Mary said crisply, "is get Woody a good lawyer. Somebody who can arrange for us to talk with him, too. I'll put Hafford onto that. He may even take on the case himself."

Sheila doubted that Aunt Mary's lawyer, who specialized in corporate law, was going to be much use. But she said nothing. She was concentrating at the moment on making certain Crystal drank large quantities of hot tea with plenty of sugar, for the young woman looked as if she could faint again at any moment.

Crystal had fainted the first time immediately after that terrified whisper: "He really did it! What are we going to do?"

Lieutenant Green had kindly whisked a very smelly something under her nose until she revived, then provided a strong officer to help her to Sheila's car.

It was Frank McGehee. "How's your dog?" he asked

Sheila. She gave him a chastening look, but instead of being chastened, he turned his attractive attentions to Crystal instead. "Hi, Crystal. You still at Georgia State?"

"I was," the girl said in a soft, toneless voice.

Lieutenant Green called Sheila to one side. "By the way," he told her, not unkindly, "we checked out that note you and McGehee found at Mr. Anderson's. The one saying somebody was desperate and couldn't stand the pain? It was written by Miss Fowler. I don't think we need to mention it again, do you?"

It was a rhetorical question, but she shook her head anyway.

Crystal's legs scarcely seemed capable of bearing her weight. En route to the car she dangled between Officer McGehee and Sheila like a limp doll. Her mind was clearing, however. She said to McGehee, "Have you been working on this case?"

He nodded, and the worried look Sheila had noticed the first day was back in his eyes. "But remember, Crystal, I'm your friend. Always remember that, okay?"

Her eyes searched his, then she slumped again.

McGehee held her tenderly, fanning her face, until she opened her green eyes and looked around. "What happened?"

"You just fainted," he said with a cheerful grin. "Like Scarlett O'Hara or somebody. But two's your limit. Next time we'll leave you on the sidewalk." He helped her into Sheila's car.

"You were at Galaxia," she remembered.

"Yep, keeping watch over the elevator by night, like shepherds of old. In you go, now. Is anybody at home to cook your dinner?"

She shook her head. "I'll be all right. I'm not hungry."

"I'm taking her to my aunt's for now," Sheila assured him.

"Then have supper with me." It was an order.

Crystal gave him a wan, hopeless smile.

"I mean it," he told her. "I get off at five, and I'll come by your place. You still live in the same house?"

When she nodded he slammed the door and came around to Sheila's side. "I hope you won't let her be alone tonight."

Sheila didn't make any promises. Between an active dog and a pile of dusty photo albums, her apartment was already getting full.

At Aunt Mary's, Mildred had met them with sweet hot tea and a plate of cookies. Seeing Crystal's pallor, however, she asked, "You had any dinner?" She didn't wait for an answer. Very soon she set a place at the table with a full plate. Sheila, who had seen Mildred do the same for her many times over the years, merely smiled her thanks. Crystal approached the table almost on tiptoe, her face as hungry for this kind of care as her body was for the food.

Aunt Mary had waited for her to finish eating before she would discuss their problem, but now that they were all back in the living room, she would wait no longer.

"I wish you had thought to get a copy of that confession, dear," she reproached Sheila.

"I knew you would say that. But we really couldn't."

"It was my fault," Crystal apologized.

"Nonsense, dear. You fainted. Sheila was the one who should have thought of it."

"Sheila was dealing with the fainter," Sheila replied. "And I doubt Lieutenant Green would have given me one, anyway. You can't just get police records by asking nicely, Aunt Mary."

"Mmm." Aunt Mary's murmur conveyed that people could if they asked nicely enough. "I don't suppose there's any chance that he is confessing out of misplaced guilt?" she asked.

Crystal looked as hopeful as Aunt Mary sounded, but Sheila shook her head. "He described in detail what happened. I'm sorry."

She didn't know if she was sorrier for Crystal or for Aunt Mary, who sat on her end of the couch like a tiny owl whose mouse has just gotten away. Sheila understood her snippiness and clutching at straws. The little woman was battling to recover a case that had ended in a disappointing, heartbreaking thud.

"I think," she mused, trying to work out in her head the way it must have happened (and talking mostly to herself anyway—the other two were lost in their own thoughts), "that Dean was really reaching for his Galaxia directory, which had his lawyer's phone number written on it. Bayard said when he took her gun, he flung it into a drawer. A top drawer is handiest for flinging."

She had been mistaken. Crystal had been listening after all. Her green eyes widened with horror. "So Mr. Anderson wasn't even threatening Daddy? It wasn't really self-defense?"

"I'm afraid not." As long as she wanted to know, perhaps it was better to hear it here than later, in court. "Dean had confiscated the gun from his daughter that afternoon, and stuck it in a drawer. I think he may have been about to call and see what could be done about transferring royalties to your dad. He would have had to move the gun to get the number."

"Daddy killed him for *nothing*?" This was more than Crystal could bear. She burst into tears again, and nothing Sheila could say would comfort her. Aunt Mary could have done it with a few astringent comments, but she sat staring into space, her lips pressed together and her eyes angry.

Mildred came in with a warm washcloth scented with lemon. "Wipe your face now and come comb your hair," she said in a no-nonsense tone. "You're not going to help your daddy carrying on like that."

Bluntness succeeded where kindness had not. Crystal rose and followed Mildred toward the bathroom.

Aunt Mary rose as well. "This is a most unsatisfying conclusion. It makes no sense. I hope, Sheila, that by to-morrow you will have thought of something to do."

She went to her room, leaving Sheila to wonder what precisely she was to do. The whole thing made tragically good sense to her.

25

There was really no reason on Monday for Sheila to go back to Galaxia. She knew that. The only plausible excuse she could give herself was that since she had to take Crystal to Georgia State, she might as well drive the few extra blocks and say goodbye.

She had suggested that Crystal take a few days off school, but the girl had vehemently rejected that idea. "I've got an exam, and besides, if I sit around, I'll go crazy."

Sheila could understand that. If she thought much more about this case, she might go crazy, too. So she volunteered to drive Crystal not merely to the Chamblee-Tucker MARTA station, but all the way downtown, stopping for her books on the way. She didn't say, even to herself, that she planned to go to Galaxia until she was inserting her official card to open the Galaxia garage and pulling into the private space Elton Dekker had arranged for her.

She dropped her keys into her purse and admitted, for the first time, that she was as disappointed as Aunt Mary. Usually at the end of a case she felt at least a modicum of satisfaction in a job well done. Today she merely felt drained.

Part of that, of course, was Crystal, whom Frank Mc-Gehee had delivered to Sheila's before nine. She had gone quietly to bed in the guest room, but had sobbed until Lady padded into her room around midnight. Sheila had found them this morning curled into a ball in the middle of the double bed.

She greeted the elderly security guard and hesitated between buttons for the sixteenth and tenth floors. She could see Mr. Dekker later, she decided. The tenth floor was beginning to feel like family.

They were all busy at their desks when she arrived. She wondered how they were taking Woody's arrest. She discovered, to her surprise, that nobody knew.

"Woody?" Elise squealed. "Woody killed Dean?"

Her cry brought Porter from his office next door. "What did I hear? Has supersleuth supersleuthed? Is all discovered? Has a villain fled for his life?"

He stopped when he saw Sheila's face. "Oh, darling, you look like death warmed over. Let Daddy get you some coffee." He bustled out and soon returned with a steaming cup. Jonah and Veronica were at his elbow.

"What's this Porter tells us?" Jonah demanded.

"Woody?" Veronica's eyes were round with surprise. "I always liked him. Are you sure he did it?"

Sheila nodded. "He's confessed." She sipped her coffee. "Could we sit down somewhere? I'll tell everybody at once."

"Maybe we ought to call Mr. Dekker, too," Veronica suggested.

Sheila nodded again. "I don't know if he's heard or not."

"And Wylene and Craig." Elise hurried out her door.

"That woman would be nice to the devil if she knew how to find him," Porter said, shaking his head. But Sheila noticed that since their race, his voice held a new respect for his assistant.

Elton Dekker was out for the day. Everyone else gathered in the foyer, cups in hand, ears cocked. Sheila looked around the circle. "Just like we looked last Monday, isn't it?"

"No," Elise objected. "You and I were by the wastebasket then. And Dean's daughter was in this chair, and poor Woody . . ." She shook her head in dismay.

"Poor Woody, indeed," Sheila agreed. She told his story for him, as well as she could.

"So it was just an accident," Veronica summed up. "Do you think they will try him?"

"Have to, I think," Craig grunted. "At least that's the law where I'm from. He can plead self-defense."

"Or temporary insanity," Sheila nodded. "Nobody knows yet."

"He looked crazy when I first saw him." Horror had stretched Wylene's mouth beyond its usual limits. "Do you think I'll have to testify?" As she spoke she moved her head in a way to set her earrings swinging.

One of them, Sheila noticed, was missing a gold bead on the end. She made a mental note to ask Lieutenant Green to return it. She didn't know if Wylene would have to testify, and said so.

"Where's Woody's daughter?" As usual, Jonah focused his attention on the people in the case.

"You planning a special?" Craig asked with a sneer. "Children of famous killers?"

"Stuff it," Veronica warned him.

"Poor taste, Craigie boy," Porter admonished simultaneously.

Sheila and Aunt Mary had agreed not to say where Crystal really was. "She's with a friend for now," Sheila told Jonah. "I don't know what she'll do long term."

They had other questions, but none of significance. Finally Craig stretched his arms above his head. "Is that it? Because if so, I have work to do. I can't spend all day wondering why a brain-damaged man does what he does."

"You are nasty!" Elise's voice was angrier than Sheila would have imagined it could ever be. "That is the nastiest thing I ever heard anybody say, Craig Stofford, and I'm not going to speak to you again until you apologize!" She shut her lips firmly and her eyes flashed.

"Your loss, my gain," Craig told her, and ambled to his office without a backward look.

"Don't mind him." Jonah reached out to squeeze Elise's shoulder. "He's mad because Veronica and I scooped him Friday."

225

"Woody didn't have anything to do with that," Elise replied. "I wish *he'd* done it. If they sent him to the electric chair, I'd pull the plug myself!"

With that pronouncement, she started to her desk. "I'll pray for him," she felt compelled to add. Sheila hoped she meant Craig, not Woody, for in her present mood it sounded more like a threat than a promise.

Everyone suddenly remembered work that needed to be done. Sheila managed one quick word with Veronica. "I take it you and Jonah got your script approved?"

"Did we ever!" Veronica grinned. "Mr. Dekker liked the idea so well he's asked us to write six weeks' worth! He told Craig to concentrate on the next six weeks after that. Maybe by working apart, we can actually work together."

Sheila went thoughtfully to her desk. Dean's desk. As she took her seat, she couldn't help thinking of that. Last week at this time, Dean had sat here, in this very place. Not in this chair, but in one very much like it. He had talked with his wife, his son, and his daughter. He had put a gun in this very drawer.

She opened the drawer, and her eye fell once again on the directory. She thought of a question she wanted to ask the lawyer herself. Could Woody receive royalties if he went to jail?

While the number rang, she swiveled the chair as Dean would have done, to look out the window. Across the way a construction worker saw her and gave her a wave.

She hung up the phone unanswered, struck with an idea. Had any of them seen Dean's death? *Could* they have seen anything that happened inside a room seventy-five feet away?

She popped into Elise's office. "I'm going out for a while. If Mr. Hashimoto calls, tell him I'll be back in half an hour or so."

pproaching a construction site was not as easy from the ground as it looked ten stories up. At one point Sheila wondered if she could get a stout rope and just swing over from her own window. It took almost half an hour to find someone with authority to give her permission to question men who had been working on the building the afternoon Dean was killed.

It took another thirty minutes to locate the right man, a burly man with curly hair at his thick neck and a mop of curls springing out of his hard hat.

"Anderson waved at me," he said. "He was standing at the window looking this way. I waved back, then he sat down with his back to me. When I heard on the news he'd been killed, I wondered if I was the last person to see him alive. Except for the killer, of course."

"What time was that?"

"Oh, three-thirty, I'd guess. Not much past."

"Maybe a little earlier?"

He shook his head. "I didn't go up there until three-thirty."

"Was he alone?"

"Seemed to be."

"And you could see him clearly?"

"Sure. It's not far across."

She eyed him thoughtfully. "I don't suppose you could show me, could you? Would I be permitted up there?"

"If the boss says so, and you put on a hard hat."

Which is why, after exercising more charm and persuasion than she knew she had, Sheila got the thrill of stepping onto an incomplete floor of a building—ten stories up.

Immediately she wished she hadn't asked for this visit. She had never had a fear of heights, had climbed taller trees and swung higher than any child in her neighborhood. Visits to the Empire State Building and the Sears Tower had left her unmoved. But within two steps of the construction elevator she found herself clinging to her guide, looking uneasily toward the vast open spaces surrounding them.

"What a difference a few inches of brick makes," she said with a nervous laugh. "Ten stories high in Galaxia feels safe as earth. Here . . ." The wind whistled through the spaces between girders and the whole building seemed to sway. "We're moving! We're falling!"

Her companion laughed as he steadied her. "We sway a little. But it's mostly the clouds. When you see them hurrying by like that, you think you're moving too. You get used to it."

"I never would," Sheila assured him, feeling a bit foolish. She took a deep breath and concentrated on her reason for being here. "Which window was Anderson in?"

"That one." He pointed diagonally across the street to the right. "He was in that front corner window with the blind flapping. See?"

She was relieved to follow his pointing finger. She could not possibly have leaned over to count floors from the ground up. She didn't feel any too secure even this far from the edge. She clung to a beam of thick steel and considered the view. She could see into both Dean's front window and, slightly, into the nearest of his side ones. To her surprise, she saw Laura Anderson sitting at the desk, going through a drawer.

Her eyes moved to the next window. Jonah was visible at his desk, too. She willed him to look up and, to her surprise, he did. His jaw dropped, then he jumped to his feet. "Hi!" he shouted, leaning out his window and giving her a wave. She waved back, then grabbed the beam for support. When she'd let go, she'd felt herself sway in the wind. Her stomach churned and she was about to turn to go when, in the next office, she saw Craig look up and stare. Good! She'd managed to surprise even old Callousheart.

She looked again toward Dean's window, watched Laura take a sip from a mug. The view reminded her of sitting in the balcony of the Fox Theater—everything small, but very clear. "You didn't see anybody else in his office? Across the desk, perhaps?"

He shook his head. "No, he was standing in the window, blocking the view. First he wiped his forehead, like this," he swiped a hand across his own, "then he gave me a big grin and a wave, like he was celebrating something. When I waved back, he turned and sat down where the woman is now."

"But you didn't hear a shot a little later? I don't suppose you could, with traffic noise."

He shook his head. "Not likely." He hesitated, then said

slowly, as if uncertain whether to mention it or not, "You know, there was a shot over there before—it nearly blew my head off!"

"What do you mean?"

"Just as I got off the elevator, something hit a girder. If I'd been in the way, I'd have been a goner. See?" He stepped back toward the edge of the building and pointed to a short scar—almost a pockmark—on the side of a girder near the front of the building.

Sheila was glad it was the side of the girder, not the outside. She could never have walked around in front of it, less than six feet from the drop to Peachtree Street.

The angle between the mark and Dean's window was a direct line. "Why did you think it was a bullet?" Sheila asked him.

"I found it later. Right over there." He pointed to a spot on the concrete floor. "Hey," his voice was suddenly worried, "you aren't thinking it was the bullet that killed him, do you? It looked clean to me, and I'd swear Anderson didn't look like a wounded man."

He was right, of course. Dean Anderson hadn't stood in his window waving after being shot in the heart. Still . . . "Where's the bullet now?"

"I gave it to my kid, who took it to Show and Tell the next day. It's in his science center at school. Second grade." His attempt to sound nonchalant was a failure. He was obviously a proud father.

"You never mentioned this to the police?"

He shook his head and rubbed one cheek in embarrassment. "I did time once, years ago. I've been clean since then, and I'm working steady. You talk with the police, they rake up the past . . ." He shook his head again. "Anderson was alive and well when I saw him. No need to bring this other into it at all, as far as I could see."

She nodded. "I see. You aren't planning to paint over that spot today, are you?"

"Nah, I doubt anybody'll paint over it. It won't do any harm."

He started to put his finger into the nick, but she stopped him with a touch at his wrist. "I don't suppose you saw anything in that office *after* Dean waved to you?"

He shook his head. "I went around to the back to tell the guys. About Anderson, I mean. Several of them are . . . were keeping tabs on how many times a day he checked up on us. He just loved watching our progress, I guess. When I got there, they needed some help, so I never came back around to this side." He jerked his head toward the nick. "To tell the truth, this baby scared me enough I was happy to work out back for a spell." He seemed a little embarrassed by the confession. "You ready to go back down?"

Was she ever!

She walked carefully to the elevator and took pride in riding down the screened cage without fainting dead away. At the bottom, she even forced her trembling knees to walk normally across the street until she was inside. Then she collapsed into a chair in the coffee shop with a cup of steaming espresso.

H er arrival on the tenth floor this time was hailed by all. Jonah, in fact, seemed to be haunting the foyer until she arrived. "You looked great! A hard hat suits you. Can you get me up there?"

She shook her head. "And I wouldn't get myself up there again for a million dollars. I hope those workers are well paid. They deserve every penny."

"What were you doing up there?" Elise scolded. "You could have gotten hurt. What if you'd fallen off?"

"I'd have gotten hurt," Sheila admitted.

"You were awfully foolish," Wylene chided.

Sheila nodded. "I won't do it again."

"What *were* you doing, darling?" Porter wondered. "Playing peeping Thomasina? If I'd known, I'd have streaked through by Jonah's windows."

"That would have been charming, Porter, but actually I

had a hunch that maybe one of those guys had seen Dean get shot."

"Did they?" Laura had come to Dean's door, and was leaning against the doorjamb.

There was silence while they all waited for the answer.

"No such luck."

"But it was a good idea." Was the look in Craig's eye the glimmerings of respect?

At this point Sheila didn't care. She wanted to talk with Aunt Mary. While she drank her espresso, she had also been thinking. She thought she knew exactly how Dean Anderson had died. Could she get Lieutenant Green to believe her? Could they prove it if he did?

26

Monday evening Sheila and Crystal went to bed early, both exhausted.

Crystal had finally seen her father, an event that had been more traumatic than she had imagined it would be. "He looks old," she kept saying over and over at dinner. "He looks so old!" The only bright spot on her horizon had been lunch with officer Frank McGehee, who had showed up at the door of her classroom after her exam. When asked how he'd found her, he had grinned. "Good police work," was all he'd say.

Sheila was at least as tired, having spent the afternoon with Aunt Mary and, eventually, Lieutenant Green, going over and over the evidence and conclusions they had drawn from it. He had been willing to agree with them early, but "Okay, so we think we know what happened. What's our proof? If I can't prove it, I can't take it into court. It's just that simple. Give me a way to prove it. Come up with one concrete piece of evidence I can show a jury."

At last she and Aunt Mary had gotten permission to talk with Woody, in the presence of his lawyer and a representative from the prosecutor's office. They asked him three questions. Two proved beyond a doubt that he had not killed Dean Anderson. The third confirmed that they were on the right track. But it was still not the kind of proof Lieutenant Green wanted.

"Give me tangible proof," he insisted. "A hair, a fingerprint. That's what I need. Not theories and ideas."

"You check the police reports again," Sheila told him grimly, "and we'll see if we can think of anything else."

But tonight, as she brushed her hair and prepared for bed, she was too tired to think clearly. She could hardly stay awake long enough to stretch her legs full length beneath her sheets.

She awoke as suddenly as she had slept, raised herself on one elbow and strained to listen. She heard nothing—or did she?

Her heart pounded until it made her weak, and her hands and feet felt numb. She told herself that Lady was in the other bedroom, that Crystal was there, too. But for a minute she lay paralyzed by her old terror of the dark.

"It's nothing," she told herself sternly. Then she heard a gentle tinkle, like falling glass. Lady gave a low growl.

Now that she knew she was dealing with a real intruder and not merely with darkness, her fear vanished. Senses heightened, she pulled on her robe and tiptoed to her bedroom door. When she had moved into the apartment, she had decided to reverse the builder's plan, using the larger front bedroom as study and guest room and taking the smaller one behind the kitchen for herself. She preferred a good view from her desk to a view from her bed.

Now, however, her view of the living room and door to the master bedroom was blocked by one wall of the galley kitchen. She hated to step out of her room. Where was Lady?

A tiny beam of light winked in the living room. A pencil flashlight. Someone was moving across the room with purpose, toward the master bedroom door!

As the light struck the door, Sheila understood why Lady had not yet barked. Crystal had closed the door, and the intruder's footsteps were silent on the thick carpet.

Now the flashlight was at the door. As a gloved hand pushed it open, Lady rushed forward with a volley of barks. Sheila watched in horror as the intruder kicked the little dog viciously across the room and rushed toward the bed.

She was almost too late. In the time it took her to get through the kitchen and into the room, hands had already found Crystal's throat and were squeezing. Hard.

In an instant Sheila had caught and flipped the intruder. She lifted his head and pulled up his ski mask, then turned from the unconscious figure toward the bed, where Crystal lay in terror.

"Out cold," Sheila said with satisfaction. She switched on a light. "Are, you all right?"

Crystal nodded, struggled to speak. "How . . . how did you do that?" Her voice was hoarse and she was pale, but otherwise she seemed fine.

Sheila smiled. "Martial arts—a woman's best friend."

In one corner, Lady lay whimpering. One side of her stomach was indented, and the dog's eyes were full of pain. Sheila's stomach churned. Could the little dog be saved?

"Go to my closet. Bring belts or scarves to tie him up," she commanded. "Then call the police and a vet. I'll watch our visitor. Hurry! Lady's in pain!"

Crystal sat up, holding her throat. "Who could it be? Why did he want to hurt me?"

Sheila stared down at the figure, dressed in black slacks, a black turtleneck and a black ski mask.

"Craig, of course. And he thought you were me." She pulled off the ski mask. "Because he suspected I knew he shot Dean Anderson. I only hope we can prove it."

27

"I thought Woody did it." Elise's blue eyes were puzzled as she looked around the circle.

"Nope." Woody beamed with pride. "I missed him."

"How's Lady?" Crystal asked.

Sheila sighed. "She'll be all right, but it was a nasty kick. I'm leaving her at the vet's for a few days."

"Who's Lady?" Now Elise was thoroughly confused.

"My dog," Sheila explained. "Craig kicked her."

"How nasty! Why?"

Sheila smiled at her friend. "Let's begin at the beginning. Woody, why did you go into Dean's office last Monday?"

"I wanted money," Woody said simply. "For my book. I thought Dean was getting rich from my book."

"Craig put you up to that," Crystal told him. She turned to the others. "That weekend when he came by, he kept telling Daddy how rich Dean was getting from the book. Daddy got all worked up."

"Surely you didn't take a gun in to see Dean," Jonah objected.

Woody shook his head. "I'm afraid of guns. I hate guns!"

"It was mine." Bayard spoke softly, and her hand reached out for Jonah's. "I had it in my purse when I went in to tell Daddy goodbye. He found it, and took it away from me."

"So that's what made him so angry." Sally's lovely eyes

237

flashed. "I wondered what would make him shout at you that way. He was always so proud of you and all."

A chastened Sally had returned to the office, but offered no explanation beyond "I needed some time off." The others seemed to accept that one so exotic might have special needs.

"We're all proud of Ms. Travis and her marvelous aunt." Elton Dekker led a small round of applause. "And of our worthy lieutenant here." Another round of applause.

It was Tuesday afternoon and they sat, as they had sat twice before, circling the foyer of the tenth floor. Bayard had flown back to Atlanta as soon as Sheila had called her this morning. Mr. Dekker had put his appointments on hold. Even Aunt Mary had left her apartment to join in the denouement.

But there were differences, too. Craig was absent, of course. Porter, too, had not yet come in. Wylene was not trying to run the show. (Aunt Mary's presence had awed her into almost silence.) And while Lieutenant Green leaned once more against the pillar, he deferred to Sheila. "It's your story," he told her.

"How did you get Bayard's gun, Woody?" Elise asked. "And why did you think you'd killed Dean if you didn't? I don't understand anything!"

"We don't know precisely what happened," Sheila told her, "but here's the way I think it may have gone. Dean had put the gun on top of his building directory, in his top drawer." She looked to Bayard, who nodded confirmation. "On that directory, he had written his lawyer's number earlier that very afternoon. I believe Dean picked up the gun to get to the book."

"I thought he was going to shoot me!" Woody said, looking around the circle. "I thought he would. So I grabbed the gun. It went off, and Dean fell."

Sheila smiled around the circle. "In his confession, Woody said that same thing. It puzzled me, because Dean had been found sitting in his chair. Woody didn't see him after he called Wylene, remember. When we asked him yesterday to describe the position of the body, he said Dean was lying face down." She chuckled. "I think Dean hit the ground automatically, as he had done many times before in battle zones. But when Woody saw him fall, he panicked."

"I thought I killed Dean," Woody agreed.

"But he didn't?" Elise demanded.

Aunt Mary shook her head and took up the story. "The bullet went out the open window. Yesterday, Sheila learned that a bullet hit the building across the street sometime around three-thirty. A workman saw Dean alive after that. He told several people that Dean Anderson waved to him from across the street."

"He also found the bullet," Sheila added, "and took it home to his little boy as a souvenir."

"Neat souvenir!" Jonah obviously approved.

Veronica regarded him sourly. "Remind me not to let you come play with Demonde. You are warped!"

Jonah shrugged. "I'll bet the kid loved it."

"He did," Lieutenant Green confirmed. "Took it to Show and Tell and left it in his class science center, where I found it yesterday afternoon. I left him another souvenir in exchange."

"To return to your story, Woody," Aunt Mary suggested, "what did you do after you thought you shot Dean?"

"I ran to Sally's desk." Woody pointed. "I grabbed some Kleenex. I wiped off my fingerprints. I put the gun and the Kleenex in the wastebasket. Then I went downstairs."

"You should have come to me," Mr. Dekker told him, putting a gentle hand on the maintenance man's knee.

"I was afraid," Woody said simply.

"That was the second thing Woody told us yesterday—that he left the gun in the wastebasket," Sheila continued. "It was found, you remember, in Dean's office. Then he went to the fifth floor, to check on a toilet. Why did you do that, Woody?"

"I told you that yesterday, too," he reminded her.

"Tell us again."

"I heard a toilet flush. On ten. That reminded me of the toilet. I thought I could check on it and think what to do."

"Speaking of toilets, where's Craig?" Porter had come off

the elevator as Woody was speaking. He checked for messages under the ceramic turtle and took the only vacant chair, beside Sheila.

"Craig killed Dean," Elise informed him, "and Sheila is telling us all about it."

"Craigie?" Porter's eyebrows reached new heights. "But he was the only one who never left the eleventh floor!"

Sheila shook her head. "That's not what Jonah said. You said, Jonah, if I remember correctly, that Craig was the only one who was never gone more than five minutes. Right?"

Jonah nodded. "Something like that. You mean he heard the shot and came down to investigate? I didn't hear anything. Did anybody else?" There was a universal shaking of heads.

"I *think* what happened was, he came down to go to the bathroom and check his messages—and heard the shot while he was in the bathroom. It was his flush that Woody heard when he came out of Dean's office. Craig could have seen Woody without being seen, so he could have seen Woody wipe the gun and hurry, trembling, downstairs."

"Good old Craig," Porter drawled. "Convicted by a toilet. What a fitting downfall."

"But didn't he rush in to help Dean?" Wylene was shocked. She dabbed her eyes with a tissue. "How could be be so callous?"

"It was too good a chance to miss," Aunt Mary told her. "There was Dean, off guard, and a gun ready-to-hand. And there was also poor Woody, who probably thought he'd killed the man. Craig could have easily shot Dean and been back upstairs in five minutes."

"He looked proud of himself!" Elise remembered. "Wait a minute!" She rushed into her office and they heard her scrabbling among papers. She returned, triumphant. "I drew his picture, because I'd never seen him look like that." Sure enough, from the center of the paper Craig stared at them, exultant.

Sheila waited for the uproar to die down before she went on. "Do you remember, Elise, what you saw in this wastebasket the day he died?"

Elise closed her eyes, seeking a mental picture. "Lots of tissues, with a toothpick and a pink message slip on top that somebody had tossed."

"And you only took one call that afternoon, Sally. Isn't that right?"

Sally nodded, catching the spirit of things. "For Craig!"

"If that wastebasket's contents had been saved," Aunt Mary said with a reproachful look at Lieutenant Green, "it would have been evidence against him."

The police officer smiled at her. "I know you don't have a high opinion of the police, ma'am, but we automatically save the contents of wastebaskets when we're dealing with murder. I've got it. And now that I've watched that man there"—he indicated Porter—"check for his messages without knowing he was being watched, I can testify that it is a habit around here."

"Of course it is!" Elise told him. "I could have told you that."

"Yes, ma'am, but I kind of like to see it with my own eyes."

"Is that why you asked me to come in late this morning?" Porter asked Sheila, eyes dancing with mischief. "If I'd known I had a stellar role, I'd have put more oomph into the performance."

"You did fine," she said with a smile.

"Are you telling us," Veronica asked, "that Craig just took the gun from that wastebasket and killed Dean in cold blood?"

"I'm afraid so," Sheila said, nodding. "Carrying it in his handkerchief to avoid prints."

"From what Sheila tells me," Aunt Mary put in, "Craig is a young man who enjoys taking risks. This opportunity would have seemed to him too good to let slip." She turned to the president. "He expected, I think, that you would promote him to Dean's position."

Elton Dekker shook his head. "He did not have a suitable temperament. Mr. Baker and I have already discussed his taking over Dean's responsibilities."

Aunt Mary gave him a shrewd smile. "For Mr. Baker's

sake, I'm glad you didn't announce that before Craig was behind bars."

Sheila walked around the circle and put a hand on Bayard's shoulder. The girl had sat hunched and silent throughout a conversation that must have been extremely difficult to listen to. Now, without a sound, she had begun to weep.

"Do you want to go, Bay?" The familiar name slipped out. She was beginning to like this tough, feisty young woman. It had started, she decided, when she knew Bayard had stolen the video to protect Neal.

Bayard shook her head. "I'm all right." She fumbled in her pocket for a tissue that wasn't there. Sheila brought her one from the new box on Sally's desk and she blew her nose, hard. "I just keep thinking if I hadn't left my gun—"

Aunt Mary spoke crisply. "You are not to blame, dear. The crime was consistent with both men's characters." Bayard's wet lashes flew up and she opened her mouth to defend her father, but Aunt Mary stilled her with a flick of one hand. "Craig was an ambitious young man. Sooner or later he was going to kill someone, for he believed he deserved to have anything he wanted, and sooner or later someone was going to stand firmly in his way. Your father, on the other hand . . ." She sighed. "A most charming man. But a law unto himself. Am I correct?"

Bayard nodded. "He always thought he knew best. And he never told you what he was going to do. It irritated people."

"It certainly does," Sheila said, with a meaningful look at her aunt. Aunt Mary ignored her and continued to speak.

"Most of our lives shape our deaths, dear. I mourn Dean Anderson sincerely, but I am surprised someone didn't try to kill him long ago."

Bayard said nothing. Sheila, who felt the meeting was getting a bit heavy, turned to the lieutenant. "Has Craig confessed?"

He shook his head. "Silent as the proverbial clam. He'll go the entire trial, I think. But we've got what we need to nail him. In addition to the contents of that wastebasket and the testimonies here, we found three of Dean Anderson's trophies hidden in his apartment. Probably saving them to incriminate somebody else. We don't know. His lawyer says Dean gave them to Craig, borrowing from Mr. Robles's story, here, but Mr. Robles's story can be backed up by several witnesses to whom he showed the trophy. Mr. Stofford does not have that advantage."

Crystal touched her throat. "Did it matter that he broke into Sheila's? Will that come out in his trial?"

The lieutenant nodded. "You can bet your bottom dollar, miss. He gave himself away. Climbed onto that third story deck, broke the glass door into the living room and would have killed you if my assistant here"—he flicked one hand toward Sheila—"hadn't known a trick or two. That's attempted murder no matter how you look at it. We've got him, all right."

Frank McGehee put his arm around Crystal's shoulders as though it belonged there. "You'll get to testify, honey. Just wait."

Crystal was too happy today to be bothered by that prospect.

"How'd he get onto a third-story deck?" Veronica demanded. "You'll make me scared to go to bed upstairs in my house."

Sheila gave her a wry smile. "It wasn't your upstairs he was entering. I'll admit I'm not as easy about that apartment as I used to be, but Craig has done a good bit of rappelling."

"He certainly repelled me," Elise agreed.

Sheila turned to Bayard. "For one scary moment I wondered if it was you. Your mother had told us what a gymnast you are."

"Used to be," the young woman corrected her. "I'm badly out of shape now."

"You're a fine shape," Jonah told her. He turned toward Elton Dekker. "Mr. Dekker, I know this isn't the right time to talk about replacing staff, but before she goes back to New York tomorrow, I wish you'd talk to Bay. She's a great writer, and we're short."

"We'll talk when we're done here. Come to my office."

Bayard nodded, a flush of excitement softening her face.

Sheila, meanwhile, had been following her own thoughts. She wanted to make that deck door more secure, certainly, but at least the obscene calls would stop. She could answer her phone in peace.

One person still wanted to talk about Craig. "Will you electrocute him?" Elise's voice was very small.

The lieutenant turned to her, surprised. "I hadn't figured you for so bloodthirsty, ma'am."

"I would hate it. And I certainly don't want to pull the plug."

His voice was grave. "I doubt it will come to that. But if it does, I'll make sure they don't ask you."

Aunt Mary bent to pick up her purse. "And now, if there are no other questions . . ."

"I have one." Bayard raised her eyes to Sheila's. "Can we find out about those royalties for Woody? I'll talk to Mama . . ."

Sheila smiled. "You won't have to. Your father's lawyer already checked on that for me. Dean had donated them to the Veteran's Administration in memory of the Unknown Photographer. Now that Woody's been found and identified, I think it will be simple to get them turned over to him."

Aunt Mary gave a genteel snort. "Getting money away from the government is never simple, dear."

"You should know," Sheila told her. "But even if Dean's royalties cannot be redesignated, the publisher is willing to divide present royalties between author and photographer, with Woody getting the lion's share. Furthermore, he wants to talk with Woody and Crystal about at least one more book, maybe several."

There was another round of applause.

Woody sat beaming in their midst. Under cover of the babble of conversation that broke out afterward, Porter whispered to Sheila, "Meet me at seven, same time, same place?"

She hesitated, then nodded. "This time I'll come early to watch the doughnuts. And I want to ask you about your aunt."

He chuckled. "I was afraid of that. I wondered if that's why you came the first time, when you mentioned aunts."

"I didn't know, then. Now I do."

"You probably know as much as I do—I never met her."

"Don't whisper in public, dear," Aunt Mary admonished.

"You're just jealous I'm not whispering to you. Satisfied at how it finally turned out?"

Aunt Mary inclined her head in royal assent.

Silence fell on the group as suddenly as applause had burst out earlier. Jonah turned to Woody and punched him playfully. "Hey, Woody, you're going to be famous, pal. Can we do a special on you?"

Woody smiled. "Sure. I'm a special guy."